Dedicated to
Arianna, Dana and Asher

May your horizons always
be open to the stars

© Copyright 2016
Neil Wooding
All rights reserved.

This Book is copyright material and any portion thereof may not be reproduced or used in any manner whatsoever without the express written permission of the publisher except for the use of brief quotations in a book review.

Hostile Realms™ is a UK Trademark.

Published by
White Hart Media Limited.
Registered in the UK #06696665
ISBN - 978-1540717580

About the Author

Neil Wooding was born in England a month after Neil Armstrong landed on the moon. Since then, has had a passion for the stars.

As an avid model kit builder, Neil has been creating scifi model kits for many years and is involved in many groups that contribute to this hobby, and making friends all across the globe.

He has 3 wonderful kids, a loving wife and is looking forward to retirement where he plans to spend more time on his hobby.

ARMS RACE

CHAPTER ONE
PROLOGUE: Three years ago...

As the cluster of needles penetrated her skin at various points on her exposed body, and the substrate liquid flowed down the thin tubes, Kath'ryn imagined she could feel every single one of the robotic nanites crawl into her system.

She struggled to stop the tears flowing from the violation, from her shame.

Kath'ryn clenched her teeth and, in an effort to redirect her mind from the sharp pain, thought back to the events that had led her to this predicament.

She reviewed her life's choices that had removed her self-respect and had ultimately led her to this low place.

Kath'ryn Jacqueline Kass was a thirty-one-year-old ex-military Junior Grade Lieutenant. Whilst she, by her own admission, would not rival any of the vid stars in the appearances stakes, she liked to think she was, well, presentable.

She certainly had no real problems gaining male friends, so no, that was not part of her burden.

She had been cashiered out of the service for unruly behaviour and had gained herself a reputation for being a maverick. Her last military op had gone badly wrong, leaving two crewmen dead and a lot of questions unanswered.

She had failed to supply necessary or sufficient answers at the military tribunal that had followed.

The tribunal had, nevertheless, concluded that her actions, though strictly not in line with Terran Task Force edicts, had not led directly to the unfortunate deaths of her companions. Despite this ruling, the outcome was one of disgrace and had only marginally given her enough legal grounds to avoid attending a military jail. So, instead, she had been stripped of her uniform and escorted unceremoniously off the base and left to her own devices for the past ten months.

With no real focus left in her life, her world during those ten months had been filled with depression, an ever decreasing set of career prospects and a growing tally of one-night stands fuelled by alcohol and regret.

Kath'ryn had tried to get work in many places on Mars, that much was true, but she had lasted only a short time in each role. Each new job she took was worse than the last, her options becoming limited each time she moved from one to failure to the next.

Mars was not a big planet however and word had got around fast, her tarnished record hanging like a badge of shame around her neck, advertising her flawed past to all and sundry. It was a burden that it would seem she would be forced to wear for the rest of her life and it was a burden she had no choice but to carry.

She had nowhere near enough credits left to book return passage to Earth or even one of the orbiting platforms now. She had contemplated suicide many times in the past few weeks, looking for ever more creative ways of stepping outside an airlock to end it all, such was her despair.

Then the message had arrived in her vmail.

That bloody message.

It had been either a godsend or the devil in disguise she was now thinking as the nanites started to enter her bloodstream, as she stared unblinking up at the cold hard steep tiles above her in the medical wing of this small, but very private, hospital.

For reasons she was still at a loss to understand, one of the very few military acquaintances who were still on speaking terms with her had unexpectedly contacted her, simply asking if she wanted one final chance to redeem herself and offering to put her in contact with an anonymous benefactor.

A day or so of soul searching the bottoms of a bottle or three had resulted in her responding to her erstwhile colleague's enquiry with a rambling and graceless acceptance of the offer. Now, here she was, just one week later, lying like some discarded puppet strapped to this cold table, enduring this clandestine and probably unapproved military experiment.

A puppet having its strings applied, rather than cut.

The offer had been simple – either she volunteered to be injected with a new style of military nanite protocol designed to create a Smart Mind inside her own, and consequently get her record expunged, or she could return to her self-destructive downward spiral.

Accordingly, she had set out that morning from her cheap lodgings in Lovell City and spent ill-afforded cash on a metro journey to the northern perimeter of the city dome, and from there descended to the lower levels in order to report to an anonymous address in an obscure side passage.

After a brief scan of her identity card, a morose looking male nurse had led her to a small ante room where, after what seemed to be overly thorough and intimate physical examination by an equally morose doctor, she had been taken back through the ante room and into a large ward where other figures could be seen lying on hospital type beds with tangles of wires and tubes attached to their bodies.

In a very short space of time, she too was hooked up to the same arrangement of wires and tubes by a bustling nurse.

Kath'ryn took a moment to take stock of her surroundings.

There was nothing unusual about the rooms and wards of this obviously military hospital or clinic, other than the fact it was tucked away like an embarrassing secret. She soon realised after looking around at the ward's other occupants however that, amongst the keen and eager group of volunteers - or lab rats, she thought cynically. She alone was the only one not currently in the employ of the Terran Task Force.

The other members of the subject group were obviously all young Terran Task Force officers and pilots and those that weren't restrained to their beds by all the medical equipment were all keeping their distance from her.

She did learn from brief snatches of overheard conversation, that she was a member of the very first group to be receiving the 'Treatment'. She could practically hear the quotation marks and capitalisation of the word in their voices.

Realisation had dawned then, and she now was now more certain than ever that she had been chosen for her expendability and that had scared her more than a little.

At five-foot-eight, she was physically a tough woman, having learnt the hard way to train her body to the rigours of military life.

She had an athlete's body, or had before the abuse of the last few months had started to have its detrimental effects. She had achieved her better than average fitness through deliberate sessions of boxing with the men when off-duty during her last military assignment. She used to keep her brunette hair short for practical reasons but had let it grow down to her shoulders during the past six months as a way of rebelling and escaping from her past.

"Try to relax a little, my dear." Said a warm voice from beside her as a motherly-looking nurse walked into her view. She was holding a data Padd reading, Kath'ryn presumed, her vitals.

Kath'ryn had not realised she'd been clenching her hands tightly into fists since that first pain from the intruding needles, and slowly opened them to stretch her fingers wide.

Her nails had dug small grooves into her palms.

"The nanite injection is proceeding well Mz. Kass and you have nothing at all to worry about."

Nothing to worry about? Oh yeah? Well how about you have these fucking machines put in you then, eh? Kath'ryn thought, transforming some of her fear into anger at the kind nurse.

They had not sedated her, briefly explaining, in terms she didn't understand, something about the need for her body and mind to be unaffected by sedatives other than the local anaesthetic where the needles, even now, still penetrated her skin industriously injecting their tiny wards.

"How...how much longer?" she asked, stammering a little as she felt an icy chill pass down her spine.

"A few more hours yet Mz. Kass I'm afraid. We'll need to perform some scans next to check that the nanites are clustering properly around your central nervous system and glandular centres and are also proceeding correctly into your brain." The nurse replied, looking into Kath'ryn's blue eyes with a smile on her face.

The brain - that was the frightening part.

The Smart Mind, as it had been explained to her, was a miniature version of the advanced Artificial Intelligence, or simply AI, technology that had surfaced after the Flexani race had first appeared to humans, nearly seventy years ago.

Kath'ryn allowed her mind, as yet seemingly unchanged, to drift away from the fearful here and now in order to recall what she had been taught about that historic moment in human history.

If she recalled correctly, first contact with the Flexani alien race had been an amazing time for the preceding generation, and the initial relationships between the two hugely different races had been positive and productive.

The Flexani were a hyper-evolved and ancient race, long ago becoming dependant on nano-technology, their organic bodies had been reduced to a much baser form through genetic manipulation of their chromosomes and DNA.

Now without a recognisable spine they were shaped like terrestrial squids, or octopuses, and with a single eye in their central mass, they possessed several lower limbs which helped them move through the waters of their own planet. Smaller upper limbs were utilised as arms. Over millennia they had developed and adopted many innovative technologies that were integrated with their bodies at birth.

Some were even equipped with exoskeleton systems attached surgically in order to enable physically movement and interactivity with their surroundings, when those surroundings were high gravity.

The Flexani, away from their normal planet's environment though, generally used exosuits, powered by cybernetic limbs, into which they inserted their invertebrate bodies. The exosuits enabled those of them not surgically altered, to walk around in heavy gravity fields and toxic atmospheres with no more effort than if they were still on their native planet.

It was known that four Castes of the Flexani existed but little more.

The Flexani were very tight lipped (or as tight lipped as a species that didn't have any lips as such could be) about their social behaviours and arrangements and, especially now, no human was ever allowed to visit Flexani Prime, their homeworld, even though several unsuccessful missions had been despatched, none returned.

Even so, the Flexani in the first few years of contact gave the humans unsolicited help to achieve interstellar space flight and within mere decades they cause human technology to advance by centuries. These unprecedented events in human history forever changed the way that mankind viewed the universe. Interstellar travel, once an unattainable dream, was transformed almost overnight, into an opportunity to indulge that most driven of human traits, exploration and exploitation of the unknown.

The first contact with the Flexani and the following initial inter-species relationships, despite initial human fears that were based in no small measure upon the influence of Hollywood, Japanese B movies and other such media channels, had been positive.

This had been especially true in the field of medicine, where the Flexani expertise in cross species medical techniques became apparent and were shared freely across the globe.

Some forms of cancer, AIDs and even the common cold were banished to the history books as a result.

The Flexani intention, it seemed, was to work with Earth to create and nurture an ally, but the rapid advancement of human capabilities caused tensions in the relationship, and factions of several Flexani Castes viewed the human race as too much of a threat, a viper in its bosom as it were, and fought to address the proceedings.

Mankind too had its dissidents among its echelons and in the masses. Religious leaders too had fought the collaboration, arguing that their God had not given the Flexani his guidance and love, and that they were a race void of religion.

This led, inevitably, to mankind's first interstellar Cold War, with humans firing the first shot.

The First Stellar War broke out in 2061. The Flexani, though a powerful race and far more advanced than Earth, did not have the resources within the Sol system to fight a prolonged battle. After several years of warfare and one final huge battle in the vicinity of Jupiter, a Treaty with Earth was agreed. Known as the Treaty of JurTan, it ratified the borders between the occupied systems as well as certain trade and diplomatic protocols.

This Treaty took longer to agree than the war had taken, taking many years of diplomacy to iron out and achieve mutual accord from both sides. But once it was established, rather than re-building the status quo, the Flexani presence on Earth which had reduced to almost nothing overnight in the build up to the war, never returned.

It was claimed that no one had seen the pre-war exodus and rumours and theories were rife trying to explain how and why they had disappeared in such a manner.

Little was heard of the Flexani again on Earth.

There existed only what could be termed a standoff, or cold war.

Kath'ryn grew tired, and still the nanites continued to flow.

CHAPTER TWO
Border Control

The signal being generated by the local subspace node angered Arbiter Gen6aC. An alien ship, identified as being apparently Terran in origin, was blatantly violating an area of space defined as belonging to the Flexani by the newly updated Treaty of JurTan.

It was the Arbiter's duty to ensure this deliberate violation by the presumptuous and greedy Terran race was dealt with in the strongest possible way, in strict compliance with the Seven Precepts of the Lords of JurTan.

He sat, or rather floated, at his Listening Post, aboard the small station, located deeper in Flexani space. The station had been designed for him and his servant and so everything he needed fell immediately to "hand". He reached but a short distance to touch a lighted panel with one of his pseudo limbs.

"Servient Gen7cD, this is Arbiter Gen6aC of the NorHan House, Watcher of the Outer Rim requesting authorisation to release drone vessels in order to intercept and deal with an unauthorised Terran interloper in sector 45H-56, as instructed and approved by the Council of JurTan."

As a lower rank than that of his Servient, he couched his request in the required terms of dutiful precision in its tone and just sufficient subservience.

"Granted and approved Arbiter."

Built into his exosuit's cybernetic components, his subspace tweeter pinged the terse response a few seconds later though subspace — using a range of space-time that the Flexani scientists had discovered and were now exploiting. This discovery had enabled their race to manipulate the very subspace strings to send and receive almost instantaneous signals through the void over immeasurable distances, albeit at a high energy cost.

However, for such a critical purpose as the guarding of the very boundaries of the Flexani empire as it was now being used, the cost was deemed affordable.

As far as the Arbiter was concerned, the Terrans were a race to be distrusted.

As he had been taught whilst still in his maceration vat back on Flexani Prime, despite the previously misplaced effort to share information with the Terran race, Flexani technology was still many years ahead of them.

He had learnt of the period of peace and prosperity between the two races that had existed for over fifty-six solar cycles, but the animalistic and destructive Terran nature had risen, and a war had ensued.

Factions within the Terran world had chosen to rebel against the Flexani influence and benevolence, treating the Flexani ambassadors with contempt and revulsion, rather than embracing the opportunity they were being offered by them. It had resulted in the Flexani withdrawing all of its diplomatic contingent from the planet many cycles ago after several skirmishes, both on and off-planet.

The last great battle had been around the Terran system's gas giant, fought above the great cyclonic eye that many Flexani thought to be spiritual in nature, since they too had one great eye in their main carapace.

Arbiter Gen6aC himself had been a product of that war, bred in the maceration vats of Flexani Prime with specific genetic and cybernetic enhancements carefully crafted to serve this one purpose. To watch and to wait.

The Flexani had originally evolved on a planet much like Earth, but possessing a higher hydrogen content in its atmosphere.

Flexani Prime possessed less landmass than Earth and it orbited around a smaller, bluer star. The evolution of life on the planet had inevitably led to a race that had originated and developed in the seas, and then advanced out into space, taking to low gravity, and then to no gravity environs with ease.

The planet was rich in minerals and the underwater mining and exploitation of them had enabled the Flexani to develop their advanced generic and technological systems. These systems allowed them to expand offworld, as well as helping to shape their culture by societal status and cybernetic changes to their young.

They rarely used their natural limbs anymore for anything more than minor tasks and only their criminals or seriously injured had their tech removed so that they were left as nature intended – before their ultimate removal from the gene pool.

In fact, it was so much of an aberration to be without tech that at first contact, the Flexani reviled, then pitied the humans for their lack of tech and initially had only engaged with the severely disabled, those with cybernetic limbs or cochlear implants or other such medical enhancements.

All these things Arbiter Gen6aC had learnt, but for now he concentrated on his given task, to protect Flexani space from these approaching Terrans.

He now activated the rest of his console and recalled the relevant sector of space onto his view screen. Along the border he knew he had access to many hidden caches of weapons, drones and other exotic technologies the humans as yet knew nothing of. There were in fact, some weapons of such destructive force that even someone of the Arbiter's rank and status did not have enough clearance to call into action without requesting from a much higher authority than the Servient who had approved his current request.

For this exercise though, he considered that just three of the Torrak class drones he had access to would be more than sufficient to deal with the intruder.

The Torrak class craft were autonomous drones measuring a little over twelve metres in length and equipped with an Infusion Manipulator Drive, or IMD. They also boasted artificial combat mind capability and six highly accurate and deadly fletchette railguns, each of which were mounted on one of the drone's six main 'wings'. Shaped like a Courach shell, four of these spiny wings jutted slightly forward of the main fuselage with two larger wings trailing back. A vented bulge at the rear of the fuselage contained the IMD that drove the ship forward in space. The only occupant, the Artificial Mind, was housed inside the shielded vessel.

The Arbiter swiftly entered the commands required to initiate the launch of the three craft from their disguised base, located in a small asteroid field near the planet designated XT-67-C.

The three drones awoke from their dormant state moments after receiving Arbiter Gen6aC's command. They nimbly leapt clear of the asteroid field, the Artificial Mind aboard each craft easily steering the craft to avoid the smaller asteroids and dust until their field was clear and they entered the void.

Their target was an infinitesimal visual dot in the vast area of space, but their advanced sensors clearly pinpointed and locked onto the small Terran ship and their Artificial Minds were already running routines and assessment protocols to optimise their attack vectors so as to cause maximum damage at the first approach and to facilitate the intended destruction of their target.

Arbiter Gen6aC watched through his link to each Torrak, recording for the Servient and his masters the closing gap between predator and prey, all the while checking the telemetry from all units in this small skirmish.

The ambush was set.

Good he thought to himself, *it seems that dormancy has not dulled the drones' assessment protocols.*

Arbiter Gen6aC had no concerns for the occupants of the Terran ship, if there were any. He neither cared, nor considered the vessels crew. He was only concerned with the certain knowledge that the vessel was violating the space around XT-67-C and it was his duty as Arbiter to ensure that this violation did not go unpunished.

++++++++++

It had been an uneasy peace with the Terran planet up until now.

After the last War between the Flexani and human races, the Flexani Council of JurTan, their main governing body and representative voice, had signed agreements with the various government bodies of Earth before it had left, agreeing to the location of borders and the rights of both parties to protect those borders.

The Terrans, as they preferred to be called, however always failed to adhere to the latest set of amendments and changes to the lines between their empires, refusing to recognise them.

The Council had grown weary of the seeming belligerence of this race, after all, the Terrans weren't the only race the Flexani had borders with, and the lines were always changing over time. The Terrans did not seem to accept this fact.

Currently, the planet XT-67-C that the vessel targeted by Arbiter Gen6aC had just departed had a small Terran mining colony situated on its surface. The Terrans were mining the ore containing the mineral Corismite, used in the Terran engines that powered their FTL drives. The location of Corismite deposits were limited to a very few known places from where it could safely be mined.

Flexani vessels thankfully did not have to rely upon this material for their power needs so XT-67-C did not have that much strategic significance to the Flexani. Hence it had not been annexed from the Terrans - there would certainly be more Flexani forces in this sector if it had been.

However, the Council of JurTan had only recently updated the border lines near this particular planet, so it was that the conscientious Arbiter Gen6aC pulled up the files on the latest data packet from the Terran government to verify their response to the change before he committing his speeding Torraks to attack.

"The people of Earth represented by the Global Federation Committee, Terran Tactical Force, the United Nations and the associated Governments around the globe, and as confirmed arbiter of the human race within the Sol System, cannot and will not accept and concur with the latest set of border amendment as per Appendix H8-C of the Flexani Accord Treaty of 2067.

The border amendments violate the right under Clause 126c subsection 12 and Clause 255 subsection 2 regulating the mining of Corismite from planet Mirral designated 'XT-67-C' and the human operation currently present on that planet. As per Clause 255 subsection 1d, we hereby reject the new border amendments until arbitration and settlement can be made between both parties as is our right under this covenant."

"And so the Terrans wilfully refused our very generous offer of resettlement and provision of Corismite materials." sneered Arbiter Gen6aC.

The Flexani offer had been considered and reasonable – because of the movement of the Border, the humans would be allowed free movement to resettle on their side of the border and they would need to stop all mining operations.

The Council would then compensate for the loss with shipments of refined ore. Obviously at a reduced output when compared to the volumes currently mined of course, this after all was politics and it wasn't desirable for the humans to get too much ore from the deal.

Interstellar politics, like those on Earth it seemed, was the same old game.

All sides playing each one off against another.

It's just that the Flexani had what some considered to be an unfair advantage, in that they had been playing the politics game for a lot longer than the humans and had refined it to a fine art within a specific racial Caste whose particular genetic enhancements made them eminently suitable for the strategy and counterplay needed in the art of negotiation.

The Terrans however, were still arrogant enough to think they could play the same game by refusing the proffered settlement.

The AM2's synthesised voice came through the subspace link and drew the Arbiter's attention back to the alien vessel. "Acquired target is within twenty frecs. Permission to proceed with target elimination?"

Arbiter Gen6aC unhesitatingly gave the command, "Permission is granted. Proceed and execute."

++++++++++

"Intrepid Star, Personal Log Update, Captain Kass reporting - start recording:

We left Earth's orbit over 3 weeks ago and are now out of the home solar system, having engaged the ships' main drive en-route to Sector 45-1 near the Flexani border. Before we left I officially expressed my concerns to Mission Control about how close our destination, the M-class planet known as 'Mirral' is to the border with Flexani space, but they have assured me that Terran military ships are in the region and it is therefore deemed safe for us to travel there.

The crew have been preparing the vessel for sublight and all cargo and equipment has been stowed and secured safely for the trip. We have just one crew unfit for duty, Flight Officer Olsen has been suffering from a mild case of flu, and I have ordered him into Stasis first, under advice from the Chief Medical Officer.

With regard to the ship's operational status, we've been having an intermittent coolant issues with cryo tank six. Engineering has assured me it's quite safe but I have decided to shut down Stasis Pod Four for home depot maintenance, so it will be unserviceable for the remainder of this trip – again! I don't want a problem with the Pods in deep space and risk my crews' lives. Coolant leaks are becoming more and more frequent, despite repeated requests to Control for more funds to repair these ageing units.

I've therefore put the ship on a three-man rotation during the duration of this mission. This will mean added shifts and less time in Stasis but I'm sure the crew will perform as well as they have done before.

Our mission parameters require us to rendezvous with the mining Station on the planet's surface and to collect 300,000 tonnes of raw Corismite crystal ore for processing. We'll commence the refining process on the journey back to Earth and aim to complete the mission in little under 5 months, if all goes well and nothing else breaks down.

I've also entered into the Ship's Log the ship's current fuel and resource status – see supplemental file Mirral-160951, as well as the crews' last evaluation report. Engineer Coulson is once again on disciplinary report but the more encouraging news is that Ensign Drexler has been progressing well with his duties in the mess-hall - fitting in well with the team although he does have bear the brunt of the crew's jokes at times. All good natured I'm glad to say.

We have a full manifest of food and medical supplies for the mining Station and I'm personally looking forward to having dinner again with Commander Terris, the mining station's manager. He was very complimentary and supportive of our work the last time we made this trip, and he was a pleasure to talk to after several months in Stasis isolation. I have stored a personal bottle of Chateau Lafite Rothschild Pauillac 2078 which, I've been told, is a very good year and I hope to share it with him. Call in perks of rank.

All relevant navigation data has been entered into the AI and I have confirmed it with Mission Control, so we now just waiting for the AI to engage the FTL drive. First shift has begun and the remainder of the crew are now safely in Stasis. I have slaved the AI controls to my own Pod and will be alerted should anything happen on the journey but will be entering stasis myself within the next 48 hours.

Captain Kass signing off."

++++++++++

Captain Kath'ryn Kass replayed her last personal log entry even as the Intrepid Star rumbled its way up out of the thick atmosphere of XT-67-C, better known as Mirral.

She was preparing to write a long overdue update and wanted to review her previous comments before drafting her new log entry.

She smiled warmly at her recent memory of the way the station commander – Andrew Terris - had flirted with her. She was not the most attractive woman she knew - her body a bit too muscular for some men and her features a little severe - but she still welcomed his flirtatious comments and felt she probably would not avoid the inevitable next time she visited, after all Andrew - she smiled inwardly at her familiar use of his first name - had issued her several of his more salubrious invitations over the past year and just the thought sent a warm glow through her as she thought of the sexual feelings it brought up.

Kath'ryn had not felt really happy in a long time since her mother's death which had coincided with the period when she was enduring the nanite treatment. She had been forced to miss her mother's funeral due to the treatment protocols and had been desperately angry at the time. The period following had been a very lonely time for her.

God, how long has it been since I last had sex Kath'ryn started to wonder wistfully.

"Captain?" First Mate Jung's voice unfortunately interrupted her reverie as he spoke to her from below.

Kath'ryn, as Captain, was sat on the main flight deck of the Intrepid Star transport ship, a Raven Ore Confederated Logistics vessel that had seen far better days and should have been decommissioned years ago she felt. Nevertheless, she was its Captain and so played her part and was grateful for the job.

After the attempt by the military many years ago to grow a Smart Mind inside her own had produced just limited results – results the TTF military medical brass ruled were not good enough to allow her back into active military service, she had taken the only job she could get at the time with a small, but fast-growing, mining corporation, Raven Ore Confederated Logistics. The only positive thing about the situation though was that the military had at least kept their promise and had her previously blemished record expunged, so she had good references at least.

Her Captain's seat, such as it was with its worn patina leather bearing the coffee stains from all the previous occupants, was located on the upper mezzanine level, and Jung was stationed below her with the pilot, Alain Brock. He was carefully checking the connection from his spinal interface to the ship's AI in preparation for taking it out into deep space for the long flight back to Mars.

She leaned forward over the rail in front of her and queried, "Yes Harry, what's up?"

"We've just received a small data packet from the TTF regarding some demands by the Octopoids on changes to the boundaries in this region of space. It's warning us about increased Squiddie activity along the neutral zone but they say one of the TTF vessels is in the local vicinity and will be on patrol. Huh, I feel safer already!" he said sarcastically.

Octopoids, Octoids, Flexies or Squiddies – all were derogatory names circulating the net and social media to describe the Flexani. They were all in common use when referring to the Flexani in day-to-day conversation, and especially on board a mining ship, the crew were pretty common in nature. Regarding themselves as simple folk with a loathing and suspicion for the unknown or unusual.

"Route it to my terminal will you?" requested Kath'ryn.

"Done." He complied, leaving the report to be the Captain's problem now. He'd done his part.

Kath'ryn digested the brief report. The Terran Tactical Force had sent an update bulletin to all Terran ships near the Neutral Border running between Flexani and human space. One section of the bulletin caught her eye immediately. Mirral, the planet that the Intrepid Star was even now pulling away from, in the process of leaving the flirtatious Commander and his team of miners behind, was the very planet the that the Flexani had just tried to annex in their latest changes to the border lines.

Shit she thought… *Why was the TTF not sending any escort vessels to her location as a precaution?*

She knew from her own past experience in the TTF, prior to her subsequent cashierment from the service, that the TTF could, and had, in the past, protected ships in less delicate situations than this.

She suspected though that since the Intrepid Star was not owned and operated by an Earth based major mining corporation , then Raven Ore Confederated Logistics, based as it was on Mars, obviously did not have the political or monetary clout to demand protection. She felt a chill run down her spine and she shivered, knowing that her ship and crew were considered expendable by the corporation. Faceless, uncaring, penny-pinching managers controlling her destiny yet again it seemed.

"Harry?" Once again she leaned over the rail to speak to him. "Can you send a message to the TTF vessel in this sector please, wherever it currently is, and request a safe vector away from Mirral? We need to get out of this system as fast as we can before the shit hits the fan."

He nodded. "Sure, I'll get in touch with them now."

"And Harry, how long until we are able to go sublight?" she enquired, knowing already the answer full well, but wanting the latest status update from her First Mate.

Harry frowned. The FTL drive had been experiencing some issues on the flight out to Mirral from Mars and because of this, the trip had already encountered significant delays. ROCL HQ had already chastised the crew about the delay so it was critical that the return journey home did not suffer any further holdups.

"You're not going to like my answer, Captain." He replied, shaking his head and shrugging his shoulders.

"Oh for fuck's sake, has Coulson not yet fixed the damn drive yet?" Kath'ryn said with a rising level of frustration in her voice. "What the fuck was he doing while we were docked and loading the cargo. Getting drunk with his cronies again I assume?"

Chief Engineer Coulson was the lead engineer on the small haulage vessel, highly knowledgeable in ship's systems and engineering, but prone to giving it to his twin vices of drinking and gambling.

Almost every time the vessel was docked he as to be found wasting most of his 'hard earned' creds on these two pursuits. He was frequently hungover but still managed to do good enough repair work when forced, which was the only reason he still had a job with ROCL. Though for how long, Kath'ryn wondered, knowing his last performance report she had submitted to HQ was not complimentary and would almost certainly result in the termination of his position as Chief Engineer aboard the Star.

God alone knew where he'd go from there as all the other shipping companies wouldn't take him on, that much was certain.

"I can't say Kath'ryn." The first Mate was trying to be neutral but understood the anger directed at Coulson. After all, he also had to deal with the man on a daily basis and on a small ship like the Intrepid Star, you just had to get on with your fellow crew or who knows what might happen on your next layover. Coulson knew a lot about the systems on the ship as well as the Stasis Pods, equipment vital to facilitate the travel between solar systems by enabling the crew to sleep in suspended animation while they travelled at sublight speeds. Get on the bad side of him and there was a good chance you might never wake up, or that's the impression the temperament of the man led people to suspect.

Captain Kass completely understood what Harry was saying to her.

"Fuck!" she exclaimed again in frustration. "Let me know what the Task Force says will you, I need to go and have a word with our so-called chief engineer."

With that, she exited her seat on the Bridge and headed down the ladder towards the bulkhead exit at the rear of the compartment.

CHAPTER THREE
Mechanical Troubles

Kath'ryn took her time and breathed deeply as she walked back through the ship, towards the main engineering room, trying to calm the anger that seethed inside her and her frustration at the problems this man caused on each and every trip.

Minutes later, Kath'ryn opened the hatch to the engineering section and immediately saw Coulson and his junior staff member, Tim Harr hard at work on the FTL drive, panels open and with tools and components strewn over the hullplate.

"Shit, this doesn't look good Coulson!" she shouted over the thrum of the main fusion drives, gesturing to the scattering of important FTL elements beneath her feet.

Coulson turned to her and she thought she saw him mutter something under his breath. "Captain!" he exclaimed with obviously feigned joy. "To what do we owe this pleasure. Come to take me up on my offer eh?" a sly grin appearing on his face.

"I'm sure Timmy here can take over while we head to my bunk for a quick tumble!"

Coulson was a man who carried a paunch from the drink but still had muscle from the work he and Harr did. Though still in his mid-thirties, his hair was thinning and he seriously needed a shower most days.

He failed to care about his appearance other than a cursory approach to cleaning up for the hookers he bedded in port.

In summary, Coulson was the kind of lowlife that every mining vessel Captain didn't want on board.

Just my luck to be stuck with him.

Unlike the Base Commander and his use of persuasive charms – Coulson, in Kath'ryn's very first week on the job as Captain had tried to get her into his bunk in a very direct and forceful way.

She however, had rebuked him in no uncertain manner with some well-learned military self-defence techniques that had brought the lecher to his knees. It had certainly made his eyes water at the time, but it had not unfortunately stopped these little jibes and pathetic attempts at sexual humour at her expense.

"Listen you shit, and listen up good. I'm only interested in you doing your job, fixing this ship – not for what you can or more accurately, cannot do in bed – OK?" She continued to raise her voice at him, her body language making it clear who was in authority.

"We have a big problem with this warning from the TTF. We have to get the hell out of here before we're the cause of an incident, I want to be out of this sector as soon as humanly possible. Now, what do you need to get the repairs done?"

"Well you don't need to worry your pretty little head about it Captain. The Squiddies can go fuck 'emselves for all I care." He gestured wildly, his hatred for the Flexani race clearly visible on his face.

"I don't care in the slightest what your narrow mind thinks about the Flexani! We need FTL as soon as we can – *Chief!*" Coulson saw her start to react at his statement and knew he'd overstepped the mark.

Holding up his hard to her he said, "But actually, me and Timmy here have just finished repairing the damaged module. T'was a faulty actuator and I can tell you, HQ better not keep buying substandard parts for the Star if they want us to make quota this month. Fuckers want me to not get my bonus don't they? Anyway, we just need to reassemble the Drive and you'll have FTL in less than an hour!" Grinning at this, Coulson smacked Kath'ryn on her hip, his hand lingering a little too long.

Roughly brushing his hand aside with disdain she questioned, "And Stasis Pod Four? You said in your last report we had an issue?"

"Err, yeah," his faced dropped. "Going to have to take Four offline as Cryo-Container six still has the hairline crack in the cylinder wall and it's leaking cryo-fluid all over the deck. It'll need a replacement cylinder and we don't have one on-board in storage."

"Will it take long to fix?" Kath'ryn enquired.

"Nah, it's a simple job – if we had the parts. Once we get to the ROCL port on Mars I'll get Tim on it to get it fixed. Should take less than a day."

"OK. Let me know immediately we have FTL capability." With that she turned on her heel and left Coulson and, knowing his lecherous eyes were watching her walk out of the room, she added, "Get on with it Coulson!"

Then, just as her hand touched the hatch handle, the warning strobe and alarm burst into her consciousness.

"Captain!" came the voice of the Intrepid Star's pilot Brock over the comms.

The panic in his voice was tangible even through the distortion of the speakers. "We've a ping on sensors. Three Flexani vessels approaching fast on a vector of two-seven-zero mark four-five!"

++++++++++

Kath'ryn left Engineer Coulson and his wandering eyes behind her. He was now the least of her concerns.

She raced through the ship, avoiding the panicked stares of some of the crew as she headed back towards the main flight deck.

"Main engines to max thrust," she shouted into her personal comms to Brock, but even as she did so, she felt the fusion drives peak and the hull begin to rattle with the unaccustomed high levels of power being applied to it as the old ship's in-system engines began to accelerate it forward, away from the Flexani vessels on approach.

Good man, she thought.

Brock had already anticipated her command and executed it.

The Star's AI announced, its calm emotionless voice cutting across the comms channel, <All crew to designated Safe Zones.>

Kath'ryn's blood ran cold at the sound.

Normally only heard before in safety drills, the alarms sent waves of fear that gripped her insides as she continued her headlong rush to the main flight deck.

The klaxon and strobes continued to wail and flash all around the small ship. The crew, trained as they were by all those safety drills, ran to get into their designated protected sections of the ship the Safe Zones, or into the single life raft located along the vessel's starboard side.

Coulson and Tim Harr were already well protected in Engineering, as were the bridge crew, being isolated as they were from the rest of the ship by airlock doors which even now could be heard slamming shut one by one, as the crew evacuated the more vulnerable areas of the ship.

Along with members of the bridge and engineering section, only the Medical bay staff had the luxury of already being in locations that were designated Safe Zones.

The rest of the crew unfortunately, did not have that luxury and were running to whatever Safe Zone they could reach.

The Intrepid Star was a simple consignment vessel, and one that was already a thirty-year-old design. It possessed quarters for just a dozen crew members; a small galley and equally diminutive recreation area; the engineering section and bridge with a limited medical facility where the Stasis Pods were contained. The remainder of the deep space haulage vessel comprised, apart from the tiny Safe Zones, the fuel cells for the trip and large cargo containers full of the raw Corismite ore.

These vast containers were housed under the main superstructure in six large external cargo pods, triangular in cross-section, which could be removed at dock and transferred to a Black Raven refining facility.

The Star had been in continuous operation for almost twenty-seven years.

It was claustrophobic, dirty and old.

It didn't even have any weapons.

It was vulnerable.

At a mere sixty-two metres in length and manned by twelve crew, the ship had twin Orion FTL V67-J drives, currently straining at power levels they were not used to handling. Normal operation usually required the ship to be in deep space for over eight months at a time, so the systems had to be simple enough for the limited crew to maintain.

Kath'ryn entered the hatch leading to the Bridge, sealing it behind her and then leaning for a second on it to catch her breath before flinging herself forward to the two seats ahead, the pilot and First Mate at the controls.

She felt the palatable tension in the air as these two junior offices looked at her for assurance, genuine fear in young Alain Brock's eyes.

She realised she needed to be strong for the crew and ordered her limited Smart Mind to repress the rising levels adrenalin and the resulting panic she was feeling. As the machine inside her took charge, an induced sense of serenity came over her.

Standing behind Harry Jung, she watched the First Mate's display showing the three angry red dots representing the approaching alien vessels. The Star's on-board AI pulling the relevant data and information from its databanks to add the identification symbols for the type of vessels they were, together with a text readout. Slowly, the information appeared, their AI being an early model with limited quantum processors was not really up to the task.

Harry Jung spoke out loud, reading the data from his screen, "Torrak attack drones, minimal range but, SHIT... they're moving fast. Loaded to the core too with Fletchette rounds apparently. What the fuck are the Octopoids doing!?" he almost shouted the question, his voice rising as stress bled through.

Kath'ryn sensed the rising panic throughout the ship and knew she needed to reassure the crew.

Her previous TTF training kicked in and she spoke calmly but forcibly. "Easy Harry, I know we have a problem here, but I need you to focus - OK?"

Harry looked at her and taking a deep breath, nodded in acknowledgement.

"Good. Now, what is the range of these ships from the Star right now. How long will it be before they reach us?"

"Err.....," he took a moment to run the numbers, the trajectories computed in near real-time by the AI. "Thirteen, maybe fourteen minutes," he read out.

"Did you get hold of the TTF vessel in this sector as I asked?" she enquired, almost before he had finished speaking, throwing him momentarily off track with the question but now Kath'ryn's mind was at full speed, racing ahead with decision trees and computational paths of possible outcomes and plans.

One of the benefits of her experimental surgery all those years ago was the implantation of a series of nanites in the core of her brain in order to construct a miniature electronic Smart Mind, or SM embedded in her neocortex, and it had worked – at least, partially.

It had taken a year or so for the nanites to assemble together, then utilise trace elements from her bloodstream in order to construct the quantum processor at the heart of the SM.

Once this had been completed, the nanites no longer existed in their original form, their hardware and software becoming the heart of the Smart Mind, but it had taken a much longer time for the SM to start to evolve and mature and to integrate itself more easily with Kath'ryn's own biological mind.

This time delay was in fact one of the very reasons the Military had thought of the experiment as a failure. They had needed and expected much faster results.

She had been shocked the first time her SM really spoke to her.

Now, it was an integral part of her mind, she thought of it almost as an old friend, but it could be a voice of irritation more often than not.

Now though, she was very grateful for its assistance.

"The TFF...? Oh yeah, I did, earlier." Harry stumbled for a moment before remembering his earlier task.

"Good. Get them on the line again. I want to speak to their Captain, NOW! While you're at it, send out the standard distress signal and then send a transmission on the Flexani subspace band that we're a transport vessel with absolutely no armament and a civilian crew, in Terran space under the JurTan treaty. If they hear and understand they may stop an attack before it starts."

She watched as Harry activated the standard Distress signal broadcast, then initiated the comms to the TTF vessel.

As Harry was carrying out his orders, Kath'ryn turned to Alain Brock, the pilot, and rested her hand on his shoulder. He turned to her, his face both concerned and puzzled. She could see the strain he was under, this young pilot fresh from the Academy.

"Alain, FTL will be online within the hour – Chief said so." She smiled at him, trying to put him at ease.

He chuckled nervously, trying not to remember that the approaching Flexani drones would be upon them long before the FTL would be available, and turned back to keep watch on the tell-tale warning lights on the fusion engines.

Designed in principle over eighty years ago in early 2015 by NASA as a way of beating the Tsiolkovsky rocket equation, the principle of the Intrepid Star's fusion drive was simple. Xenon gas was fed into a circular channel into which was then injected a accelerated stream of electrons excited to around half a million degrees Celsius, the accelerated electrons then literally annihilating their counterparts in the xenon gas atom nuclei, converting them into highly positively charged ions which were ejected out through an exhaust cone which in turn pinched the stream of ions using a steerable magnetic field, resulting in the ship being thrust forward.

Whereas the fusion drives of the Intrepid Star were based on that principle, they were much more efficient in output than the early prototypes, possessing the capacity to produce around 450 kilowatts of thrust per engine.

Thrust that was right now being applied in an attempt to accelerate the Star in an attempt to not so much gain distance as time before interception by the attackers as humanly possible. All aboard new the Star did not have anything like the ability needed to outrun the Torrak drones even now closing rapidly on them.

Unfortunately, pushing them the engines hard at full power for as long as possible was going to be a risky manoeuvre but they desperately needed that extra velocity to give them time. Time that might possibly furnish them with the help they would almost certainly need.

So far, the engines whilst intimately close to their redline, had not yet exceeded it, so they were steadily increasing their velocity by the second.

For now.

The pilot, Brock, was a young man with only a few years' inter-stellar flight experience under his belt, so he had gone to work for Raven Ore Confederated Logistics as it gave him the chance to log many deep space flight hours, a chance that a lot of his academy buddies would not get.

Most of the his Flight Academy graduate colleagues had chosen to fly the Sol in-system ferries and the private luxury shuttles of the rich and famous, very few selected hauling deep space freight around or, alternatively, the Terran Task Force as their career. He had always yearned for adventure in deep space though, and when the opportunity had arisen to venture there, albeit as a lowly freighter pilot, he had jumped at the chance and so it was he now found himself now occupying literally the hot seat as he sweated in his flight suit. He was now considering perhaps whether he had made the wrong career choice.

Harry spoke up, interrupting his thoughts, "Captain, I have a Captain Middleton of the TTF Kydoimos on subspace, putting him through now to your terminal."

Kath'ryn quickly returned to her own seat above the two younger officers. As the call was routed through, she looked down at her display screen and the face of the TTF Kydoimos Captain appeared.

At around fifteen years older than her, she subconsciously estimated, with greying temples and some lines around each of his eyes Captain Middleton looked the archetypal deepspace warship captain.

Hardened by years in the service, his green/brown eyes betrayed every year of his military and combat service. She knew instinctively that this was a man who understood loss and pain in battle and he obviously had had to make some hard decisions along the way to earn those facial lines.

"Captain." He spoke in a mild Australian accent as he recognised Kath'ryn's status on the Intrepid Star. "We've received your distress call and we're responding. What is your status?"

"Captain." She acknowledged back. "We've detected three Torrak drones on our vector and closing at very high speed, approximately ten minutes from our position."

He frowned slightly, the lines around his eyes deepening. "Three?" He paused and turned to one of his subordinates who was handing him a digital Padd. Reading quickly, he turned back to her. "We do have them on sensors but we are currently too far away from you to respond with our Reapers."

Reapers were human fighter craft, designed and battle hardened during the first Stellar War against the Flexani, for use in mainly vacuum but possessing some atmospheric flight capability. Manned by a crew of two, they were the equivalent to the fighter craft of the previous century that had flown in the atmosphere of Earth. The Reapers however, were much faster and far more deadly, using as they did, a fusion of Flexani and human technologies. Their pilots were cybernetically connected with their craft through spinal taps allowing them a much faster combat response than using traditional touchscreen commands.

They simply thought, and the fighter responded.

With powerful fusion drives and a range of weapons and countermeasures, the craft had finally helped win that first war.

"Are you able to defend yourselves until we arrive or can you escape to our position by FTL? If not, we are en-route but will not be in your local vicinity for at least sixteen hours." Middleton was consulting with his staff who fed him the information he needed to impart.

"Negative Captain." She shook her head sadly, "the Intrepid Star is a Gorgon-class ship - we're simply a cargo transport vessel with no armament or defence capabilities. The bad news is our FTL drive is offline and whereas repairs are currently underway, it cannot be fixed in time. We're already at maximum thrust on the fusion engines but they could go redline at any moment... Our plan, such as it is, is to try and maintain or increase the distance between ourselves and the drones if we can." She knew this was an impossible plan given the drones speed capabilities but it was the only one they had.

"We've also tried to contact Flexani Prime on subspace, but you know how long diplomatic communication can take with them." Her exasperation was visible on her face for all to see at the futility of that approach to the situation.

"Drones will be here in eight minutes!" Harry shouted from below her.

Captain Middleton heard the cry across the comms and looked Kath'ryn in the eyes. He saw a strong woman facing a premature end to her life, but resigned to her fate. She had no illusions as to what the outcome of this encounter could bring.

Knowing that he and his ship were helpless to do anything in the coming minutes and hours that could offer her any solace.

"I'll see what I can do Captain, meanwhile I can only suggest that you hold your course and get the hell out of that system as fast as you possibly can. We will make all speed be with you in sixteen hours. Good luck Captain, Kydoimos out." With that, he signed off, leaving Kath'ryn's screen showing the digital representation of her approaching potential doom.

++++++++++

Captain Middleton turned to his First Officer and they both knew without exchanging a word that the Intrepid Star was already lost cause.

"Sir, I don't understand it, why are the Flexani so clearly in violation of the JurTan Treaty?" asked First Officer Brookes She was clearly confused, the Flexani *never* made mistakes on this level unless, of course, it was planned.

"I can only guess that they truly believe we have accepted this sector is now annexed and that our appeal does not warrant any changes to the Treaty.

Either way, this so-called Cold War has just got a hell of a lot hotter." Captain Middleton replied.

"Make sure that all Flight Wings are prepped, fully live armed and ready for launch. I want to go to Red Alert as soon as we enter the Mirral system," he ordered.

He leaned forward, his hands pressing on the long holographic display table as he studied the latest intel displaying in real-time 3D, hovering above the table surface.

Turning to his Comms Officer he added, "Get me TTF Earth Command ASAP, I need to speak to Admiral Varnava as a matter of priority. Route it to my terminal in the conference room."

With that, he turned and headed to the conference room, off the main bridge, to report on this devastating news to his superiors.

CHAPTER FOUR
Violation

"Two minutes to engagement!" shouted Harry, the emotion in his voice betraying his rising panic.

"Starboard Engine at 104 percent, Portside Engine at 103 percent, both now starting to redline and I keep getting warnings from the AI to reduce the power to 85percent unless we want to permanently cripple the ship!" came the unwelcome announcement from Brock, the pilot, as he struggled to maintain sufficient coolant flow into the overheating fusion engines.

He was feeling harsh vibrations through the ship now, as did everyone else on-board, and he was sure he could hear the old girl starting to complain about the abuse he was forcing her to endure.

Coulson's voice burst in over the open comms to join in the cacophony of noise, "Captain, I've re-routed all the coolant I can and Tim and I are trying bloody hard to squeeze every last fucking drop of power from the Star."

"Shut down any non-essential systems if you need to." Kath'ryn told him.

"I've already fucking done that!" came the insubordinate response.

Thinking fast, she yelled down to her First Mate, "Harry, jettison all cargo pods."

"What!?" Harry exclaimed, "At this velocity?"

He reeled at the thought of ditching the cargo pods and the potential damage they could cause if one struck the ship as it separated.

The Intrepid Star was carrying over three-hundred thousand metric tonnes of ore.

This was bloody suicide!

"Do it!" she demanded, all the time watching the countdown clock at the top right of her screen display. "Ditching those pods might not only help our mass ratio slightly but we may be able to disrupt the Torraks' weapon tracking systems if they have multiple targets to acquire." She explained to the shocked First Mate.

[00:01:14]

Harry frantically scrolled through lines of drop-down menu items on his touchscreen terminal for the right command protocols that would activate the explosive pivots securing the cargo pods. It was a command most First Officers had ever used outside of a training simulation, and he stumbled to find it amongst the menus and submenus presented to him.

[00:00:57]

There. Nested deep within the emergency command tree, the button highlighted as he pressed it, and more precious seconds ticked by as the twelve explosive charges on the pivots primed.

"Come on Harry, what's the hold up?" Kath'ryn queried urgently.

"I've never done this before!" he retorted, stress overtly apparent in his voice and she forgave him. She too knew this was a risky strategy.

[00:00:46]

THUD. The dull thump of twelve charges detonating simultaneously sent a wave of panic throughout the uninformed crew who, ensconced away in their Safe Zones believed that they must already under attack by the Flexani drones. For now, it was simply the charges around the cylindrical cargo pod structure underneath them detonating and causing additional noise and vibration throughout the Intrepid Star.

The six eighty-foot long triangular pods containing all of the precious Corismite ore material floated away and back from the Star as her engines drove her forward with a small gain in acceleration.

"Pods released!" Harry exclaimed with relief, punching his fist into the air.

"Redline reached on Engine One!" Brock announced to Harry and Kath'ryn, "I'll have to throttle back otherwise we'll be do more damage than the Octopoids ever would."

"Ok Brock, do it." She commanded, eyes on the clock.

[00:00:20]

Harry watched his screen with mounting dismay as the three alien drones refused the bait offered them and manoeuvred gracefully on flames of fusion past the six tumbling cargo pods, "Oh no... the drones are ignoring the cargo!"

Oh shit. Kass cursed to herself, it had been a long shot at best and it just hadn't paid off.

"OK, all of you, get your arses to a better Safe Zone! Now!" she ordered.

[00:00:18]

Time to look after herself now.

She turned towards the ladder and slid down it, hands and feet on the outside of the rungs and leapt desperately to the rear of the flight deck, and lunged for the entrance hatch.

Jung and Brock had already cleared the hatch and were running headlong down the corridor by the time she reached it.

[00:00:12]

She ran down the port side of the ship, towards the Medical Bay.

Jung and Brock had headed to the only life raft on the starboard side of the ship, but she knew there was limited room in it and Coulson would have sealed the Engineering section, selfish bastard he was. He'd not let anyone else inside if doing so would prove risky for his own sweaty skin.

[00:00:01]

...

[00:00:00]

What happened next was as clean and precise as it was brutal. The Artificial Minds in the Torrak drones had already calculated the numerous attack scenarios available to them and coldly executed the one that would cause the most damage to the alien ship, whilst husbanding their ammunition expenditure and energy output.

Safely remote from the unfolding drama, floating in his Listening Post, Gen6aC marvelled at the efficient nature of the Torraks' minds and how they had been created for this single minded and deadly task.

Though his subspace link, Arbiter Gen6aC had a ringside seat, so to speak, as he watched through the eyes of all three of the drone attack ships, augmenting his perception from the long range sensors on his own vessel, so the scene seemed to unfurl in his mind in multiple dimensions.

With the speed only capable from the cybernetic enhancements provided to him at birth, he was able to view and assess the destruction as it occurred.

He slowed the subspace feed to present him with the data in real time, and watched as the weapons fire from the three Torraks tore into the hull of the intruding ship and saw fire explode from its engines, mortally wounding it.

He slowed the subspace feed to present him with the data in real time, and watched as the weapons fire from the three Torraks tore into the hull of the intruding ship and saw fire explode from its engines, mortally wounding it.

The Terran vessel had no weapons, that much was obvious and had tried to turn and run, its engines executing maximum thrust as its own sensors had seen the approaching Torraks but it was cumbersome, slow and lacked any grace.

It had not even yet climbed out of the planet's gravity well, and was still on the leeward or unlit side.

One Torrak fired all four of its front fletchette weapons in a single torrent of fire into a side compartment of the vessel, tearing a long gash in the metal and the Arbiter saw with the sensors of the Torrak as it flew past the vessel, several human forms ejected from the breach, along with debris and containers from the interior.

He saw what he guessed was terror on the fleshy face of one of the victims as the cold vacuum of space froze its silent scream. *Ugly four-limbed creatures* he thought.

++++++++++

Kath'ryn had just reached the entrance to the Med Bay when the first of the fletchette rounds from the leading Torrak drone struck the ship and she felt as well as heard, the metal scream as if in agony as the rounds ripped through outer skin, panelling and conduits alike.

The ship creaked and groaned from the attack. The metallic rounds, fired at hyper velocity from the magnetic railguns mounted on the Torrak wings, tore holes easily in the thin outer surface of the Intrepid Star like angry wasps with the sole intention of searching out and killing those who disturbed them.

The very structural fabric of the ship was losing integrity from each round as system after system was struck in a propagating wave of destruction as the fletchettes disintegrated into smaller pieces on impact, the shrapnel then becoming a secondary weapon that caused further havoc and damage.

In the Engine room, Engineer Coulson and his mate Tim Harr cowered by the fusion drives as they felt the ship take damage around them. They heard the rattle of death upon the hull as the metallic rain struck vulnerable targets. The Torrak drones had calculated with ruthless efficiency their fire patterns on their journey towards this slaughter.

Tim curled himself into a tight ball, weeping and pissing himself as several fletchette rounds struck one of the external fusion drive exhaust ports at the aft end of the ship, the impact energy of the projectiles so high as to almost vaporise the nozzle bell, and to render the engine useless in an instant.

Coulson stood, arrogantly drinking rum from a hip flask, his only regret being that he didn't have a bigger bottle when a single fletchette round passed through a tiny seam in the hull that was not as well protected as the rest of the ship, losing practically no momentum as it did so, and effortlessly removed his head cleanly from his shoulders in an explosive mist of tissue and brain matter.

His body remained standing for a few seconds, still holding the flask to lips that were no longer present to sip from the rim, and sent a wide arc of arterial blood to coat the ceiling of the engine bay, before dropping heavily to the deck, still pumping blood until his heart slowly stopped, the blood flow trickling from his neck.

His hip flask clanged to the floor beside the decapitated body, cheap rum mixing with the red blood on the deck-plates.

Tim screamed almost as loudly as the Intrepid Star herself was screaming, as the internal atmosphere found numerous escape routes to the vacuum outside.

He kept at his screaming, staring at his colleague's body just inches away until he was hoarse, still curled up on the floor under the failing engines. As the atmosphere continued to thin, his cries of fear gradually ceased in a choking, bubbling wheeze of departing consciousness.

Kath'ryn stumbled through the doorway of the Medical Bay, the power fluctuating now and some major circuits exploded around her.

Small pieces of hot metal landed on her skin, burning it and she gasped in pain.

Her Smart Mind was beginning to become overloaded by all of her sensory inputs and was unable to repress any more of the rising levels of cortisol in her system now as she felt the end coming.

The ship suddenly lurched to one side and instinctively she knew they'd had a rapid decompression in one of the compartments. Anything not bolted down tumbled around the ship and flew toward the source of decompression causing yet more damage.

The ship was still under acceleration, but was now at the mercy of unregulated thrust from its terminally damaged engines. The now riddled hulk started to rotate around its central core as atmosphere vented uncontrollably, and the Intrepid Star's horizontal axis also became destabilised. With many systems offline the movement became unchecked and the Intrepid Star danced drunkenly in the heavens above the planet.

Kath'ryn was convinced that felt one of the engines totally lose power, but with everything happening so fast, how could she tell. It could be her imagination.

Gravity also started to shift as the ship's tumbling spin increased and the artificial gravity generators on the old ship failed to compensate.

She felt even more pressure as they span and stumbled again, thrown by the wild changes in gravity.

The Intrepid Star's AI was failing to compensate for the wild venting that was the root cause of the spinning - that much was obvious. With no pilot at the helm, the AI was the only input trying to stem this wildness and it was fast losing the battle.

Now Kath'ryn felt her ears pop and her breathing become more laboured through the loss of atmosphere and knew that the Star was dying.

++++++++++

Brock and Jung didn't stand a chance.

The fletchette rounds tore a gash in the corridor of the Intrepid Star as easily as if the supposedly tough outer hull was just a thin veil of cloth.

The hypersonic pellets of matter struck with terrific force, at over seventy-thousand miles per hour, and within an instant created a huge hole in the side of the ship large enough for almost instant atmospheric decompression of the corridor section.

Both of the bridge crew members had been racing down that very corridor towards the Safe Zone when the breach materialised in the hull and they had no chance to even register the pressure differential before both their bodies were flung into the vacuum of space.

Jung was the first of the unfortunate pair to be expelled through the hole in the side of the ship.

The First Officer experienced extreme agony in his extremities and joints as embolism took hold - the formation of bubbles in his body's fluids as their boiling point fell to below his body heat in the vacuum outside the ship.

Within moments, Harry's lungs had collapsed, releasing plumes of water vapour that turned instantly to ice crystals as he tried to scream in the sudden silence. The fluid left in his lungs also turned to ice from the extreme cold of dark space.

Fifteen seconds later, as he wildly tumbled away from the ship, Harry lost consciousness, his brain no longer receiving the oxygen it needed to keep him awake.

It was merciful that Harry was unconscious, for in the last forty seconds of his fleeting life, all the remaining water still in his system rapidly evaporated from the exposed areas of his body.

His eyes literally froze solid in their sockets, his mouth and tongue cracked and split from the loss of water and blood. Frost formed all over his exposed arms and face as the effect of almost absolute zero from the black-body radiation temperature - together with the lack of convection or conduction of body heat - caused his life to cease.

Harry then simply became another piece of debris from the cloud of matter being flung into the void from the wildly spinning carcass of the Intrepid Star.

Brock however, did fare a little better than his colleague.

A split second after Harry had been forcefully ejected from the Intrepid Star, Alain followed him out of the breach.

Providence prevailed for him though, for, as the ship's pilot, he was wearing his flight exosuit, which afforded him a level of protection the First Officer did not have. The exosuit was a basic model, with all the necessary cybernetic links to fly the ship but it also was designed to maintain his life in an emergency – it was the same as the suit the Captain also chose to wear.

Even so, Brock felt a moment of searing agony as embolism started to take effect through his exposed facial skin as he exited into vacuum in the moments before his suit could seal the emergency helmet and faceplate over his head. As soon as it had, he found himself still able to breathe and the pain receded somewhat. The exosuit therefore reprieving him, at least for now, from the death that had befallen his colleague only moments before.

As he slowly tumbled away from the ship, Alain had the unique opportunity to watch in horror as the Torrak drones fired their deadly weapons again and again at the Star until the ship split apart in a massive explosion as its fuel cells were ruptured. His faceplate barely had time to darken in response to the sudden flare to shield his eyes from the intense light from the explosion.

He watched mute and alone as large sections of the ship started to succumb to the planet's gravity well and fall toward the planet, coffins for the crew that still remained on board.

As he floated away from the scattered debris, with nothing but the sounds the pumps in his suit and his own ragged breathing to accompany him, Alain knew he was as good as already dead. Destined to either remain in orbit around the planet or to eventually join the ship's remains in a fiery plunge to the surface below.

He would never observe himself suffer that fate though, his oxygen would be depleted long before his current orbit decayed... he cursed his life choice to explore the unknown and now wished he had taken a boring job flying luxury shuttles in the Sol system after all.

++++++++++

Coughing from the acrid smoke now being drawn through the ship, Kath'ryn stumbled and crawled over medical equipment that lay scattered on the floor. Her eyes were streaming from the toxic stench of plastic materials burning even in the dropping pressure somewhere close, she could hardly see and her lungs were bursting with the effort of breathing a rapidly thinning atmosphere.

She struggled over the loose items of strewn equipment to the one and only MECS70-B Stasis Pod that was still prepped, lit and open, and just hoped and prayed, that the engineering crew at Moneta Engineering Consortium that had manufactured such a wonderful piece of technology had done their job well.

That the Pod would work under extreme situations such as this.

That the Pod would function even with a loss of power.

That one of the bloody fletchette rounds would not crack the crystalline glass and kill her.

That the Pod would survive where she unaided could not.

Deep into the emergency as she was, she couldn't stop her Smart Mind communicating a burst of data to her own, struggling biological mind.

<The Stasis Pod,> her Smart Mind told her, <is another product of the amalgam of technologies and meant that deepspace travel by FTL was possible with fragile human flesh protected from harm on long journeys.>

<First released in 2078, engineers from MEC perfected the design and functionality of the unit for use on commercial starships. By 2095, the latest bio-pod model was used extensively by most of the main starship operators for deep space incursions. Mainly used to preserve life for critically-injured or terminally-ill patients until their conditions could

be stabilised in a fully-equipped medical facility back on Earth or Mars.>

<The function of the MECS70-B Stasis Pod unit is to suspend all cellular activity and disease processes, keeping the patient from succumbing to their illnesses or injury for an indefinite period.>

<In 2092, a law was passed by the Global Federation Committee to ensure that Stasis units became standard equipment on deep space starship vessels, but was optional for short range ships within the Asteroid Belt.>

Fuck off! Kath'ryn screamed in her own mind to the Smart Mind, *I don't need bloody adverts, I need a fucking miracle!*

She was already well aware that the Pods were never meant for use in combat situations and certainly never for the reason Kath'ryn needed it for now – a life raft. A sanctuary from the destruction she saw outside.

Looking through one of the port windows she saw a Torrak drone flash past, its very shape a thing of horror with spines and almost organically grown panelling that gave it the look of a mutated alligator.

Several of her crew must have had the same idea as her, and already occupied the other Pods in the Bay, she was lucky one still was vacant and open. *Fuck, hope it isn't Pod Four I'm getting in to,* she thought, as she desperately threw herself inside the Pod and activated the control panel, near the glass door. *Coulson would be more than happy to see my frozen arse!*

It was required by any crew on a deepspace flight to study and read the specs on these Pods, and all knew they had an independent power supply capable of supporting life for several days.

<*In fact the MEC S70-B Stasis Pod typically consumed 0.9MW of power and has a fuel cell that provides up to fifty-six hours of backup power before terminal life support failure.*> her Smart Mind provided dryly.

Hopefully that should be more than enough time for the TTF Kydoimos crew to rescue us, provided the pod integrity is maintained and this part of the ship doesn't totally ripped apart by the ongoing attack. She thought desperately.

It was her only chance to live.

She hoped it was enough.

The Stasis Pod itself was a utilitarian structure formed of a large cylinder made of alloy and carbon fibre weave, and stood approximately ten feet tall. Inside this casing was housed the human occupant in a glass-panelled tube at the front, a large door sealing the occupant inside.

The rest of the bulk of the machine contained the cryoliquid tanks, medical monitoring equipment computer and a medical Smart Mind as well as the simple mechanical pumps needed for the Stasis Pod operation.

During her time in the TTF, she'd also seen the newer models in operation but all were big, bulky machines and took a lot of power from main vessel operations so she was glad Coulson deemed these earlier models 'essential' to the Ship. The one thing that bastard had done right. Now she was going to have to depend his assurances.

The Stasis Pod came to life, even, as all around her, the Intrepid Star was dying.

As the large glass door closed and sealed in front of her, she took one last breath of the rapidly vanishing air from outside the Pod, smelt the acrid stench of burnt plastics and rubber as the faint antiseptic mist invaded the chamber she stood in.

Coughing slightly, she stood and let the medical Smart Mind check her vitals even as tears formed in her eye. They were not tears caused by irritants to her eyes, they were tears of emotion.

Her life aboard the Intrepid Star had come to an end. Was her life likely to continue anywhere, or were these her last thoughts?

Cybernetic leads and connector ports snaked out of panels behind her back to connect with the specifically designed interface ports in her suit.

As had Alain Brock, she had donned the suit earlier this morning as they had left the mining colony, planning to enter one of these Pods once they had repaired and engaged the FTL drives. She was now glad for the foresight to dress in the suit earlier than she would have at any other time. Again, she had something to thank Coulson for. If he had repaired the FTL engine when he was supposed to have done, she wouldn't have bothered with the suit until just before the FTL acceleration..

Most crew tended to suit up at the last moment, just before getting into their Pods but as their Captain, she needed to support the pilot and AI until the moment the Drives engaged, so had felt it necessary because of the delay caused by Coulson's laziness, to wear the suit to save a little time.

Her vision blurred as the drugs and cold cryoliquid entered her bloodstream, slowing her body functions until they were negligible.

As she drifted, she hoped that Alain and Brock had made it to either the life raft or the Safe Zone along the starboard side, she was worried about her two young wards.

The medical Smart Mind inside the Pod would monitor and regulate her functions from now on, her own mind now separated from her body by the spinal shunt at the base of her neck, isolated and secure from damage – provided the Pod could itself survive..

Captain Kath'ryn Kass of the Raven Ore Confederated Logistics vessel, Intrepid Star lost consciousness.

Almost at the same instance, and after twenty-six years and two-hundred and eighty-four days of uncomplaining service, the Intrepid Star ceased to exist as a coherent device.

No longer capable of maintaining structural integrity, it exploded from deep within, spilling its entrails into the void.

It ripped itself apart into three main sections.

First slowly, then with ever increasing speed, these parts tumbled down the planet's gravity well, the atmospheric friction barely slowing them, but absorbing some energy as they commenced their fiery descent towards the planet surface.

++++++++++

"Drone AM1 reporting to Arbiter Gen6aC. Threat assessment now judged to be minimal. Vessel has been eliminated and is falling into atmospheric descent. Return to base or continue with destruction?"

Arbiter Gen6aC thought for a moment, reviewing the preliminary reports all three drones were sending him.

"Return to base." Arbiter Gen6aC ordered all three drones.

It was clear that the catastrophic breakup of the Terran vessel followed by the atmospheric entry and subsequent impact with the planet surface of the remains would destroy any remaining human lifeforms on board even if the explosion had not already done so. The violator was no longer any threat.

The drones complied with mechanical efficiency, each turning gracefully on jets of ionised plasma and setting course to return to their clandestine base in the distant asteroid field.

All that was left for Arbiter Gen6aC to do was to file a full report to his superiors and to once again, return to his watch over the now empty reaches of his space for any further violations of the border.

CHAPTER FIVE
Searching for a needle

"Three Flexani ships you say?"

Admiral Varnava leaned forward in his green leather Chesterfield office chair, placing one elbow on his rare antique teak desk and resting his angular chin on the back of his hand. His display screen illuminated his face, giving him a distinctly unsettling appearance, a fact he was well aware of. He checked the display was in its encrypted setting as he conversed with his Captain aboard the TTF-200869 Kydoimos warship.

Their link was via subspace tweeter - the same technology the Flexani had graced to the humans over sixty years ago and was still in operation today.

As each of the paired subspace strings sang in harmony with their counterpart, the secure connection between the two Terran Task Force officers was as near instantaneous as if they had been in the same room.

"Yes Admiral. Three Torrak attack drones are currently in what seems to be attack mode rapidly approaching a Terran civilian vessel in designated

Terran space. That must mean that a Flexani Listening Post is out there too. They obviously have a base secreted somewhere in that area in order to have been able to launch these drones. They are not known to have a vast range," Captain Middleton responded to his senior officer back on Earth.

Middleton himself had swiftly appraised the situation with his own more than capable military mind.

He'd seen combat many times and knew most Flexani strategies.

To aid him in his assessment, the AI aboard the Kydoimos was an advanced model, birthed at the Diona Shipyard facilities near the main city of Palmerston North, located in the Manawatu-Wanganui region of the North Island of New Zealand. At his request had furnished him with multiple threat analyses and decision trees to help him finalise his own conclusions, but it was down to Middleton himself to choose the most logical in order to share it now with the Admiral.

Admiral Varnava called up on his display the latest known intelligence the TTF had regarding the specifications of the drones, so as to refresh himself on their capabilities before he gave Middleton a terse order. "You are to protect that civilian ship in any way you can Captain, and you have my authority to engage and destroy those drones. Find that Listening Post, and if it's in Neutral Territory, you are to also destroy that. Are my orders clear Captain?"

"Yes sir."

"And Captain, we must keep that mining route secure regardless of what the Flexani have decided. It is imperative you do what is needed to guarantee Task Force protection to the mining operations on the planet surface, as well as safeguarding all travel to and from Earth in that shipping lane. I will issue immediate orders to have the Vanguard and the Imperial Rose rerouted to your sector and if the situation demands it, placed under your command" he said. He nodded across his desk to his aide who was standing opposite him, frantically tapping on his personal Padd, preparing the orders to be issued by the Admiral.

"Thank you Admiral. It will be of enormous help if we can bring those two warships to what looks more and more like turning into the frontline," replied Captain Middleton.

Both the TTF Vanguard and the TTF Imperial Rose were powerful vessels captained by colleagues he respected, but he knew that while he may well privileged enough to be Captain of the very latest, and most modern equipped ship in the Terran Task Force fleet, those two other vessels were much larger and much more capable of defence than his.

Even so, because they were both older and slower than the Kydoimos they would take valuable time, even at FTL, to arrive on scene.

Until then, it looked like he was going to have to defend a very long and very thin defensive line.

"I will also convene a meeting of the Admiralty Board immediately, Captain. I want you to prepare a more detailed report of the situation, as no doubt it will be seen at the highest levels by all our governments globally. My aide will be in touch. Good luck." With that, Admiral Varnava closed the encrypted link and sat back in his chair, swivelling to look out of his office window to the seascape beyond.

His aide remained silent, knowing from his years of working for the Admiral, when to speak, and when not.

Varnava stared out of the window for a few more moments, watching the waves rolling into the shore.

The weather outside was becoming very unsettled, promising a storm later, a good analogy for the stellar storm that was brewing, many parsecs away.

He spoke quietly, never taking his eyes away from the ocean, "Matthias, get me the SECDEF's offices on the line will you?"

"Yes Sir". Matthias stepped out of the office, leaving the Admiral alone with his thoughts and walked back to his own, more utilitarian desk.

He felt a chill down his back, knowing of the Admiral's actions during the first Stellar War, many years previously.

A highly decorated Veteran of the Vesuvian and Jovian battles, Admiral Varnava – who was then merely Captain Varnava, of the TTF Interceptor – understood only too well how tenacious and ferocious the Flexani would be in battle. If this present crisis near Mirral meant another war between the two interstellar races, then this crisis could lead to the end of one race's existence. Matthias feared it could be their own.

++++++++++

Captain Middleton left his private quarters and as he walked back onto the bridge of the Kydoimos, he pondered the readiness of his ship and crew.

The Kydoimos was the very latest warship in the Fleet. It was a more modern design than the older Legatus-class destroyers which had been the state of the art vessels prior to Kydoimos. Named after the Greek character representing the personification of the din of battle, confusion, uproar and hubbub, she was an Imperator-class ship, the newest design of vessel to leave the TTF construction hub in Earth's orbit. She featured the latest human advances in weapon technology and engine design making her more effective and certainly faster than her forerunners.

At four hundred and twenty metres in length from bow to stern, the Kydoimos had six decks, packed with equipment and a crew complement of around three hundred and eighty personnel, including twenty-four bridge officers and twenty-two Reaper pilots. She was protected by the latest in hull technology and possessed advanced medical facilities, including the new MEC S70-Hx Stasis Pods.

Externally the Kydoimos was sleek and purposeful. Even though not designed for atmospheric operations, she still looked streamlined, with two 'wings' containing crew quarters and weapons batteries, and a smaller ventral fin on her forward underside. Four NovaCorp DX5 Sublight Drives for deep space FTL travel propelled the ship through space, their power coming from four independent nuclear hearts located deep inside the main superstructure, and each one was a hundred times more powerful than the reactor on the poor Intrepid Star.

The warship was also equipped with eight short-range Reaper attack fighters and four shuttles for missions to planetary surfaces and for ship to ship transfers. Not as many as the Vanguard nor the Imperial Rose it was to be admitted, but considered enough to deal with any threats to the vessel.

The Kydoimos' multi-layer hulls, like most other Terran warships, were very thick, manufactured from carbon-bonded laminated metals, carbon nano-fibres, and self-sealing smart plastics materials amalgamated in them to seal hull breaches. The super tough material gave sustainability and survivability in a battle scenario, enough to make up for the limited shield technology. While all fleet ships used some form of energy shielding, it was still very rudimentary when compared to Flexani vessels which was believed to utilise magnetic disruption harmonics that was able to slow plasma and solid projectiles before their collision with the hull. That was a technology the Flexani had been very careful not to share in the past. This meant that the push to advance the effectiveness of physical shielding had been prioritised.

The Kydoimos' weapons though, now they were a very different story altogether.

Since the first war with the Flexani, all efforts had been applied to advancing weapon design technologies, and many weapons system manufacturers on Earth and Mars were now profiting from the advances that they had made in the advanced weapon designs now installed on board the Kydoimos.

Powered by individual compact fission nuclear reactors, two large magnetic railguns mounted amidships, one on each side, fired small pellets of pressurised carbon at thirty-five thousand metres per second – achieving around Mach one-hundred during tests in vacuum performed at sea level on Earth. This gave a few hundred grams of matter incredible penetrative capability. Railguns were designed to be highly effective against the more advanced Flexani shield technology and earlier versions had served the fleet well in the first war. It had proved to be a good balance between simplicity and reliability when ranged against more cutting edge designs. Kydoimos also boasted ten smaller railguns mounted to hardpoints on the underside of the vessel.

The biggest advancement in weaponry since the first Flexani war though, was unique to this class of vessel. This was the installation of focused Plasma Beam emitters mounted on the two main wings of the ship, and the lower ventral wing. Each emitter was capable of firing directed energy beams of 1.21GW at their targets over a significant distance and still slice through the hardest alloys with ease. With just a thirty-five-degree arc firing range in both the horizontal and vertical axis they weren't the most versatile weapons on board, but packed an enormous punch when deployed. They also had the advantage of causing energy shielding to become disrupted and when used in combination with the projectile weapons were extremely effective. Middleton hoped to use them soon against the Flexani, he was sick of firing at asteroids. Yes, he thought, the ship is more than ready. The crew though – we will see.

As Middleton headed towards the group of officers clustered around the helm as they waited in anticipation of his orders, he was addressed by the ship's AI.

<Captain Middleton, my sensors are detecting that the Intrepid Star - designation ROCL-XM-78KL – has undergone a catastrophic loss of integrity and I am detecting significant localised debris in the vicinity of its last reported position.>

"The drones?" he said to the room, for the AI was everywhere.

<Currently on a return vector to an asteroid field orbiting the third planet in the system.> came the instant reply.

<I have detected fragments of the Intrepid Star on a decaying orbit towards planet XT-67-F - appellated Heimdallr – and I determine they will intersect with the surface in four minutes and 30 seconds. The re-entry angle is too oblique to confirm whether the vessel will survive the atmospheric re-entry and survival rate for any crew remaining onboard the fragments is less than five-point-six percent.>

Fragments. Middleton thought. *Shit.*

He felt sorrow for the woman he spoken too on his screen less than fifteen minutes ago knowing in all certainty that she was either already dead or soon would be.

"What is known about this planet?" he asked the AI.

<Captain, for your information Heimdallr is Old Norse for World-Brightener. It is an L-Class planet, similar in mass and diameter to Earth, rich in mid-range minerals and with an atmosphere relatively high in CO_2, and. The planet is inhabited by many forms of life including an intelligent species called the Dall. According to TTF records, this alien sub-species is not considered to be very advanced, and it would appear that they have not yet achieved flight of any kind. However, from the limited contact there has been between their race and humans it is concluded they are extremely hostile, very little more is known about their race.>

"The Dall... I think I've heard of them. Insectoids correct?" he enquired, remembering some limited reports on this species he'd read last year as he'd prepared for his mission to this sector.

<Correct Captain. From the little information that is recorded about this species, it is believed they have three main categories, or Castes – Warrior,

Drone and a Leader type. No data is recorded about the latter, on the statement of their existence. They are known to form small tribes or clans and form strong bonds with their clan mates. They are ritualistic in nature, much like the ancient indigenous Earth races in the Amazon basin on Earth. We have some records of metal working, advanced manual skills and construction of dwellings but none indicating advanced technologies. They also have agriculture and trade of sorts.> The AI finished the limited report.

"Thank you" Middleton said. "But that is not going to help the crew of the Star unfortunately, even if they survive crash landing on the planet. Most likely they've all been killed in the attack anyway. We have new orders from Admiral Varnava. Record these in the Ship's Log please AI." He transferred the new orders from his own personal data Padd to the main ship's database.

<Confirmed and logged.>

"Our orders Captain?" came the query from his First Officer who strode over to join him, a questioning look on her face.

"Prepare and lockdown the ship for battle Brooke. Our orders are to find those Flexani drones that have just destroyed the freighter. We are then to search out any Flexani bases or Listening Posts in Terran space and to eliminate them." He responded. At the same time, he was mentally considering the strategies and calculating the resources that would be needed to destroy the three known drones as well as any other resistance in the local sector.

"The good news is that we'll have fleet support in the form of the Vanguard and the Imperial Rose within a few hours to assist in the search. I want you to consider our orders and to prepare a briefing for all senior staff in the conference room in fifteen. Understood?"

She nodded, understanding the urgency. "Of course Captain."

"What do we do about the Intrepid Star sir?" she added gently. She had heard the AI's report on the fate of the Star and the description of the Dall and knew this was going to have a large bearing any mission to recover the wreckage – if there was any.

Middleton thought for a moment then said with more authority than he currently felt, "Have Flight Leader Boakai prepare an S&R, ensure adequate medical teams are on the shuttle to search for survivors, you never know – but, I only want them out for eight hours before they are to return. We can't afford to have them attacked as well. Share the AI's intel on the Dall and make sure Flight Leader Boakai keeps an eye out for any of their presence when they land."

S&R – Search and Rescue, the standard practice for any rescue mission was to fly in a specialised search pattern within the designated zone of space and by monitoring the advance sensor nets on the shuttles. Even debris as small as a VR headset floating in space could be detected.

On the surface of a planet though, the sensors were not as accurate, mainly due to atmospheric scatter, so surface searches were limited to flybys using radar and lidar, with drones deployed to investigate potential finds.

"Something about this just doesn't feel right though Brooke," mused Middleton, "why send two more warships into an already sensitive zone and risk further provoking the Flexani?"

"We do have more than sufficient manpower to conduct a scan of the sector and carry out any search and rescue operation on our own, that much is true Captain. I am also confident that we can deal with those drones and any Flexani listening posts as well" she said in response to his comment.

"Ok then, let's brief the teams and discuss this later in my ready room. It's bugging me that I just don't feel comfortable about these orders, and I'm not sure why."

++++++++++

Arbiter Gen6aC floated in his private sphere onboard the Sentinel Post ship and let his mind wander where it would. It decided to cogitate his current surroundings.

His Sentinel, or Listening, Post ship was secreted on the surface of a barren moon, a world void of ocean, orbiting far from the systems' sun. The vessel was positioned well away from prying eyes under the shadow of a crater wall. From the safety of the ship, he could observe and study the neighbouring systems using its passive sensor net with very low risk of detection.

The vessel was an oasis of Flexani homeworld comforts in an otherwise desert environment. Like all Flexani, the Arbiter enjoyed liquid around his limbs and in his lung, but he felt completely at home in this artificial environment.

He had been rewarded well so far in his life, earning him the right to be granted the title Arbiter through his demonstration of skills and successes in the hotly contested Competition of Skills held every full yearly cycle of Flexani Prime. That cycle equated to five-hundred and twenty Terran days, and so each competition was eagerly awaited and treated with great ceremony. His competition success had brought him financial rewards as well. He was now in a position to own his own personal exosuit, built to his own requirements, rather than having to use the rather more utilitarian suits he had been forced to wear during his earlier service.

It was only when he exited his Post that he had to wear an exosuit. For now, he simply used his own limbs to drift around the chamber.

Many different versions of the exosuits were available, each custom made for the wearer and environment in which it was expected to operate.

Each Flexani exosuit design was equipped with adaptable ports and was modularised to facilitate upgrading. The exosuit connected directly into the spinal node at the back of the user's skull to facilitate seamless cybernetic integration with his own internal nervous system.

Whole industries were involved in exosuit design and manufacture all over Flexani Prime and on other worlds where Flexani influence had been established. These industrial societies and states - formed over centuries - had created more and more elaborate and fascinating suit permutations.

The Arbiter had his favourite creator of course, each Flexani with the means to pay for bespoke manufacture did, but often style had to be sacrificed for function and exosuits sometimes had to conform to a common standard.

There were typically many different types of exosuit configurations available, from those designed to operate on high gravity worlds to, at the other extreme, gossamer material suits for mating purposes.

The Flexani did not bond for life, choosing instead to copulate simply in order to generate the complex mix of genetic materials before transferring them to the maceration chambers for embryonic implantation in the hatchling egg sacks.

This was the civilised method and it had been done this way for centuries, each Caste of the Flexani controlling their own maceration chamber to keep their line pure.

The Arbiter had been disgusted to read the reports of casteless Terran sexual behaviour. Video feed and sensor data had been shared among Flexani of various interactions between male and female Terrans, and it shocked many on Flexani Prime.

'Breed True to your Caste' was the common saying among the Arbiter's species.

At the beginning of their encounter with humans the Flexani had shared their exosuit technology, in exchange for medical technology (one of the few areas in which humans had almost as much knowledge as themselves), oceanographic data and some species of native fish that the Flexani found delicious, so it had been a bitter pill for the Council of JurTan to swallow when they were betrayed by the humans.

For it had been Flexani skills and knowledge that had aided the Terrans in creating their own battlesuits and cybernetic enhancements. Ironically that knowledge had helped the humans to oust the Flexani from the Sol system, with the loss of the Great Eye.

Gen6aC knew all these facts in detail since it had been taught to him from when he was a hatchling. He had learnt all about the Great War with the Terrans and about their betrayal.

His inner timer pinged, letting him know his duty cycle was due to start, and Gen6aC gathered his thoughts. He rotated to face the exit of his personal chamber, reluctantly silencing the music of Paetron GenRx9, one of Flexani Prime's most famous musicians and singers. Her melodies usually managed to calm him after a long cycle, but now it seemed he was not going to enjoy the calming affect her music afforded him after all.

He floated down the main corridor towards the sensor chamber.

He was joined by one of his minions, a small race of aquatic animals looking very much like the stoat of Earth, its fine sleek fur allowing it to travel efficiently underwater.

Through Flexani genetic manipulation, the species no longer needed to breathe gaseous oxygen in the traditional way, having been genetically modified to develop gills in order to extract oxygen from the liquid passing over them - so they no longer had any use for lungs.

Larger than the stoat they resembled, at around a metre long, the Vorrax were excellent attendees to the Flexani, and kept their personal spaces clean.

This one was his personal valet, and was by his side most of the time he was not relaxing.

Speaking through a small subspace tweeter embedded in its brain, the Vorrax spoke to its master "My Lord Arbiter, I have been informed that the drones have returned to the asteroid belt without damage and with minimal use of assets. However, preliminary report scans do show that the alien vessel was not fully destroyed upon re-entry to the planet as was forecast."

The Vorrax floated below his master in a subservient pose, averting his eyes and curling its tail between its rear legs in a sign of dishonour at reporting this bad news to Gen6aC.

"Not destroyed?" Gen6aC responded angrily at this news.

"No my Lord, not fully. Large pieces of the vessel have crash-landed on the southern continent across one of the more rugged mountainous regions and are still recognisable."

Arbiter Gen6aC immediately accessed the datafile from the ship's onboard system and reviewed it in his mind as he and the Vorrax continued towards the main sensor chamber.

"Mighty Hixx!" he exclaimed with irritation after seeing that the sensor image transmitted from orbit around the planet, did clearly show a large debris field on the mountainside.

His ire grew as he saw in the image, several large structures of the Terran ship remaining intact and relatively undamaged upon the surface.

Settling himself into his control position and accepting the connector port into his own interface, he joined the advanced systems and became one with the sensor net.

His vision expanded beyond worlds as the network of hidden subspace satellites conveyed their multitude of images to his consciousness.

There he experienced a comprehensive view from orbit as if he were floating in space above the wreckage site on the planet Heimdallr.

His virtual vision penetrated through the clouds and plummeted down to view the crashed vessel in greater detail.

Arbiter Gen6aC saw the elements of the alien ship strewn across the rocky surface, smashed open like so many Surlak eggs.

However, three main sections of the vessel still remained identifiable, although the front section had clearly melted, having been the section that had borne the brunt of the heat from atmospheric re-entry and was a misshapen hulk, glowing in the pale light.

Despite high levels of carbon dioxide, fires were alight everywhere – presumably from the fuel cells and other combustibles, producing thick smoke which was clouding his scan.

He switched to other frequency bands – from UV to Infrared – all in order to try and establish if any of the Terrans had survived the fall from space.

There were many heat sources however and with no clear visibility he could not ascertain the existence or otherwise of crash survivors from the scans, even with the advanced Flexani technology at his disposal.

One thing was abundantly clear though. The report he'd filed to the Servient Gen7cD only five frecs ago was wrong.

This is not good he worried as he paused to consider his options.

If any of the Terran vessel crew were subsequently found alive, then Gen6aC would be stripped of his rank and most likely reduced in status at the next Caste meeting. He could not afford this dishonour, it was imperative all the Terrans had been eliminated. There was only one choice of action he must take to be completely sure.

"Vorrax, prepare the shuttle. I have to travel to this planet to ascertan for myself whether any Terrans survived the crash."

"By your orders my Lord." The Vorrax swam off.

Gen6aC fretted, knowing he was about to take an extreme risk. The Sentinel Post had also detected subspace wave fronts from deep within Terran space - clearly indicating another vessel was coming toward this sector.

Quite possibly a rescue or punitive mission.

The Arbiter was going to have to put himself in a perilous situation, but he needed answers. He must safeguard his position.

He could always launch the drones again in his defence if he needed them, he considered, so that would mitigate the risk - probably.

If it proved necessary, he would eliminate any alien survivors on the planet himself. That way, his report would remain accurate and he would avoid any reduction in his Caste status.

Gen6aC opted for a little caution though, not being one for rash decisions, and ordered the Vorrax to ensure his own battle exosuit was loaded on his shuttle for the mission – just in case.

If he had to go down to the planet, he wanted to be protected as much as possible.

Within quarter of a frec, the Arbiter's shuttle had launched and was accelerating away from the protection of the hidden Sentinel Post vessel, out into space and following a complex course to ensure it could not be traced back to the frozen regolith of a small moon above the sixth planet in the system.

CHAPTER SIX
Broken & Bereft

The first sensation was of pain.

The second was of more pain.

Fuck.

That fucking hurts.

Shit, I'm alive, Kath'ryn thought as she struggled to gain a sense of her body through the haze of pain clouding her consciousness.

She lay at a slight angle with her face pressed against the cold glass door of the Stasis Pod, and she felt bruised all over. Kath'ryn struggled to open her eyes as the last vestiges of soporific left her system and she knew that something was terribly wrong with the Stasis Pod.

Her Smart Mind interjected her thoughts with a clear statement of fact <*Kath'ryn, it would appear that the Stasis Pod's power unit has failed. Body functions have been restored to normality.*>

Normality.

Fuck that.

She felt anything but normal right now.

<I detect a fractured rib on your left side and an atmospheric leak in the Stasis Pod, through which outside atmosphere is entering the Pod environment. It is not toxic, however oxygen levels are very low and the external temperature is currently at 4 degrees Celsius.>

She took a deep breath and felt the rib stab her with pain. *Damn, that hurt.*

"Can you suppress the pain for now?" she asked the Smart Mind.

<I will comply.>

Within moments, she felt the pain subside but knew that her relief would not last for long. By now her vision had improved somewhat, so she looked out of the glass and observed the scene of horror around her.

The Pod itself lay just outside a section of the Intrepid Star's infrastructure, most likely the Medical Section, although there was very little left of it to identify with any degree of certainty.

She saw four more Pods scattered around her immediate vicinity but thick clouds of smoke plumed in the air and obscured her vision. There was little natural light illuminating the scene, only that filtering through all the smoke, coming from an indistinct faintly glowing sun. The lights of the fires surrounding her Pod gave her enough hellish light to see by though.

The Intrepid Star lay broken. Dead. With its charred bones scattered across this seemingly barren and mountainous place. That she would never fly again Kass knew with absolute certainly.

Reaching over, she touched the control panel interface and thankfully, the glass door slid shakily open, power to achieve that much still left in the Pod's batteries thankfully.

Shit! That's cold.

Bitterly cold, harsh air blasted her, the wind was blowing embers and smoke into her face as she exited the Pod, jumping down and holding her rib in pain as the SM inside her failed to control the pain suppression levels quickly enough.

She had to see if there were any other survivors.

Carefully skirting around some of the larger fires, she moved towards the nearest of the other Stasis Pods.

It lay on its side some seven metres distant, and as she scrambled slowly and painfully over the rocky terrain, she tried to consider her options.

A body lay inside the Pod.

Well, what remained of a body anyway. The Pod itself had obviously been ripped apart after being ejected upon impact from the crashing ship and had tumbled over and over before coming to rest here.

It was hard to tell if the body was that of a male or female due to the extensive damage to the upper torso, but when Kath'ryn saw the tell-tale ring on the left hand, she knew it could only have been the ship's physician, Doctor Teodoro Pizzino.

She bowed her head in loss and grief over the Pod that was now his coffin. She had always liked the senior medical man and his debates about politics over dinner in the mess had always been knowledgeable and entertaining.

After what seemed like an eternity, Kath'ryn managed to collect her emotions and move on.

Cruelly, the next two Pods were the same - destroyed along with the bodies inside.

A waste of human life she had tried so hard to save.

Fate had decreed that only Kath'ryn would cheat death for now it seemed.

For just how long for in this cold, dark and desolate place she didn't know, her only hope for continued survival lay with the TFF Kydoimos arriving soon.

To maintain her sanity, that was the only thing she must focus on.

She continued to pick her way through the wreckage, collecting a few items that had survived the descent and may have some use in easing her plight. She needed to find shelter above all though, to get out of the biting wind, to keep warm. As she cast around trying to find shelter away from the devastation, she heard the noise.

A horn?

She cocked her head into the wind to try and listen, but the blustery wind was not going to give up its secrets that easily.

But, there it was again. Definitely a horn.

But the question was, what was blowing it?

Would they be friendly? That could be the bigger question.

She frantically looked around the immediate landscape for a place to hide. There! She saw a small rocky outcrop and glimpsed an opening.

A cave?

She came to a decision.

Running across the ground as fast as her fractured rib would allow, and panting from the thin air she sucked into her lungs, she heard the clatter of what sounded like animal hooves on the ground coming from over the adjacent ridge.

Kath'ryn spurred herself to run faster and slipped on the loose shale around the entrance to the small dark opening in the side of the mountain and fell headlong.

Cursing and suppressing a cry, she rolled, slipped and tumbled down a slope into the cave, the darkness within enveloping her like a shroud.

She lay as quietly as she could, panting from the exertion and low oxygen level, keeping as still as she could in the darkness, straining her ears to hear the noises outside. Her side was burning in agony and salty tears were blurring her vision.

There were the snorts of what had to be beasts of some sort and the sound of what could be the jingle of metal harnesses – riders and their mounts then.

And voices – well, voices of a sort.

Clicks and low-pitched whistles and squeaks of several different tones came from outside her hiding place.

She could not discern how many creatures there may be, and did not want to risk climbing back up the bank she had just slid down in order to alleviate her curiosity, but she was sure there were at least four distinct voices she could distinguish, maybe more.

Kath'ryn was unaware of any sentient race anywhere in this system but then, her knowledge was woefully inadequate. She wished she'd reviewed the datafiles on this system a just little more thoroughly before leaving ROCL HQ.

She lay back against the frozen rocky ground and listened to the alien shouts, clicks and noises as the mysterious unseen figures tore apart what remained of her ship for trinkets.

Should she reveal herself to them, and trust them to be friendly?

She heard a sudden surge in their piping chatter and she surmised they must have discovered the bodies of her dead colleagues. The sounds of what was obviously a fight broke out, of that much she was certain.

A fight over what, she feared to know.

Her tears flowed freely as she wrapped her arms around her cold body and tried to stop her teeth from chattering.

She lay there for what seemed like hours until she heard the chattering noises fall silent and the clatter of hooves once again.

Kath'ryn listened as the riders left the scene of disaster.

She remained motionless until she felt it safe to move again, her limbs now very stiff from the cold that had seeped through her suit.

Pulling herself awkwardly to her feet, she clambered back up the slope, and stumbled awkwardly out of the entrance to the cave. She stood and surveyed the scene below. The sun was now much lower in the sky and the cold was really biting into the exposed skin of her face.

The flames from the wreck had died down now, and were merely smouldering embers.

However, from her vantage point, she could see evidence that the mysterious figures had indeed searched the wreckage and near one of the broken Pods, in a gruesome diorama, one of the bodies of her colleagues had been disembowelled and strewn across the ground like carrion for the vultures.

She felt sick to the stomach, vomit burning the back of her throat.

+++++++++

"Turn around slowly, Terran" came an obviously artificially generated voice from behind her.

She twisted around to face a large metallic object – a Flexani exosuit.

Oh God, no! She thought in abject terror, her Smart Mind failing to to respond quickly enough to repress the levels of fear flooding her biological system.

The dark metallic exosuit was shimmering slightly in the pale sunlight. It stood on four powerful cybernetic legs, with another four pseudo limbs holding an array of weapons, all pointed at her. A single green glowing eye watched her balefully as the Flexani slowly advanced towards her.

"I have been looking for you, Terran. I do not like loose ends." It said venomously, raising one of the weapons.

"Wait!" she screamed.

She needed time.

Time for the Kydoimos.

Time to be heard.

Just time to live.

"Why should I wait, Terran? You violate our Flexani space and flout the new annex rules as per the Treaty. You are therefore now my prisoner of war and as such, I am within my rights to dispose of you."

Flexani rules regarding the treatment of prisoners was very much different from those of humans, and the Flexani had been shocked that humans still incarcerated their criminals. On Flexani worlds, all criminals were stripped of their tech and then destroyed, so to cleanse the race of bad genetic material that might taint the bloodlines. A criminal's genetic offspring could be terminated if their crime was sufficient to warrant it.

"Wait, please. We tried to explain that the changes you made to the Treaty needed review. So far as we were aware, we have not transgressed your space at all! We are innocent victims of your Flexani terrorism!"

"No, you do not obey the Treaty. You will be executed and my status will remain unchanged within my Caste."

With that, he aimed his weapons and Kath'ryn closed her eyes.

The ground exploded and she was thrown backwards.

As she landed on the rocks her head exploded in stars from the blow. *Aghh!*

As her senses returned, she struggled to clear her vision, shaking her head. A movement in her peripheral vision combined with instinct and her Smart Mind drove her to throw herself to one side as a lethal spear tip nearly pieced her throat.

Shit! What the...? That was close!

Above her, with the pale sun glowing behind its head was an insectoid figure. It had a blunt triangular-shaped head with six eyes - black and emotionless. It was really an odd looking creature. Kath'ryn's first impression was of a super-sized praying mantis. This creature however had two sets of eyes, three on each side of what Kath'ryn assumed was its nasal cavity. A mouth filled with small razor-like teeth showed her a vision of future horrors.

Standing around seven feet tall, it had a bulky carapace and what seemed to be very tough muscle sinews visible on his exposed body, and apart from a small belt and thong covering what she assumed was its genitalia, the beast did not seem to be worried by the cold atmosphere.

What the fuck was it!?

She saw the Flexani also lying on the ground about ten metres away, a still-smoking crater between them. The Flexani was struggling. It seemed he had been restrained by some bonds of rope-like strands, and was clearly unable to move. Three of these insectoids held the strands around the Flexani who also seemed to have been stunned by the blast.

Obviously, she reasoned, what she and the Flexani had not been aware of was that the creatures she had heard scavenging the wreckage earlier had not left the area but returned on foot.

Unknown to Kath'ryn, these creatures were known as the Dall, the insectoid race indigenous to this planet. The creatures had first fled from, and then watched the Flexani's ship fly down to review the wreckage.

The four warrior caste Dalls had in fact watched Kath'ryn crawl back out of the hole like a grub and had then had observed the encounter unfolding between her and the Flexani.

The leader of the Dall warriors had then lobbed one of their precious Gorsac grenades at the two aliens, its powerful explosive created from the volatile minerals around Homecave and the crushed juices of the Lillan worms. Contained in a clay shell, the mixture itself was not activated until encountering a third agent in the centre of the grenade. As the grenade struck the ground between Kath'ryn and the Flexani, a small pellet of vossimite crystal was broken on impact. The three components of the grenade then reacted together violently with explosive force.

The beast looming above Kath'ryn spoke in the strange clicking language and bent down, still holding the razor thin spear against her throat.

He grabbed her by the arm and pulled her up sharply. She cried out in pain from her fractured rib as he forced her to stand. The creature turned toward the other beasts, saying something which made them react with what she assumed was laughter.

The blow came fast and she was totally unprepared. The Dall's other fist, still holding the spear, smashed into her face with force and she blacked out.

Gen6Ac on the other hand still remained conscious, but his exosuit systems were malfunctioning. The explosion had contained such concussive force that it had knocked him from his feet.

The battle exosuit had, of course, not been damaged from the blast. It had been designed to withstand far greater ordinance than that of the Dall grenade so he was uninjured and was still safely sealed inside the suit. However, the suit's Smart Mind link with his own was not functioning well and the suit systems were trying to reboot using their default settings.

Arbiter Gen6aC thrashed and screamed in futility as he watched his exosuit being trussed like an Orfin pup and hitched to one of the lumbering mounts to be dragged along behind it.

Curse the Hixx!

<Reboot sequence corrupt. Bypassing...>

"Activate subspace link to the Torrak. I order all drones to converge on my location for the urgent recovery of a Flexani citizen in distress."

<Subspace link to shuttle currently offline. Damage detected. Estimated two frecs to repair Arbiter.>

Holy Hixx, two frecs until he could contact help.

This mission was not going well.

Not well at all.

Gen6aC could do no more as he observed the other Dall warriors throw the limp body of the Terran over one of the mounts back and then climb up onto it himself.

His translation matrix was one suit system that remained undamaged and so he was able to hear and understand every word the Dall exchanged with each other on the journey back to the Dall camp.

Anxiety gripped the Arbiter.

++++++++++

The warship TTF Kydoimos translated back into real-space with a ripple of warped space-time, her stern-mounted NovaCorp sublight drives slowly reining in their power so that the vessel slipped through the membrane of subspace and back into normal space, like a dolphin breaching the surface of the sea.

<Warp field now at full standby status.> The Kydoimos' AI said, <Translation to the Mirral sector has been confirmed, we are within thirty-six

minutes of the planet Heimdallr designation XT-67-F..>

Captain Middleton stood from his chair on the main bridge and watched his efficient crew working around him. Brooke, his second in command, stood attentively nearby, talking to one of the junior bridge crew.

"Captain to Flight Leader Boakai," he said, speaking directly into his wrist comms - a sub-function of the ship's AI which instantaneously directed his voice to the Flight Leader.

"Yes Captain, Boakai here," came the immediate response. Boakai was obviously keyed up and ready to go.

Good man, Middleton thought.

Born and raised in the Ewe region of Ghana on earth, Afryea Boakai had been recruited into the South African TTF training academy after graduating from his university with honours. He had excelled in strategy and aerial combat techniques, especially in space combat sims. After Captain Middleton had seen his scores and credentials, he had pulled a few strings – and called in a few favours – to have the man lead his flight crew. He had not regretted his decision to this day.

Boakai was now in command of the Kydoimos' entire complement of twenty-two Reaper and Shuttle pilots.

"Are you prepared and ready for the Intrepid Star S&R Flight Leader? We've just exited subspace and will be entering the reported location of the attack within the next half-an-hour."

"Yes we are Captain. All shuttles and crew are ready. We intend taking two shuttles with one Reaper for protection, along with a small medical contingent in case there are any lucky enough to have survived the crash."

"We have received updated telemetry from the AI and the latest scans from the Sensor Teams, so we know this will be a surface based S&R."

FL Boakai again was proving himself a very competent officer and he had prepared his team well for the task awaiting them.

He also understood the futility of the 'rescue' part of the mission but he had his orders and would follow them until they had positive confirmation of the demise of all the Intrepid Star's crew.

"We are able to launch in ten sir." He stated matter-of-factly.

"Excellent. I want regular updates every thirty minutes during this mission Boakai."

"Understood Captain."

"If you do find any survivors, let's get them home safely and quickly Flight Leader."

"Of course sir, we'll certainly do our best." With that, Boakai signed off and, sighing to himself in the certain knowledge that all they would be bringing back would be body bags, if anything, left his quarters, heading for the Kydoimos main hanger bay.

Ten minutes later, after their pre-flight checks, two shuttles accompanied by a single Reaper left the main hanger bay and set a parabolic course toward the planet.

Preliminary scans submitted by the Sensor Teams on-board the Kydoimos had clearly shown wreckage which could only be what was left of the Intrepid Star, scattered across a mountainous three by three kilometre area of the planet surface - creating a possible search zone of nearly ten square kilometres to be covered.

Boakai had prepared an optimal search pattern, spiralling out from the perceived centre of the main crash site. He was piloting Shuttle One – called

Starburst – and would land at the centre of the site and deploy the medical team.

The remaining Shuttle piloted by Lieutenant Jerris would stay in the air and follow the defined search pattern to look for possible survivors in other sections of the downed transport vessel.

The Reaper piloted by Lieutenant Hawkes and his co-pilot Frick would fly a protective net over the two shuttles should the Flexani drones come looking.

That left seven Reapers with their crew remaining on the Kydoimos to protect the warship.

Within twenty minutes of leaving the Kydoimos, all three vessels had slowed to safely enter Heimdallr's atmosphere and, descending to around twenty thousand feet above the surface, cruised on a vector to the crash site location shown on their scanners.

Boakai and Jerris initiated a gentle descent toward the site. He ordered the activation of radar, FLIR and other sensors on both of the shuttles to begin the search for metallic debris that would indicate unseen pieces of the destroyed ship.

"Negative on tracker scans Flight Leader," one of the officers working the sensor net said from the depths of the shuttle behind Boakai.

Tracker scans had been initiated as a matter of course, since crews of transport vessels had PDTs or Persona Data Transmitters about their person most of the time, but it seemed that either no one from the Intrepid Star had them, or more likely all PDTs had been destroyed, along with their owners. It had been a longshot but was standard procedure when on a search and rescue mission.

"Coming in on approach vector, buckle up for landing." Boakai said to his shuttle occupants as he slowed their descent.

On small pillars of flame, the shuttle Starburst hovered gently over a patch of stony ground, several hundred metres away from the wreck and descended slowly until the landing struts took the weight of the shuttle and she settled to the rocky floor.

Close by, the second shuttle landed, stirring up a brief flurry of dust that quickly dissipated in the chill wind that blew across the scene.

"Commander, atmosphere is thin and cold so I'm recommended helmets are closed for the mission," came the call from the Chief Medical officer.

"Understood. Ok, let's do this."

Boakai's fingers played across his console as he shut the shuttle engines down and activated the controls to lower the main hatch at the rear of the shuttle, allowing the medical team and crew to troop shivering down the ramp to the planet surface to join their equally chilled colleagues from the second shuttle.

Each of the three ship's officers carried short-range but highly sensitive scanners that could pinpoint the electrical activity from lifeforms within a few hundred metre radius. The medical team did not carry these scanners, but did have the necessary medical equipment boxes with them for emergency treatments.

As the team left the shuttle and began to fan out around it, they started to scan the area for signs of life.

"Nothing here, moving off in a westerly direction," said one.

"Same here, negative on the scan. Moving north," stated another, moving behind the bulk of the main piece of wreckage.

Boakai's scan too came up negative. He started to head toward the east, towards one of the Stasis Pods he'd seen visually from the cockpit during the shuttle's descent. Something had piqued his curiosity - something not quite right about it and he wanted to investigate.

As Boakai approached the Pod, the first thing that he noticed was that the door was open and the chamber inside was empty. However, what had caught his eye from the shuttle was that the control panel inside the pod was still active, lights glowing gently in the dusk.

Someone had survived the fall and exited this Pod he thought, as he scanned around seeing if he could pick up any sign of life.

Negative. *Damn it. Where the hell were they?* He asked himself.

"Sir!" There came a sudden shout from one of the medical team searching to his left, about forty metres away standing beside another of the Stasis Pods, this one lying on its side.

Boakai headed towards her, moving cautiously over the rocks and debris scattering the ground.

As he came closer, he saw she was kneeling down next to what appeared to be a mess of macerated meat and blood. She was probing the body with one of her pieces of equipment.

"What have you found?" he said, not really wanting to know.

"I believe this was one of the Star's crew sir, but - this body has been tampered with."

"What? Tampered with? What do you mean?" His curiosity was piqued.

"Well sir, the victim was most obviously killed during the crash - the Stasis Pod was ripped clear of the main ship's structure, but it hadn't been able to sustain their life as they re-entered the atmosphere, that much is clear. I would guess the Pod itself failed, but……. it appears that someone, or something has hauled the body out from the Stasis Pod sometime later and then… well… eviscerated it." She looked up in confusion at him though her faceplate.

"I'm sorry. What?!" he exclaimed.

"Here sir," she said pointing to the remains of the torso, "the body has been forcefully ripped open post-mortem, and the inner organs exposed and well, torn away - quite violently too sir."

Opening his comms to all of the team he ordered "Heads up all personnel! All teams back to the shuttles! I want dust-off in five, we have dangerous native life or hostiles in the vicinity!"

Grabbing the medic's arm to pull her up, he looked around the ridgeline frantically searching for any signs of movement.

This was unfriendly ground and he needed to have backup before continuing with this mission.

Boakai had a strange sense they were being watched. He'd have to conduct this S&R from the air, it was far too risky to have unarmed crewmembers on the surface without any protection from whatever had performed this, this barbaric act.

He switched his comms to the ship to ship channel, and called "Reaper One, come in. Hawkes, we need an immediate aerial sweep of the area, potential hostiles on the ground". "Roger Flight" came the response. "I am currently overflying your position now, but cannot detect any movement or technology in use in your current vicinity. Keeping watch."

"Thank you Reaper One, please escort both shuttles back to Kydoimos."

Minutes later, the shuttle left the surface of the planet for the safety of the airless void. No pursuit followed them as Boakai reported back the disturbing find to the Kydoimos Captain.

++++++++++

Alain Brock was going to die.

He was certain of that fact.

For the past few hours his body had drifted, weightless in the vacuum of space, the insidious cold seeping into his suit even as it tried in vain to heat him using its dwindling energy reserves.

He didn't know whether it was going to be the cold that would kill him, or though or whether it would be because of the reason his oxygen level alarm had just started to sound.

In the few seconds before his suit had sealed to protect him from the effects of rapid decompression, he had been exposed momentarily to the vacuum of space. His body had felt the initial symptoms of embolism - as micro-bubbles formed in his bloodstream - so he was in racking pain from the bubbles trapped in his joints.

His lungs in particular felt ragged and torn, ice crystals formed as his lungs had started to freeze had obviously severely damaged the lung tissue and he struggled as his chest flamed in pain with each breath.

<Ten percent oxygen reserves remaining and falling.> His suit computer reported.

Damn.

Trying to suppress the shivers that invaded his body from the low temperature, he glanced at his wrist monitor and saw that his CO_2 count was very high - nearly eighty-nine percent - and that meant his suit re-breather must not be processing the levels of CO_2 as effectively as it should.

Alain adjusted his breathing to make each chest expansion a little shallower but knew he was only delaying the inevitable.

He would start to suffer from either hypoxia or hypercapnia and would certainly be dead within the next twenty minutes or less.

Brock and his fellow candidates at the pilot academy had undertaken classes and even a practical exercise - under safe conditions - to study and experience exactly what happened to the human body in the event of oxygen deprivation. They had learnt that asphyxia or asphyxiation is a condition resulting from a severely deficient supply of oxygen to the body. A situation that could certainly occur in space.

Well, that bloody well defines my current situation, Alain thought bitterly.

Asphyxia causes generalised hypoxia, which affects primarily the tissues and organs and he knew that this would be his fate as the build-up of toxic carbon dioxide would slowly poison him.

Oh great, he thought, *now I remember all these details!*

He'd most likely experience hypercapnia - commonly known as CO_2 retention - as the abnormally elevated levels of carbon dioxide currently entering his bloodstream from the closed system that was his flight suit, increased to toxic levels.

Since the suit's basic re-breather systems were already failing to process the levels of CO_2 he was expelling by replacing it with the oxygen needed to survive, he knew he would start to feel the main symptoms soon.

These symptoms he knew from his classes would include flushed skin, racing pulse, muscle twitches with shaking hands unable to perform effectively any task he wanted to undertake, and more importantly, reduced brain activity. He already was experiencing some of the lesser effects including the onset of a headache.

Next would come levels of disorientation as his brain was starved of oxygen.

Finally, asphyxia combined with the effects of hypercapnia would cause his body to shut down.

All these lessons he had learnt well, *and a lot of bloody good just knowing exactly how painfully I'm going to die* were his present thoughts.

Alain knew these would be his final moments and he tried to suppress the anxiety and fear coursing through him. He turned his mind away from those classroom lessons and instead thought fondly of his parents and his two baby sisters whom he'd never see again.

He started to cry gently in his suit, tears welling in his eyes and floating like spheres inside his helmet. His suit, having failed to keep him alive, would now serve to preserve his dead body a coffin his body would be entombed in for the rest of eternity, drifting forever on stellar winds.

"Oxygen reserves now at 2.5% and dropping," the computer dispassionately stated, "CO^2 levels now at 93%. Please seek medical attention immediately."

He laughed bitterly at that statement, curling into a pain racked ball and hugging himself tightly.

There was no way to turning off these warnings so it would his fate to have to listen to a running commentary of his last moment, counting down his life, until he passed from this plane of existence.

He drifted in this way until eventually he lost all consciousness.

Hearing the warnings no longer.

CHAPTER SEVEN
Clandestine Plans

Admiral Varnava and the Secretary for Defence, Joshua Stormont, shook hands firmly, before sitting down in a matching pair of the informal and comfortable chairs in the SecDef's Washington office. The Admiral had boarded the first shuttle to the Capitol as soon as his call with Middleton had ended.

The SECDEF's office was decorated in typical Washington decor, with original walnut panelling and a large picture window overlooking the back of the White House.

It had beautiful ornate crenellations around the high ceilings that secretly carried a wealth of hidden anti-bugging equipment and sensors to protect the SECDEF from prying eyes and ears.

The picture window was actually toughened plexi nano-glass, capable of withstanding high impact ballistic rounds. Invisibly woven into the fabric of the glass was privacy screen technology to prevent microphones and spying technology from picking up conversations held inside the room.

Embedded within the very fabric of the office, a private Smart Mind watched silently over the SECDEF and his guest.

Joshua Stormont was a fifty-six-year-old veteran of the Flexani Wars, like the Admiral. He had risen in the political arena soon after the War's end, working tirelessly toward his avowed aim to ensure that Earth would be safe from future interstellar invaders.

Now, as the new Secretary of Defence, he held a lot of power across the globe.

At the time, the war with the Flexani had been a hard-won struggle for mankind, but since those turbulent decades many plans had been drawn up and put in place. Large resources across the globe - in all of Earth's militaries – were now dedicated to defending the human race.

It was perhaps ironic that the most lasting legacy of the War was that now, at last, mankind had come together and united in a single goal with collaboration and resources being assigned to the newly formed Terran Task Force, beholden to no one country.

The Secretary of Defence for the Terran Task Force was also a senior member of the Global Federation

Committee, whose core responsibility was overseeing the strategic plans for the future advancement of mankind into the stars, as well as governance around defence.

"Welcome José, it is good to see you again. How is Rose, your lovely wife?" Ever the statesman, Stormont was sympathetic to his subordinates, especially those he had fought alongside in the Great War.

"She is forever telling me to retire Joshua. She keeps telling me she has found a lovely house in Montana for us to retire to." replied Varnava smiling.

Chuckling, the SECDEF commented, "Well I'm sure she will be able to find things to keep you busy."

"Yes Joshua, I'm sure she will, although she'll look hard to find me when I disappear to go fishing eh?"

"So," hastened Stormont, "I understand that the Flexani have not taken to our Treaty rejection well. From your dispatch, it would seem that we have a dispute to face in the Mirral sector."

"Yes, they have carried out an unprovoked attack with three of their Torrak drone craft on a small transport vessel and have destroyed it with what seems to be the loss of all on board." Varnava reported.

"Hmmm, so, what have you done about it?" Stormont enquired.

"Well, I've dispatched the Kydoimos to find the Flexani Listening Post and I have ordered her to destroy both it and the drones. Kydoimos will be joined by the Imperial Rose and the Vanguard soon so we will have a substantial heavy force in the area within a couple of days."

"Good. Now, is the Captain of the Kydoimos aware of the plan?"

"No," said Varnava, shaking his head, "our good Captain Middleton and his crew know nothing other than the orders they have been given."

"Good, I need for Project Valkyrie to be kept 'Eyes Only, Top Secret' until we have no other choice than to reveal it." The SECDEF was vehement in his demand, his eyes ablaze.

Clandestine research into the backgrounds and beliefs of all of the Captains within the Admiralty that could possibly have been assigned to Project Valkyrie had been carried out in the months before now.

Once candidates likely to be compliant had been identified, a team of analysts within the SECDEF's own offices had run further covert searches into their intimate personal lives.

An AI had then created a detailed psychometric profile for each candidate.

Middleton was one of the Captains that had failed the test - he score too highly in the morality stakes to be considered for any active role in the implementation of Project Valkyrie.

He was a perfectly good Captain, but it was considered that he would not be prepared to take orders that were questionable at this stage, so he had been quietly left out of the project, unaware he was had even been considered.

"Don't worry, Middleton will remain in blissful ignorance until we need him to know." said the Admiral in return he said with a sneer.

"Have both the Rose and the Vanguard now been retro-fitted with the new Valkyrie weapon technology?"

"Both have, yes. They each spent around three weeks in dry-dock at the Phobos orbital military base. Each of the vessels have been modified to accommodate the dedicated power systems and the new hardware for the weapon hardpoints. It was a simple process to remove some of the older railguns and to replace them with the new hardware. To all intents and purposes, to the unknowing observer – and we have ensured there weren't any - both vessels have just been off line for routine maintenance and no one who has no need to know will be any the wiser. Both vessels have completed the weapon trials – well out of range of any sensors on Earth obviously. The tests went exceedingly well I am pleased to report. I was onboard the Rose when both ships undertook the tests, so I can personally confirm that we have a new and effective firepower to use against the Flexani - should we need it of course." he said slyly.

"Good, I can't afford for my fellow council members to know anything about this - just yet. I want these secret weapons to remain just that for as long as possible José, do you understand? The Flexani can't know that we have this type of ordnance in our arsenal."

"Completely. Each of the Captains has strict orders to keep comms silence and to censor any crew chatter. Only on my authorisation or that of your office will the weapon be deployed and used. Likewise, the development base on Mars is also under lock down for the time being. I have a visit planned in the next few hours to check on Project Black Snow, no one will be permitted in or out of the complex after I depart."

"Good. Well if you have nothing else to share I'll get back to my next committee. The defence of Earth doesn't uphold itself you know." He said grinning as he rose to his feet, shaking the Admiral's hand once more before moving towards the door. "I hope you enjoy the fishing." he smiled as he left the room.

++++++++++

Kath'ryn awoke with a jolt.

It took her several moments to acclimatise to her location.

It was dark, but a small amount of flickering light near a roof showed that she was in some form of dry cave, made of dirt or plaster with some stones embedded in the walls. There was a large rock blocking what was probably a doorway, almost certainly too heavy for her to move, especially in her injured state.

She attempted to stand, and quickly became aware that her hands and feet were bound. Not only that - she was not alone.

The Flexani, or at least its exosuit was lying on its side, encased in ropes like hers, its pseudo limbs also bound.

Shit. She thought. *I'm not in Kansas anymore.*

She jumped when the Flexani spoke to her through its suit comms.

"Terran, you remain alive?"

Surprised at the question she replied simply "Yes."

"Good, then I can kill you later and my status will remain clean."

"What, you fucking Octopoid!" she shouted at the alien laying trussed up just a few feet away. "In case you haven't noticed you bastard, you're not actually in any position to do anything right now are you?" Her tone was icy and cold.

Her Smart Mind started to send reports on her body's status to her conscious mind, apparently her fractured rib was still hurting but she was otherwise alright.

"That may be true Terran, but when I am rescued by my Torraks in less than two frecs then I will delight in seeing your corpse upon my blade."

What the fuck is a frec? She wondered.

"Kath'ryn Kass, my name is Kass you Octopoid."

"Kass. Well Kass of Terra, I am Arbiter Gen6aC of the House of NorHan, Watcher of the Outer Rim and also your executioner."

"You are completely fucking mad!?" she swore at him, "If you're the bastard who attacked a non-military vessel with no provocation, under the terms of the Treaty of JurTan I rather think that you're the one who needs executing, not me."

"Your words are meaningless Kass of Terra. The Treaty annex submitted in the latest update was correctly ratified with the Council of JurTan many cycles ago and it was confirmed that the Terran Committee had failed to place sufficient argument on the latest annex to have it amended. You therefore despoiled our space and thus, you will forfeit your life." A slight smugness came in his voice through the speaker.

"Listen, Gen6 or whatever you fucking call yourself, your precious Council of JurTan deliberately failed to respond to our argument, you fucking idiot! We weren't the ones who broke the agreement."

Arbiter Gen6aC faltered for a moment. Surely this Terran female was not right? The Council never made mistakes and most certainly not on this scale.

"No, you are misinformed Kass of Terran," he said, "The Flexani Council of JurTan does not refuse to discuss any amendments under review as per the Treaty. We are an honourable race."

"Well I think you need to ask some hard questions of your bosses Gen6. I was flying a civilian crew and a cargo of raw ore away from the planet quite legitimately when your fucking Torraks made the unprovoked attack on us and destroyed my ship and killed my crew. That is a gross act of war in my mind." She spat the words out, hating the alien for the loss of her crew - the grief of losing so many good and kind people - with one noticeable exception - to this single wanton attack was just too much for her. She started crying again, sobbing into the dusty ground.

"Kass of Terran." Gen6aC directed a question to her once again. "What is the nature of this sound you make?"

"I'm crying you bastard!" she said between sobs.

"Why?"

Laughing mirthlessly between her tears she said simply "I don't want to die."

Before the Arbiter had any chance to respond, there was the sound of scrabbling and the large stone in the doorway rolled to one side. Three insectoid figures filed into the chamber. Two dressed as what Kath'ryn surmised were warriors carrying lethal looking spears and one altogether smaller, lither figure, holding what appeared to be a totem stick, adorned with semi-precious stones and the skulls of small animals.

Kath'ryn scrabbled with her bound legs, pushing herself up against the wall in an ineffectual attempt to escape the alien beasts, but one of the warriors swiftly strode over and grabbed her leg firmly in its hand.

"Aggh!" she screamed, the Dall's hand pinching her flesh, hard claw-like nails digging into her skin through her boot.

"Do not panic Kass of Terran." said the Arbiter calmly from his position on the ground.

Kath'ryn was beyond calm now however. The attack, the crash of her ship, the loss of her colleagues, the threat of death from the Flexani and now these weird alien insects wanting God knows what pushed her over a mental edge and she screamed, thrashing to get away.

Just what happened next wasn't at all clear to Kath'ryn in her panicked state, but the insectoid warrior gripping her leg suddenly crashed to the floor, its arm severed at the elbow, the hand still gripping her boot.

She stopped screaming then and became aware that the Flexani was free from its bonds with its exosuit in full attack mode and the three insectoids were all lying dead on the floor.

Gen6aC turned to her and she cowered back, closing her eyes so as not to see the death that was about to enshroud her.

"Take my limb Kass of Terra."

She opened her eyes in shock to see that not only had the Flexani stowed his weapons, he was releasing her from her bonds. The Arbiter held out one of his psuedo arms for her.

"I don't... what...?"

"Take it, we do not have much time. I hear many more Dall coming."

She looked at him incredulously before taking his proffered arm.

"Climb onto my back," he said, "you will be able to safely sit there."

She did as he ordered, despite the pins and needles in her hands and feet as circulation was restored and the stabbing pain in her side. She noted that the Flexani's suit had already adapted to form a small seat with hand and foot holds for her to grasp. She swung herself painfully into the seat – and not a moment too soon, for the Flexani launched itself into a full speed sprint, through the door opening and into a dimly lit tunnel beyond.

He engaged his weapons once more and began firing at a band of approaching Dalls.

Behind her, Kath'ryn felt the seat form a hard panel that shaped itself to protect her back.

The next few minutes passed her by in a blur of motion, noise and confusion as the Flexani raced through tunnels and chambers, obliterating the insectoids as they launched themselves at the fleeing prisoners.

His fletchette guns spat hypersonic death – each round that encountered a Dall simply shattered its body into blood and gore before passing almost unchecked through several more warriors until its kinetic energy finally spent itself against the tunnel wall.

The Dall were legion. They came swarming as a vast horde from all around, pouring out of tunnels and openings in an attempt to halt the fleeing fugitive pair. As the Arbiter raced up pathways towards the exit of their hive, many loosed spears and arrows at him and Kath'ryn, his passenger.

While most of their weapons just bounced ineffectively off his tough exosuit, some of their primitive spears actually did find purchase.

The hardened alloy tips those few spears possessed had been fashioned from an alloy of metals mined from a distant volcano and the Dall prized these spears above all others with only a few of the Warrior Elite carrying them. The metal itself was valued for its ability to slice through rock itself without wear. It was unfortunate for the Flexani Arbiter that it was several of these unique spears that struck home, piercing the outer surface of his exosuit.

Finally, after many long minutes of running battle with the Dall, Arbiter Gen6aC saw light from the exit of the hive brightening the rock corridor.

His internal Smart Mind was sending him multiple damage reports and he could feel precious fluid from his safe compartment inside the exosuit leaking away. He didn't have long before he'd be breathing void.

He himself was physically exhausted, even with the battlesuits' cybernetically enhanced power. Carrying the Terran on his back during battle was costing him too much of his precious energy reserves and he was confused as to why he had chosen to rescue her.

Maybe she is right about the Treaty, he considered, *is that why I had saved her life?* It may be a decision that would cost him his own.

"Arbiter?" he heard her ask from behind, curious as to why he had stopped.

"Yes Kass of Terra... I need to pause for a mi-frec. My systems are...damaged, but still functional. I ...am losing fluid from my inner chamber."

"Can I do anything? We must get away from this area just in case more of these disgusting insects come."

"Fear not, my scans indicate that... I have removed the immediate threat and no other Dall are within the vicinity for... several gals." He had linked via subspace to his observation satellite in orbit high above and had scanned the area as soon as he had exited. They were safe for the moment.

"Err.... Well that's ok then."

"You can however, get off my back now." He said.

"Oh, yeah sorry." said Kath'ryn. *Had this squiddie just made a joke?* She questioned herself.

Kath'ryn eased herself off the back of battlesuit and walked around to face him.

"Thank you for saving my life" she said. Then she saw the extent of the damage the Flexani had received, and rushed over to look closer at a spear, still protruding from his main torso.

Fluid was leaking profusely from around the broken spear shaft, the run through the tunnels must have severely exacerbated the entry wound, causing more damage.

"Hold on, I'm going to remove this," she said, gripping the spear's shaft and bracing her other hand against his armour.

"No! Kass of Terra, do not...remove the spear!" he shouted but it was too late, she had wrenched the spear free.

Warm fluid spurted from the hole, splashing onto the ground and immediately the Arbiter's AI informed him of the increased leak. He could actually feel the level of fluid reducing in the chamber around his headsac and panic crept into him.

"What have you done Terran!" he shouted at her, turning one of his weapons on her as he tried to see what she was doing.

She was killing him!

"Give me a second you fucking stupid Octopoid." she said, as she grappled with a canister on her belt.

All the crewmen on the Intrepid Star had had a small canister on their belts, just like this one. It held a sealant under pressure for closing small hull and suit breaches and Kath'ryn now applied the canister nozzle to the rent in Gen6aC's armour and pressed the button to release the sealant.

Within seconds the liquid sealant had hardened over the breach and immediately Gen6aC's AI notified him that the fluid leak had been staunched.

He dropped the weapon aimed at her head and stood surprised.

"You have performed an honourable act, Kass of Terra. I am ...in your debt." He bowed slightly at her.

"You are welcome Mister Arbiter. Maybe now you won't feel quite so inclined to execute me?" she cocked her head and smiled cheekily.

++++++++++

Captain Middleton and Flight Leader Boakai stood in the main hanger bay on the Kydoimos, discussing the aborted S&R mission.

Unusually, Middleton had made his way down here to speak personally with the Flight Leader, rather than summoning him to his ready room.

"This is concerning information Boakai, you were right to abort of course."

"I know sir, we just didn't have the manpower to hand to afford the medical team sufficient protection whilst the rest of us found and recovered bodies. We had no idea about what we might be up against. The only good news is that we did manage to complete our initial scans and I can confidently report that all but three of the Intrepid Star's crew can be accounted for."

Handing over a small data Padd to the Captain, Boakai continued, "As you can see sir, we scanned the full debris field from the air and while we saw no hostiles, we did get indications however that someone, or something, had been in the vicinity of the wreck within the past few hours."

"And the missing three crewmen. Do you know who their identities?"

"It's in the preliminary report sir, but I'm not at all sure all three might be missing after all."

"Explain what you mean, Flight Leader." The Captain was confused by his Flight Leader's statement.

"Well sir, the three crew we cannot account for at this time are Captain Kass, First Mate Jung and the pilot, Alain Brock. Since they may have been located in the front of ship - presumably at the helm as she crashed - we can presume that all were vaporised upon re-entry, or possibly ejected out into vacuum as the bridge shields failed. However, there is one thing that disturbs me about accepting that scenario. I discovered that one of the Stasis Pods had actually survived the crash and was still active

– its power cells were virtually exhausted though – but the cylinder was open. I only had a quick glance at the pod computer, so I can't be a hundred percent certain, but it would appear that someone was occupying it during the crash and may have survived."

"Hell. Even if it's only an outside chance that one of the crew is still alive, we need to get to them and bring them back here." Middleton stroked his chin a moment before making a decision.

"OK, I give you full authority to mount a second S&R, this time with a full complement of armed officers in each shuttle. Take three shuttles back to the surface this time and be watchful for these 'Dall'" he ordered. "Make sure you get everyone back – whether they are dead or alive. Understood?"

"Perfectly sir. We will be prepped to depart within fifteen minutes."

CHAPTER EIGHT
Black Snow

Admiral Varnava, and his aide Matthias, stood side by side in the elevator as they descended deep into the bowels of Mars. Neither spoke.

They had chartered a private shuttle for the journey from Earth to Mars, hiring it under the cover of a shell corporation so to avoid a traceable digital trail and were even now, dressed in civilian clothing to avoid drawing unnecessary attention to their presence.

The shuttle had landed about an hour earlier, the Admiral and his aide taking the public hyperloop transport across the Sisyphi Planum basin, part of the Sisyphi Montes mountain range. At around two hundred kilometres in diameter, the basin was a prime location for many of the industrial operations on Mars, utilising materials mined on site to manufacture many of the components for the starships and warships of the Terran Federation alongside the more mundane manufacturing for the freighters and passenger yachts for the merchant services.

Mingling with workers and support staff employed by these industrial corporations the two men had headed unremarked into a nondescript building, one of many anonymous, standard factory units located in this location.

This was one of the main reasons the Admiral had chosen this site for his clandestine military researches.

It was secure, private and quiet.

Somewhere that Project Valkyrie and other top secret projects could be developed, away from prying eyes – those of the Flexani and especially those amongst his political and military rivals on Earth.

The lift silently came to rest and its door slid open. Varnava and his aide exited the lift and walked past men operating bulky machinery and turned towards a plain nondescript doorway, similar to several others at the rear of the factory. Entering a code in a secure panel to the side, they quickly exited the factory floor and headed into a room that had just a few basic features including a simple plastic table on which sat a coffee machine that held a half-pot of stale coffee.

Still in silence, both headed over to another single elevator door. Pausing to key in yet another code on the elevator keypad and to ave his biometric signature taken from his fingers, Varnava waited until a second later when he was granted a green light. Pressing the single button to summon the elevator, he and his aide waited until the door slid open silently for them to enter.

They had been knowingly observed throughout this whole process by hidden eyes - both human and digital. One slip or any suspicion of subterfuge from either of them and lethal force would have been applied, not only to prevent them from proceeding on their journey but to completely eradicate their existence. For no one without the very highest authority could ever enter this part of the building.

Despite the bland and innocent outer appearance of the factory, this location housed one of the most secure buildings used by the Task Force. It was not listed however on any military manifest, database or record, and only those in the very top levels of power had access to its interior.

In essence, this building did not exist.

Almost each and every person in the clandestine building was combat trained and part of a very select group that the Admiral had personally recruited after enormous effort had been expended on exhaustive personal and background checks.

Of the men and women machine operators they had passed on their way through the outer factory, around 10 percent were not really factory workers performing inane tasks, but in reality trained military professionals equipped with concealed weaponry. The remaining ninety percent were employed simply to produce finished goods in order to maintain the facilities façade of being a simple manufacturing plant.

It was several minutes before the elevator reached its destination and its doors re-opened to reveal a corridor hewn from the planetary bedrock. Two men wearing the latest battlesuits barred the Admiral's passage as they turned their stubby weapons on the two men as they exited the elevator.

There was a moment's pause before the guards, listening to a hidden AI voice, lowered their guns, saluted briskly and allowed the two men to pass safely by.

During the elevator's descent deep into the Martian surface, inconspicuous, but intensive, scans of both of the men had been performed by hidden scanning equipment built into the elevator's walls. These scans were capable of detecting - down to the microscopic level - any modifications to the men's physical state as compared to recorded reference scans, as well as checking for weapons, explosives or other tech that could compromise the hidden base. If one of the scans had detected anything untoward, the elevator would have halted in its descent immediately and lethal action would have been taken — any occupant within that lift would be subjected to an intense radiation burst designed to kill within seconds. Controlled by a dedicated AI, it was totally independent of the core systems in the building and very clinical in its work. There was no room for error in its decision-making processes.

This then, was the Admiral's Black Ops base - known simply as The Nest.

Past the scans and the guards, Admiral Varnava nodded wordlessly to his aide as headed off down a separate corridor towards his new project, code named Black Snow.

Many projects had been developed here at the Nest by scientists and engineers he had secreted away over the past three years. They were given an almost unlimited budget, whatever resources they demanded with the sole purpose of developing and creating weapons and equipment that could give humans the upper hand should they one day ever enter a war again with the Flexani. That day was now rapidly approaching.

The project, Black Snow, was the latest brainchild of an elite amongst elite team of men and women whose sole task was to consider worst case scenarios.

Admiral Varnava headed towards one of the science bays and entered confidently, each of the scientists around their desks looked up from their work, startled by his unannounced entrance.

"I need to speak to Doctor Kluska now. Where is she?" He demanded of the room.

A large woman appeared from one of the side rooms and started to walk towards him. She was wearing the standard medical jacket, but wore smart civilian clothes underneath.

She possessed short blond hair, slightly greying at the temples and hinting at her maturity. Her eyes were hard, she was obviously someone who had known personal pain but did not let it affect her personal and professional life.

Iranian born, Doctor Amita Kluska had worked in various government think tanks after graduation and then her degrees in robotics and artificial intelligence had led to several lucrative posts working for a few of the larger military defence contractors across the globe. After studying for her doctorate, she had been head hunted by the Admiral a few years previously. Her expertise in cybernetic systems and Artificial Intelligence were highly prized by her employers. Unfortunately for her though, her latest project goal was proving elusive in the extreme, and had generated failure after failure. Failure was something the Admiral despised and didn't tolerate for long.

Amita Kluska was one of the doctors tasked with creating a Smart Mind within a human subject's brain over three years ago. She was the same doctor that had been responsible for the experimental operation on Kath'ryn Kass, although Kath'ryn had never met the Doctor herself - only the kindly nurse and a few other anonymous doctors as part of the follow-up session. The work she had done in those early stages with Kath'ryn and the other 'volunteers' had led on to this new project, and her current incarceration in The Nest, deep within the bowels of Mars.

"Ah, my good doctor, I trust you are well?" the Admiral said with far less warmth than his words implied as they met together in the centre of the room. The remainder of the scientists turned back to their own work - but each was keeping one ear on the conversation. Gossip was a rare commodity within The Nest.

"I am sir, thank you for asking," she replied, thinking hard about how she was going to put a positive spin on the latest set of negative results.

"And, what of the project?" he asked, his face impassive, looking into her hazel eyes as she tried to avoid his intense stare. The Admiral was not a man to be trifled with.

"Errr...." She hesitated a little before continuing. "Well the nanite configuration for batch 17A has been confirmed as viable for the purpose of the trials. We've done several tests now on the actual nanites and their assembly processes code and can confirm that they will be expedient for the next phase in the project."

Varnava frowned slightly, recognising the hesitance in her voice. He asked, "So, how long before you have prepared sufficient nanites? You were made aware we need a vast quantity of nanites for the next phase of the project, weren't you?"

Known to the SecDef and a very select few people in the upper echelons of the Terran Task Force,

Operation Black Snow was a bold plan. It comprised a series of smaller projects, each one critical to the main project's success. Doctor Kluska's team was a key component of the overall goal. The overall task was to create and develop a type of bio-weapon, capable of infiltrating any Flexani exosuit and then the epidermis of the alien itself. The weapon would commence spreading throughout the alien's body and would mutate and destroy cells as it did so, killing the creature from within. The delivery methods and stealth technology capable of avoiding detection had to be made to work as did the ability of the delivery payload to work intelligently so as to adapt to circumvent any defence the Flexani might have at cellular level.

Unfortunately for the Doctor and her team inside The Nest, they had what was turning out to be the most complex part to the project to undertake. Its slow progress was the reason why she was facing the scrutiny of the Admiral right now.

She had single-handedly devised and produced a small batch of hyper-stimulated helical nanite components with complex molecular-based neuroprocessors, far faster than the current technical standards. Her team were desperately trying to perfect the practical working models. The morphology of these new model nanites should be more than capable of infiltrating themselves undetected into the Flexani's physiology, penetrating fibrillary material. Then, once inside the host, they would use predefined and dynamic algorithms to adapt themselves to mimic the environment, chameleon-like, within the alien's bloodstream.

The nanites would then proceed onto the second stage of the strategy, using the host's own biomatter to replicate sufficient quantities of themselves until there were sufficient numbers of them to proceed with the final, deadly part of their programming.

That, at least, was the theory - the Doctor had had very limited results with the final phase of this plan.

The deadly third phase called for the nanites - once they had reproduced themselves in sufficient quantities needed for critical mass - to begin a concert of death, converting any surrounding protein and biomatter into a resinous, fast-mutating 'crust' that looked superficially like black snow. This crystallisation process and conversion of flesh to a tetravalent metalloid substance would cause acute agony to the Flexani host whilst interrupting any and all bio-neural transmissions to their Smart Minds and within hours, end all lifesigns.

In truth, Doctor Kluska and her team had achieved very poor results with this last part of the plan but she did not dare let the Admiral to know this bad bit of news.

"We began mass production of nanite batch 17A yesterday Admiral. We should, no will, have sufficient volume within ... aaah – I estimate twenty-six days." she volunteered.

Pursing his lips and furrowing his already creased brow, he asked, "And did you repeat the trials on batch 17A to confirm that it was capable of penetrating Flexani exosuits?"

"Yes Admiral, we did. We ran several trial on the test subjects you supplied and batch 17A is by far the most effective batch so far against their internal biological defence systems. Not one of the test subjects was aware of the violation."

Doctor Kluska had initially been perturbed by these trials on live Flexani subjects either still held from the first Flexani war - the older specimens - or presumably kidnapped somehow by the Admiral and his team. It surely went against the Treaty of JurTan and the general handling of prisoners of war, even given the fact that at this time, she was sure they weren't yet at war with the Flexani again.

It seemed though that the Admiral had been given special dispensation from the very highest levels of authority to conduct the experiments. She had initially railed at the idea of, what to her seemed like vivisection but she had eventually been 'convinced' that it was for a greater good. Convinced, it has to be said, by coercion and certain veiled threats regarding her family.

She and her small team had worked day and night for the past year trying to perfect a batch of nanites capable of attacking the Flexani physiology. They had faced many almost insurmountable challenges and had worked through each set-back methodically and relentlessly towards the final goal of Batch 17A. At each stage, the doctor and her team had tested the latest experimental batch on the live Flexani prisoners, reviewing their results and considering new paths to take should they encounter dead ends. It was the only way to be certain of eventual success.

Amita herself had not slept the first time one of the prisoners had died on her operating table in the most excruciating way. She had been violently sickened by the result. The Admiral had been delighted at the gruesome result though, demanding her team pursue their work with renewed vigour.

Now though, she had become hardened to the cruelty and accepted it as an unavoidable consequence of the work they did.

She was surprised however, at how many Flexani prisoners the Admiral kept supplying and she secretly wondered just how many Flexani had been captured in the war. Maybe she was being naïve but deep down she wanted to believe this was the only way the Admiral was getting the test subjects.

"Excellent, the nanites must be ready for weapon deployment within the next month, so I can ill afford any more delays Doctor. Do you understand?" He said, pointing a finger at her.

"Of course Admiral, my team are working all hours to ensure that batch 17A will be ready."

"What about your progress on the final stage of the weapon. We need those nanites to perform as required for Black Snow to be one hundred percent effective."

The doctor dreaded the question, but knew she had to tell the Admiral the truth.

As her eyes lowered to the floor she mumbled, "Limited effectiveness so far I'm afraid Admiral."

She steeled herself for the retort.

Glancing up she saw the anger and violence on his face and recoiled slightly, taking a step back.

"My good doctor," he snarled through clenched teeth, as he stepped forward into her personal space, "I think you fail to grasp the extreme gravity of the situation, so let me make it very, very clear to you once and for all. In one month's time missiles will be launched with the payload on board and you WILL ensure that the nanites perform their function as specified. I think we can both agree that if you need further test subjects..." he said looking her in the eye, "... then you may well find yourself strapped to a table instead of one of the aliens. I will NOT tolerate failure and nor will the executive offices funding your little experiment, so Black Snow will be ready. I will be back in one week's time to re-assess your progress and I want daily reports from you in the meantime. You will NOT rest until you and your team have done as I have ordered."

He held her gaze for a few moments and in that brief period, Amita Kluska felt her pact with this devil had sealed her fate.

"Oh... yes, of course. Of course Admiral." She stuttered, her mouth dry.

"Good. There will be no more excuses." He spat.

"No. I will get onto it now Admiral," she almost whimpered, wishing hard to see the back of him.

"See that you do."

The Admiral took one last look around the room, seeing the other members of the science team trying hard not to appear to be listening into the conversation, all of them glad that it was Amita and not them facing his wrath.

He stood for a moment, took one last disdainful look at the doctor and walked out of the door, back to the main elevator out of the complex.

As his aide, Matthias, re-joined him in the corridor outside, and as they waited for the elevator to arrive at their floor, he spoke briefly to him. "That fucking woman! I want her eliminated as soon as she successfully delivers me Black Snow. She has been an inefficient thorn in my side for far too long and I can't afford to have her derail the plan."

"Doctor Kluska?"

"Yes, the bloody doctor. Who else? Listen Matthias, I want extra security put on her research files and vmail account. I want to know every word she types or says."

"Of course sir." Matthias nodded as the elevator door opened and they stepped inside.

"On another matter, how is project Red Horse proceeding?" he enquired, his rage subsiding slightly as he turned his attention to the other aspect of Black Snow.

"Very well indeed Admiral - the stealth missiles are almost ready. All of the sensor-masking technology has been tested against what we know of Flexani sensors and we are confident that the missiles will be completely safe from detection."

This aspect of the project was known as Red Horse - named for one of the four Horsemen of the Apocalypse - was the ultimate method by which the Admiral believed he would win the inevitable war. The missiles were now equipped with the capability of shifting into and out of subspace at random intervals, as well as other novel countermeasures. By equipping the missiles with a suitably destructive payload he was confident they had more than a good chance of defeating any method of defence the Flexani might have - should war come.

"We need to test this system Mathias" he mused, "we just need a suitable target. You know, I'm sure one will present itself soon…"

CHAPTER NINE

The right to survive

Kath'ryn stumbled again for the third time in less than an hour and cursed under her breath.

She grimaced in pain. Her strength was failing her as she and the Flexani Arbiter, Gen6aC, headed towards his hidden shuttle, on the run from the Dall warriors.

The planet's surface was rocky and almost devoid of vegetation and as they both clambered over the interminable rocks toward their goal. Kath'ryn was almost totally exhausted – she had eaten her last meal almost ten hours previously during breakfast on the Star with her crew, seemingly in another lifetime. She felt extreme thirst, the air was thin and dry on this planet and every so often, gusts of wind blew fine grit and dust into her face.

What with the disaster that had befallen the Intrepid Star, the subsequent crash-landing on this god-forsaken planet, a painful fractured rib, her capture by the insectoid Dalls - and now their attempt at escape - Kath'ryn was nearing the end of her limits.

Each movement she made sent needles of torment down her side, and she limped with each step.

Likewise, the Flexani - despite being in his exosuit - was not working at his optimal specification because of the damage sustained from the strange spear-like weapons the Dall had wielded.

Both of them were covered in a fine layer of the wind-blown dust.

Almost every breath Kath'ryn took of the thin atmosphere and dust sent her into a paroxysm of uncontrolled coughing, exacerbating her injury even more.

"Can we take a break a moment?" She coughed this request to Gen6aC as she collapsed on a large rock without waiting for his response. As she paused for breath, she noted a small hardy plant growing in the sun's weak rays next to the rock, and could only focus her attention on that to distract herself from the pain in her side and the increasing ache in her thigh muscles. Still staring at nothing in particular, she rubbed her legs in an effort to calm the fire burning in them. Taking deep breaths of the thin air offered little relief and she felt ragged and drained.

The sun was near its zenith, high in the sky but its pale warmth did little to penetrate the skin on her upturned face. Even so, this brief respite from physical effort was welcome.

"For a moment then." replied the Arbiter eventually, as he stood watching back over the plains behind them for pursuit, should it come. He too, took this moment to rest and recharge.

"We must return to my vessel within the demi-frec though."

Gen6aC had meanwhile been in continuous communication with his personal Vorrax valet aboard the shuttle who had reminded him that time was running short. He was concerned that not only was he already grossly overdue with his expected report to the Servient Gen7cD, but there was now the not inconsequential matter of his failure to eliminate the Terran now resting in front of him.

If the Council of JurTan or his Caste Leaders ever discovered his indiscretion, he would be stripped of his holdings on Flexani Prime, his rank reduced and he'd be extremely lucky if he managed to avoid criminal proceedings before a full and open court. He shuddered at the thought of this and wondered again why he was helping the Terran.

I owe her nothing he thought. But even as he thought this, he knew it to be untrue. She had saved his life by sealing his suit and preventing him from suffocating.

Gen6aC was in emotional turmoil.

He knew it was his duty to watch for and eliminate any Terrans daring to intrude in his sector, but this one intrigued him. Especially now, since she had sown seeds of doubt in his mind over the ruling from the Council.

Either way, Gen6aC knew he needed to reach his shuttle in order to check the records.

He could always contact Servient Gen7cD by subspace tweeter he knew, but he felt justifiably nervous about approaching his Caste Leader unless he had indisputable information to hand.

The Servient should always be above reproach and, as one of his mandarins, an Arbiter must always obey the words of his leader. Gen6aC was acutely aware of the dichotomy of his situation. He may soon have to make a choice that could have long lasting repercussions on his life and Caste position should the information that the Terran had stated, was proved true. But if it were a lie, she would die at his hand, of that he was sure.

"How much further until we reach your shuttle?" Kath'ryn asked suddenly breaking his train of thought.

"Not far," he stated, pointing towards the ridge-line. "Over that ridge is my shuttle where we can gain escape from this Hixx forsaken planet."

As if on cue, a low note sounded across the plain behind them and they both turned in unison to face the way they had come.

A horn...? *The Dall!*

In the distance, both escapees saw huge plumes of dust thrown high up into the air but it was only the Arbiter who, with his genetically enhanced vision and cybernetic lens in his exosuit, could see the approaching force in any detail.

A large posse of Dall warriors rode on the backs of massive four-legged beasts - most likely the last of the clan they had escaped from — and they were racing on a direct path towards them. In the front of this pack, several of the Dall rode ahead at a greater speed, obviously trackers who had their trail.

Kath'ryn got quickly to her feet, wincing at the pain that the sudden movement triggered and started to run as best she could toward the previously observed ridge, cradling her wounded side and gritting her teeth.

Gen6aC knew she would not make it unassisted.

"Kass of Terra, take your perch upon my back again and I will carry you the rest of the way to my vessel."

She faced him, tiredness and pain visible on her face, her eyes shrunken and drawn. He could see her questioning his suggestion. She made the decision and stumbled back to him, climbing slowly onto his back to sit once again in the seat.

Gen6aC knew his own energy levels were low but he dare not share this information with the Terran. He was acutely aware of her unstable emotional state and could ill-afford to harm it even further right now in the midst of the pursuit.

Arbiter Gen6aC set his suit moving as fast as its limbs were still capable of safely achieving and headed once more towards his hidden ship.

He had also withheld from Kath'ryn the other information his Vorrax had shared with him. Terran ships had been spotted flying around the crash site. He was determined to escape the planet without any confrontation. If she knew of the Terran presence, she would insist he took her to them, with all the repercussions that would bring.

No, Gen6aC would conceal this crucial piece of data for the simple reason that, whether either of them liked it or not, she would be good leverage with the Council should he need it. He was playing a dangerous game now and needed to question her on board his Sentinel Post vessel to validate some of the reports if she was able. But before he could do anything he needed to get the both of them off this planet safely – something the Dall were equally as determined to prevent.

++++++++++

During the next twenty minutes of the chase, saw the pursuers gaining ground rapidly on Gen6aC and Kath'ryn.

The mounts that the Dall rode were much faster than the reduced speed of the Arbiter's exosuit, and he knew it would be a close call as to whether they could reach his craft before being caught.

It was quite clear now, from the hurried glances Kath'ryn was able to take rearward, that each of the alien beasts ridden by the Dall had four long limbs and a humped back which made them vaguely resemble the Terran camel, but that was where the similarity ended. They had short shaggy hair over most their sinewy bodies except for their heads, which had a tough bone-like structure covering their skull for protection. Small nostrils poked forward and three sets of eyes - like those of the Dall themselves - sat along a ridge of bone on either side of the skull. The creatures seemed to also have a small mouth before the nostrils, through which both the fugitives could hear the creatures occasionally emitting a strange high-pitched yowling noise.

The Dall warriors crouched low upon their backs on a strange saddle, gripping a rein in one hand and a weapon in the other.

The beasts' hooves had three toe-like structures that clove the ground, digging in and pushing their bodies forward with speed that belied their size.

This was the cause of the dust cloud that followed the troop as they raced ever closer.

As the Arbiter at last crested the ridge-line, Kath'ryn saw the Flexani vessel and was immediately impressed at the design and quality of the ship. Her trained eye taking in its compact and sleek design, powerful looking engine and sturdy shielding.

It was nearly eleven metres in length - a small shuttle - with the single compact short-range engine at the rear, set in a configuration she had never seen before.

But then, Flexani technology had rarely been seen this close in recent times. She was acutely aware of her unique position and despite her fatigue, drank in the sight of the ship as they closed in on its flanks.

"We must enter the airlock, please dismount Kass of Terra - quickly." stated the Arbiter politely but firmly as he drew to a halt near to the side of the ship.

She clambered down from her mechanical mount just as the loud chittering language of the Dalls reached their hearing range and the first few scout warriors rode into view.

"Shit!" she cried in alarm, as the Dall loosed a volley of lethal-looking shaped stones from slings that they wielded with impressive skill, even as they rode their mounts at unchecked speed. They poured over the same ridge that Gen6aC and Kath'ryn had just climbed over just moments before.

Many of these missiles struck the outer hull of the shuttle, breaking apart as they struck the hard alloy, but creating deadly shrapnel that rebounded and struck the ground all around them.

Kath'ryn was struck by some of these smaller fragments which bruised and hurt her, but fortunately failed to break through the material of her flight suit. Even so, they stung and she tried to duck behind the Arbiter for cover from further missiles.

"For fuck's sake, hurry!" she shouted.

As the door irised open, the Arbiter trained his armament on the approaching Dall and opened fire, directing death once more on this clan. Any warriors' mates left at their hive would be singing songs of mourning after this battle was concluded.

It really was an unfair fight.

The Dall's chitinous armour, though hard bone, was absolutely no defence against the Arbiter's weapons. Their stones, arrows and occasional standard spear no match for his hardened alloy exosuit.

Luckily for Gen6aC there seemed to be no Dall warrior in this mob equipped with the exotic tipped spear that had proved so effective against him back at the hive.

The Dall and their mounts fell down the ridge in a torrent, like a cascading waterfall, the screams of the dying beasts drowning out their war cries.

Still they came.

As this was going on behind her, Kath'ryn had climbed inside the airlock but was unable to open the inner door. The controls were totally hidden from sight. She slammed her hand against the door in a futile attempt to gain entry.

"Arbiter!" she shouted over the cacophony of battle, "I can't get in!"

Gen6aC ignored her.

He walked calmly backwards toward the airlock, all the while firing fletchette rounds from his arm mounted guns until he had almost expended the last of his ammunition reserves. More missiles struck his exosuit but he shielded her from most of the shrapnel now.

As he neared the airlock, he fired a final volley at the approaching horde and in one motion, quickly turned, bent at the knee joints and sprang forward into the airlock. As he did so, the outer airlock door rapidly closed at his unseen command, just clearing his exosuit as he passed through.

As the door sealed behind him and he crashed to the wall beside Kath'ryn, narrowly missing her, she heard the dull thud of the crude missiles still striking the outer hull but they were now safe.

"Kass of Terra, my apologies for the delay in entering the ship, but you must realise that the ship is aligned to my personal subspace transmitter and will not open for anyone other than myself or my Vorrax."

Vorrax? What the hell is a Vorrax? She wondered, never before hearing the term.

"I will need to adjust the internal environment for you - it is currently configured for myself - so I will need to create a small space in the ship for you to breathe your gaseous atmosphere. I doubt very much that you will be able to breathe Flexani water....It will be a few mi-frecs."

"Thank you Gen" she said simply as she stood exhausted and emotionally drained.

"Do you need medical assistance Kass of Terra?" he said, seeing her hold her injured rib and watching a small trickle of blood from a cut on her brow, most likely from one of the rocky shrapnel fragments.

Just as she was about to reply, Kath'ryn's adrenaline reserves became exhausted, and her abused body quit on her. She collapsed to the floor in a faint.

With a level of compassion and care, Gen6aC picked up her unconscious body from the floor and waited until the door opened into his shuttle.

His personal Vorrax stood inside the inner door, its fur still wet following the change of environment, and followed him silently into a side room where a very human-looking bed waited. Gen6aC carefully placed Kath'ryn on the bed and waited for a scanning unit to move over her inert body.

The Vorrax spoke. "My Lord. I have information regarding the Terran vessel in this sector. They have dispatched craft once more to the planet in a search pattern around the crashed ship. I fear they may soon discover our presence. What are your orders - shall we deploy the Torraks?"

"No, no Torracks this time. We must leave this world unobserved... I have most disturbing news which may affect the Council of JurTan but I will need proof from this Terran before I dare to confront my Servient. Please care for her while I pilot the shuttle back to the Sentinel. Ensure she is given the appropriate medical care and if needed, any sustenance she desires. Ensure the gaseous environment is maintained."

Gen6aC started to leave when his servant asked "My Lord, what of your own injuries?" The Vorrax was linked by subspace Tweeter to his master and knew only too well that the Arbiter had sustained a lot more damage than he had let Kath'ryn know about.

Looking down at the sealed breach in his armour he said simply, "I will see to this when we are safely returned."

Walking his exosuit slowly to another small chamber at the shuttle's bow, he entered the small bridge. The bridge had no visible flight controls, each Flexani tied to their ship by the subspace interface link provided by their subspace Tweeter.

As the door sealed behind him, fluid began to fill the space, and within moments a Flexani watery environment allowed him to discard the damaged sections of the battlesuit. They peeled away in graceful segments, and he floated free within the viscous fluid to begin the start-up sequence.

He was disappointed, for the battlesuit had been of a high quality and it had cost him dearly - he dreaded the investment needed for a new battlesuit.

It might be possible to repair the damage though, he would enquire as to the cost when he had less pressing matters to hand.

One thing was sure though, he wanted some of the metal that the Dall had used for some of their spear points - it had potential as a new alloy and he considered the possibilities of selling the metal to one of the corporate Castes for a comfortable profit.

++++++++++

Again Kath'ryn awoke, a little disorientated and confused, until she realised where she was. This time she was lying in a comfortable bed rather than lying on a rocky cave floor, presumably on board the Flexani shuttle.

The small compartment was only dimly lit and she was aware that there was no movement - were they docked?

How long have I been asleep!?

As soon as she thought this her SM interjected, *<seven hours, twenty-four minutes.>*

Christ!

It was then she was shocked to see that her well-worn flight suit had been removed and placed at the end of the bed. It looked to have been cleaned. She was lying in her under garments under warm sheets, her wounds dressed and, as she felt gingerly at her ribs, she could feel no discernible pain.

Kath'ryn sat up slowly, trying to fill in the gaps around the last moment before collapsing in the airlock and struggled to understand what had occurred since.

Before she could think any further on her situation, the door chimed quietly.

"Come in?" She said tentatively, drawing the bed coverings up to her chin, and was shocked to see a very strange creature indeed enter the room.

It walked in on all fours, but then stood suddenly upright on its hind legs. About a metre tall, it had soft grey fur and looked for all the world like a large stoat to her. She was therefore absolutely dumbstruck when it spoke in perfect English, "Mistress Kass of Terra. I am Vorrax, personal servant to the Arbiter Gen6aC and I have been tasked with your care and wellbeing. Please feel free to call me at any time and I will be honoured to serve." The Vorrax said this with a little bow of its head, forearms clasped in front of its torso.

Despite the incongruity of speaking to something that looked as if it had just stepped out of a child's book, she managed to simply stammer "Err.. Th.. thank you."

"I have performed some medical procedures on you while you slept my Mistress. I am sorry for the gross invasion of your privacy, but my Lord ordered the procedures to repair your fractured bone. I can now tell you that your injury will no longer present you with any discomfort."

Kath'ryn was amused by the statement about her privacy being violated without her permission, thinking back to her experiences during the nanite procedure she had endured back on Earth.

However, bearing in mind the well-known fact that that the Flexani were very skilled in genetic manipulation and medical procedures, with the ability to alter a person's DNA, she began to become concerned. While she had been unconscious, what other procedures could the Vorrax have performed on her body?

She sent a command to her Smart Mind to verify that bone setting was the only operation undertaken - it would have a record of her life-signs and bodily functions during the period she had been unconscious.

"Will you require sustenance? I have programmed our food replicators for a sample of Terran cuisine from our records of Earth."

"Yes, that would be lovely," she said, becoming suddenly aware of the tightness in her stomach from the fact she'd not eaten in almost twenty-six hours.

<Kath'ryn, from my logs I can detect no invasive changes other than repairs to your fractured rib and cellular regeneration of damaged parts of your epidermis layer during the past eight hours.>

That was good news.

The Vorrax had been true to its word then. At least about this.

"Please follow me to an area where you can consume sustenance."

Conscious of not wearing much, she quickly reached for her flight suit and put it on. As she had first thought, it had been cleaned and she could see some quality repair patches that closely matched the material the suit was made from.

"Where is the Arbiter?" she asked the small alien creature as they left the confines of the compartment.

She was keen to thank her rescuer and to have him explain things.

"My Lord is currently engaged in his private chambers and does not wish to be disturbed at this time."

They traversed a very short corridor to an area that looked totally alien to her. *But then this whole place is an alien vessel, isn't it* she thought. Suddenly, the smell of food wafting through the open doorway brought her up short – this was very familiar indeed however!

Her stomach growled in anticipation - she was starving!

She suppressed the desire to throw herself headlong at the amazing buffet she now saw laid out before her, in order to ask the Vorrax one more question.

"Excuse me Vorrax, where are we?"

Bowing apologetically, avoiding the question, he explained. "My Lord will disclose all."

"But…" she hardly had time to blurt out before the Vorrax disappeared out of the doorway, back down the corridor.

God, he moves fast.

Cursing at the fact she would have to wait for the answers she craved, she could not avoid the fact that her longing for food was stronger than the desire to pursue the creature for further explanations. Kath'ryn turned to the table of bounty laid out before her. With no cutlery or plate seemingly made available, she reverted to using her fingers to sample succulent chicken wings (well, that's what they most resembled) and almost recognisable vegetables that had been duplicated by Flexani technology with amazing detail - each food she tasted had an incredible taste and texture. The protein strand manipulators that the food replication technology used were obviously far more advanced than the human food replication technologies back on Earth.

Kath'ryn felt like a kid let loose in a sweet shop, trying out each of the different savoury and sweet foodstuffs and relishing the way that each unique flavour burst upon her taste-buds. Even back on the mining colony, the meal she had enjoyed with Andrew Terris - the base commander - hadn't tasted this good. Most mining colonies survived on packaged foodstuffs - not from naturally grown vegetables or real meat, but it was real, unreplicated. Notwithstanding that, even knowing this food was replicated, she blatantly pushed that thought to the back of her mind and savoured every mouthful.

It didn't take long however until she was satiated by the food and stood back from the table, looking around the chamber she was standing in. What was clearly the advanced food replicator was located along one of the chamber walls, and some blank monitor or control screen faced her on the opposite wall on the other side of the table, but the room was otherwise devoid of meaningful features.

The door led to the small corridor, so she assumed that the bridge, engine room and other spaces, including her erstwhile bedroom also led off it. The shuttle she knew from her first observation was only around eleven metres in length and seemed to only have one deck. Therefore, it was clearly a ship designed for a very small crew - most likely just the Flexani and his servant creature.

And she had no clue where the Vorrax had gone...

Kath'ryn felt no motion of the craft. She certainly could not feel the thrum of the engine that she would have expected, so it was clear they were docked somewhere. Without windows though, she was blind to the outside world and was frustrated and increasingly frightened at not knowing more about where she was, or where the Arbiter was.

CHAPTER TEN
Listening Post

Arbiter Gen6aC was floating freely within the main control area of the Sentinel Post and speaking with his Servient master by subspace.

He had left Kath'ryn on board his shuttle docked with the Sentinel Post, his Vorrax tasked with ensuring her comfort and well-being. She had been asleep when he had docked his shuttle to the Post and he had left her to rest, knowing she was exhausted from their trial on the surface. He also did not dare to risk her presence on the Post.

He had started by having his own injuries attended to first though, before finally carefully preparing to speak to his Servient about the operation on XT-67-F.

"Servient Gen7cD, this is Arbiter Gen6aC of the NorHan House, Watcher of the Outer Rim with an updated report regarding the Terran interloper in sector 45H-56."

"Proceed Arbiter Gen6aC," came the formal response.

"I can confirm that the Terran vessel was eliminated by the three Torrak drones in a strike attack which has removed the vessel from Flexani space. The vessel crash-landed on a nearby planetoid designation - XT-67-F - and I proceeded to search for survivors. All Terran lifeforms were eliminated." He felt the lie weigh heavy on him but he just had to know more about why the Treaty was not being complied with.

He was bred to be a Watcher and he saw past the presented facts to reveal the hidden reality. He wanted to know if the order given to destroy the Terran ship had been approved despite the Council knowing that the Terrans had argued the Treaty amendment changes as was their right.

"Excellent Arbiter. You will be rewarded I'm sure by the Caste Council at our next round of competitions, and you can expect further benefits being provided to your House."

"Servient, I thank you, and humbly request an answer to a conundrum I have faced during this task."

He had to know why the Treaty of JurTan was not being honoured and why he had been ordered to violate its strict precepts.

He walked a dangerous path now.

"This is most unusual, Arbiter to question your task. However, because of your recent work, I am moved to grant this boon. Ask."

"I am honoured my Servient. My Caste is my Life." He had thought long and hard about the question he was now phrasing;" My Servient, I am perplexed by the Terran response to our annexing of the planet Mirral, designated 'XT-67-C' and the human operation currently present on this planet," he ventured. "From my research, I have read that the Terrans rejected our exceedingly generous offer, but I see no further correspondence in the Flexani data records."

"That is because you do not have the right to access the legal changes yet Arbiter," came the terse response.

A lie! He thought in shock. *My Servient has lied to me, for I know that no Flexani can ever be denied access to historical records - it is in the First Rules of the Council!*

"Servient Gen7cD, I humbly enquire why it is that I am not permitted to access these records at this time."

There was long pause before Servient Gen7cD replied via subspace, "We have information gathered at great cost to the Flexani gene pool that shows the Terran Federation are taking action against the Treaty in cooperation with our main competitors, the GurKaav Protectorate. I am not at liberty to share the data with such a low Caste member as yourself but I will impart this... the Terrans are now threatening the very fabric of our society. They have stolen our technology and have now abducted some of our own kind for purposes unknown in sure contravention of the Treaty. As a member of the Flexani Caste you are, your task is to protect our borders, not to question your orders."

The GurKaav Protectorate was a race whose territory bordered Flexani space but was nowhere near Terran space. It was not even known whether the Terrans knew anything about the GurKaav race - certainly the Flexani themselves only dealt with them briefly every few cycles or so and interaction was infrequent and not very productive at best. This was most certainly a further falsehood, as the Arbiter had not recorded any ships of any race proceeding to this sector of space - any vessel would have had to pass his own Sentinel Post in order to cross Flexani space on their way to the GurKaav

Protectorate. He was feeling very uncomfortable with this insight.

He pressed on. "My lord Servient. I wish no disrespect," he continued, "I simply am confused as to why the Council ordered the destruction of the Terran vessel when it was clear to all that the Terrans had asked for review under Clause 255 subsection 1d, as is their right under the covenant."

"Arbiter, are you questioning the will of the Council?" the Servient asked incredulously. This disrespectful line of questioning was clearly angering the Servient.

"My lord Servient, I merely wish to clarify the order, and certainly not to question the will of the Council of JurTan."

This was not going well. Something is definitely wrong here, he thought.

"You speak above your station Arbiter! If it was not for your record I would have you penalised for this insubordination against the Council!"

Holy Hixx!

"My Lord, I beg forgiveness if I have spoken out of turn. I obey the will of the Council in all things." He tried to sound contrite.

"See that you do Arbiter. I have one further task that you are ordered to undertake Arbiter. There is a second Terran ship currently violating our space in the system - it too must be destroyed. The Council wills it."

Pausing a moment the Arbiter said simply, "I will comply."

With that, the link was terminated and the Arbiter was alone with his thoughts again, floating at his Sentinel Post control deck with confusion and conflict raging through his mind.

There was something else at play here. He knew for a fact that he had not seen any signs of Terran or any other ships on a vector to GurKaav space. In fact, all the Terran ships seemed to do was to either patrol the Border itself or fly to the mining planet XT-67-F as the ship now lying in ruins on XT-67-F. No other ships had ever been detected, bar the searching vessel he was now ordered to also destroy, and he was good, very good at his role.

No, this was not all as it seemed. Why too did the Servient order the Terran vessel in the system destroyed. Surely that is a blatant act if war against these Terrans!?

He decided he needed to know more. Accessing his vast repository of data, Gen6aC quickly queried all the data his Sentinel Post had accumulated during the past few years, running analysis on the information to specifically identify any vessel at all shown to be on a suspicious vector that was not standard for other Terran vessels. His Smart Mind told him this would take several frecs to compile, so he decided to pay his Terran guest a visit.

He needed to talk to her and find out what she might know about this.

Floating out of the chamber where the bulk of Flexani listening technology fed silent data to his monitoring terminals, he headed for the shuttle dock and another exosuit.

++++++++++

Kass had been left aboard the shuttle for one simple reason - she would have been unable to breathe the Flexani water that made up the fluidic atmosphere in the Listening Post and the remaining parts of the shuttle.

The Arbiter had instructed the Vorrax to fill the area of the shuttle where Kath'ryn now languished with an atmosphere she was capable of breathing, so she would have somewhere to recover from her injuries – not that there was much healing to be done now, bearing in mind the Flexani skills in medicine. Kath'ryn, of course, was not aware that this was the reason for her present confinement, but the Arbiter was very aware he had to keep her alive for the time being, and this was the safest place for her.

He also did not want her prying into the Sentinel Post and perhaps learning more about this clandestine base than was wise, so had instructed the Vorrax to ensure Kass was sealed inside for her own protection. He was acutely aware that if his suspicions about this whole stinking affair proved to be unfounded after all and if this was indeed an illegal move by the Terrans, he would need to dispose of the Terran Kass efficiently. Therefore, all it would need was one command from him to the shuttle and it would be flooded with the Flexani water and the Terran would drown within minutes.

Safe she may be for now, but she was bored.

Kath'ryn had explored the accessible areas of the small shuttle after her repast and found that a few other areas were definitely off-limits.

She had been unable to enter the shuttle's bridge or engine room. The rest of the small vessel was at her disposal but frankly it was not worth seeing. There was nothing to do, nothing to read, certainly no data terminals with which to access information or communication systems.

She was *exceedingly* bored.

She even contemplated devising ways in which she could break into the bridge to see what the controls were like - professional curiosity more than maliciousness or a desire to leave driving her desire. She wanted to see just how the Flexani vessels were flown. She was just contemplating forcibly dismantling the bed to find something to use as a pry-bar when the shuttle airlock irised open and the Arbiter walked in wearing his exosuit.

This suit was noticeable different from the one he had worn in the escape from the Dall though. Firstly, it had no puncture wounds in the main shell. Secondly, it was of a slightly different colour and shape to the previous suit and Kath'ryn realised it was far less bulky. She surmised that this exosuit was probably more akin to normal every day Flexani exosuit designs than the battlesuit worn previously. After all, she either dressed in her flight suit or alternatively sometimes wore casual clothes when on duty for long periods aboard the Star.

So they have must keep different suits for different purposes. She surmised. *That's an interesting piece of information to know. So there may be less Flexani types than we previously thought.*

Current Terran scientific understanding had categorised the Flexani based on their exosuit frames, not on the Flexani within.

"Hi Gen!" she said cheerfully, as way of detracting his attention from the fact she had been staring. She was also aware she was still in the act of lifting the end of the bed. She lowered it to the floor as surreptitiously as she could and realised that she was glad to have someone to talk to after the tedious hours of being cooped up on this bloody shuttle.

"Gen?" He responded, confused.

"Oh, err… I was referring to you, Arbiter Gen6aC," she said embarrassed, using his full designation. "It is the way we humans tend address someone - to use a diminutive of names when we feel we know someone well."

"Ah I see. I will accept you calling me Gen if you prefer Kass of Terra."

"Kath'ryn. Not Kass, please," she replied.

"Ah. Then I am corrected Kath'ryn of Terra. In future conversations, I will know you as Kath'ryn and you will know me as 'Gen'."

She smiled warmly at this alien attempting to actually be convivial.

"I am very sorry for your... incarceration. It is due to the fact my main ship and areas of this vessel are currently filled with a Flexani atmospheric - a fluid much like the seas of Terra and you would have been unable to breathe. I therefore had my Vorrax create this sanctuary for you in order for you to remain safe on the shuttle. I hope this was to your comfort?" he enquired.

Nodding she said, "Yes, thank you Gen."

Changing the subject she asked, "The Vorrax - I've never seen their kind before. What are they?"

"They are our servants. We have known of the Vorrax for over six-hundred of your Terran years. We encountered their colony on a dying planet a few systems away and rescued them. Back on Flexani Prime our scientists enhanced their genetic and physical capabilities, and in return the Vorrax pledged their honour and support as our attendants. They serve us well and we reward them for their duties."

The Flexani sounded proud.

And so he should be I guess, thought Kath'ryn. Servants on Earth had the nasty experience of being mistreated as history had demonstrated time and time again.

"I have disturbing news I am afraid... Kath'ryn. We need to discuss this, as it affects my position... and yours." Gen6aC studied her alien features closely for the first time, trying to read her expression. *Hixx, they look so ugly these Terrans, no grace in their form!*

Her skin suddenly developed goosebumps.

"I have been speaking with my leaders back on Flexani Prime and they are concerned about the Treaty breach."

"But, you violated the Treaty..!" she started to shout before he held up a pseudopod and stopped her.

"That is exactly what we must talk about Kath'ryn. Please can we discuss the matter without perturbation of our emotional states, as it affects both our races deeply? I am disquieted by the fact that the Global Federation Committee on your planet had, in fact, as far as my research has concluded so far, complied with all the rules and regulations of the Treaty in that formal change was requested to the appendix change to the border annex."

He stood for a moment letting her digest this piece of news.

Confused, she said, "Sorry, but what does that actually mean in terms someone who is not a diplomat can understand?"

"A very serious and deeply vexing situation. Let me explain the reasoning behind my concerns and then you can then possibly enlighten me from a Terran's perspective. It may be you can more fully comprehend the complex issues here about which I have a growing concern."

"OK. Go on."

"To begin, my superiors gave me implicit orders to monitor the zone of space around sector 45H-56. That is the area of space in which the planet you picked up your cargo from is located. As you know, your ship was detected and I was granted the use of appropriate force to eliminate the perceived threat to our zone."

Appropriate force! She bit her tongue, anger mounting.

"At my command, my drones then attacked and subsequently destroyed your ship - but not, it seems, before you had sent out a distress signal. My sensor net in this sector then detected a Terran warship vessel - designation TTF-200869 - enter the system after a subspace jump. This was a vessel I had detected and had been tracking over the past few krecs. I was observing with passive sensors so as not to reveal my presence here. The vessel seemed to be simply on a similar patrol to those I had observed several times before and was not actively looking for Flexani ships – that is until after you sent out your distress signal.

"Soon after, your vessel crash-landed on the planet. I felt it was necessary to assess the situation myself. I was bound to confirm the elimination of all the ship's occupants as per my explicit orders. Please... Kath'ryn, you must remember that at this stage, I was not aware of any complicit act against the Terran Global Committee and its citizens. My orders had emphasised to me that your vessel was breaching the terms of the agreement and was deliberately flouting them."

"As I promised, upon returning to my Sentinel Post I have undertaken extensive research into the records of the legal changes under dispute in the Treaty. I also felt it prudent to instigate recent scans of the local system in order to observe any recent vessel deployments."

"I hope you are aware from our shared experience on the planet with the Dall creatures, and how you have managed to help me back to my shuttle, for which I am eternally grateful by the way, that my battlesuit was damaged far more than I was initially aware of in the encounter, I would not have survived long without your assistance."

"I mention that now because I have to tell you that the Terran TTF-200869 craft has sent out what seems to be many search parties now landed on the planetoid close to your crashed vessel. I have seen from my sensor net that many of your fallen colleagues have been recovered."

"But... they don't know I'm alive and here!" She started to rise, desperate to get back to her own kind.

"Please sit Kath'ryn. I fear there is more to discuss before you make a decision here. If, at the completion of what I have to tell you, you still wish to return to your own kind, then I will facilitate that."

"I need to tell you something of our history – it will not take long. You may not be aware," he continued, "but in our long cultural history we learnt that through the mistaken ancient beliefs in the inevitable ascendancy of the rich and powerful, life could become a one-sided battle aimed at protecting just the wealthy individuals' interests at the expense of the remainder of the Flexani race."

"Our Elders, however, had the foresight to foresee that this situation would escalate and result in the inevitable destruction of our culture and way of life. So, over one thousand jraf ago, the Elder Elite of each of our four Castes met together and agreed to ensure that this ascendancy could not be allowed to continue. They passed laws and began the plans that eventually led to the manipulation of our genetic code to make us more suited for each of the Castes, blending talents and experiences together to ensure that every individual Flexani worked for the benefit of the Caste, rather than for personal gain."

He continued, "At the same time, the Elders defined changes to the very fabric of our society and to the way that we Flexani were allowed to be mated, bred and partnered. These same rules still even now drive every aspect of our lives and we strongly adhere to these Codes. To go against these rules would effectively alienate a Flexani from society forever. It would an inconceivable and terrible criminal act!"

"So you say this is an age-old cultural thing... why do you now believe that things have changed with this attack?" questioned Kath'ryn.

"I have to believe that it is because of what must be at stake. I followed the orders assigned to me because I truly believed that Flexani lives would have been at risk from Terran attack if I had failed in my duty. It is my sole role in society. Because of our culture, I had no reason to doubt these orders. You understand therefore, I would be lost without my responsibilities as Arbiter of this sector."

She nodded. "But you are now starting to question these orders, aren't you?" she pressed, realising they had reached a pivotal point in the conversation.

"Yes. I believe that I am. My personal morality is at stake and more importantly from your perspective, I now believe that all life on your planet as well as my own is also at risk. If my feelings are right, for some reason that remains unfathomable to me, the current Council of Elders on Flexani Prime wish to enact the extinction of human life."

"You think it will come to that?" she gasped, shocked at the Flexani Arbiter's clinical assessment of the facts.

"No. But this is my doubt" he replied. "I am facing a crisis of my breeding that does not sit well with me. I cannot deny the facts I have uncovered - I have been given orders which may place many Flexani lives at risk, and those orders have come from the very leaders I have been bred to respect, obey and defend."

"But how do you know this?"

"Because I have been ordered to destroy your race's vessel, TTF-200869." He said simply.

She looked stunned, "The warship?!"

"Yes Kath'ryn. The Terran warship that is currently looking for you in this sector."

"But... but why?"

"Ah, therein lies the root of my moral dilemma, as I have stated. It is clear to me that the warship is not currently engaged in any hostile act against the Flexani race, nor is it technically violating Flexani borders, although the Council would have me think otherwise. I therefore float at a juncture in my life where I find myself woefully ill-equipped to determine the right course of action. I am lost in the shallows."

"What will you do?" she asked, fearing for the crew on the warship.

"A good question. It is one I have no clear answer to. My orders are immediate and direct. The warship must be eliminated - but I stand in a position of disharmony right now, knowing that you have dissuaded my compliance by your simple compassionate act."

She felt humbled at this admittance of truth from Gen6aC whilst secretly withholding the guilty knowledge that she had very nearly left the spear in him.

"But what can we do?" she emphasised, adding herself into the equation with a clear acknowledgement of it now being her problem, as well as the alien's. A shared challenge for she certainly did not want to see yet more lost lives attributed to her involvement.

"I have postulated a few scenarios. In all of these, the only conclusion I can draw, is the simple fact that I must go against my breeding... and let you inform the Terran authorities of this deceitful order."

Kath'ryn thought for a moment then said quietly "But what about you Gen?"

"My life is surely forfeit. I cannot, with good conscience go against my Caste breeding and obey an order that clearly violates the Treaty. I will return you to your kind and then return to Flexani Prime to lawfully place accusations against the Council as per the Codes laid down by our Elders."

"But from what you've said, the Council seem to be the ones who are actually trying to call for war."

"Yes. Even so, I must register my complaint within the correct channels even if those channels are the same ones that are being so deceitful."

"I'm sorry Gen, I can't allow that! You will surely be silenced or killed!" Kath'ryn almost shouted, "There has to be another way!"

"Please Kath'ryn of Terra. You have been kind to me considering my original intentions toward you, but you know nothing of Flexani Caste life. I will face this matter with my life as a citizen of Flexani's seas. I will ride the storm."

She looked crestfallen.

Despite, or perhaps because of all that had happened between the two, she felt a connection with this Flexani.

He was showing her a side to the Flexani psyche that she herself had never before understood - compassion and honour.

"I cannot change your mind can I?" she questioned, already knowing the answer.

"No Kath'ryn of Terra. You cannot. I will deliver you back to your people and then deliver myself to mine."

CHAPTER ELEVEN
Recovery

"Flight Leader, this is Shuttle Cephisso. We're currently scanning grid 4-D and have a small ping on our scanners we think could be a body. We're on an approach vector to the location at max thrust, as the life signs are very faint."

Boakai listened to the communique from the shuttle high above the planet as they performed their search of the crash site for the second time.

"Thank you Lieutenant. Lifesigns? So we have a live one? In space?" he enquired.

"Affirmative Flight Leader. We have confirmed that the scans are indicating that the person is alive, but the signal is intermittent, so we're not sure if their suit's power supply is failing or something worse…either way sir we'll be there within the next ten minutes."

"Inform me the instant you get there. We are in desperate need of some bloody good news on this mission."

"Agreed sir. I'll contact you once we have determined their status." Came the response from the pilot of the other shuttle.

Boakai turned his attention back to his own co-pilot who was currently flying their shuttle in a grid pattern above the crash site.

They were now around twenty-five kilometres distant from the centre of the disaster, spiralling out from the centre point and performing their own scans from the air.

Boakai had ordered the shuttles not to land unless they really needed to, and he himself had a compliment of armoured men in the compartment behind him to deal with any hazards they might encounter.

"Sir!" his co-pilot said turning his head to talk to Boakai, "I think I see something, there at your seven o'clock, on the ground." He pointed to a point on the port side of the ship, just out of Boakai's vision through the front plexi-glass screen.

Boakai raised himself in his seat against his straps to see what his co-pilot was referring too and he felt the shuttle dip slightly, the co-pilot banking the shuttle and providing him a better view at the same time.

What he saw was like a horror VR scene.

Below a small ridgeline lay devastation and of destruction of life of an obscene level. Bodies - at this range too small to tell who or what they were in any great detail - were clearly dead.

As the shuttle approached, it became clear that these bodies were probably not human. Too numerous to count, Boakai instead observed details and noted with guilty relief that they were most definitely not human.

So these must be indigenous to the planet - the Dall he thought. What the hell had happened here?

As the shuttle flew a few metres above the bloodied ground, the gruesome details came into view and he could now see clearly the array of countless insectoid creature bodies in a distinct pattern upon the ground.

Interspersed amongst the bodies, lay many strange four-legged beasts - their mounts he presumed - also dead.

It was clear that they must have ridden over the top of the ridge towards something in the centre of the basin and that they had been totally and entirely annihilated.

He needed to investigate to see if there was any connection with the missing crew, so he ordered the co-pilot to land nearby.

As soon as the shuttle doors opened, the five-man combat team ran out, fanning around the ship with their weapons held high, searching the immediate vicinity for any signs of attack.

Boakai and his team had been told to wait by the combat team until area was secured and bearing in mind the witnessed carnage outside the shuttle, he was not going to have any difficulty in complying. He was acutely aware that whatever had killed the Dall in such vast numbers must be a formidable force and was not to be underestimated.

He ordered his co-pilot to keep the engines ready for an immediate dust-off should any order come from the combat team leader outside.

"All clear Flight Leader." Came the call a few minutes later from the combat team leader - a Canadian infantry officer known as Wail Campbell, or to his squad simply as 'Bay'. Some nickname variation on his first name it was believed.

"Thanks Campbell." Responded Boakai.

Moving out of his seat and standing to face the rest of the S&R team who were seated at the rear of the shuttle forward compartment, he said gave the order - "OK team, you know the drill - let's find out what the hell happened here!"

Everyone immediately jumped into action.

As they all filed out of the shuttle's rear - past the infantry guards still watching for anything suspicious - they broke off into two-man teams and started scanning the site of the battle.

Boakai had only just stepped outside the shuttle himself when his comms unit pinged.

"Flight Leader, this is Shuttle Cephisso again. We have recovered one of the Intrepid Star crewmembers - we believe it's the pilot and the good news is that he's still alive - although only barely. One of the medical nurses on board is attempting to stabilise him but another few minutes and he'd have suffocated. He was out of O^2." The voice of the other pilot sounded happy at delivering this report and Boakai too felt cheer at the fact that at least one of the crew had been recovered alive.

"Get your shuttle back to the Kydoimos. Get him into Medical as fast as you can pilot. That's an order."

"Roger that sir. See you back at the bar for a drink - you're buying!" came the impudent reply.

The crew of the three shuttles had had an unofficial bet going between themselves, and it now seemed the Cephisso crew were the ones to win it.

There will be sore heads in the morning Boakai thought with a wry smile.

But, for now he needed some answers and to find the remaining crew members - the First Officer and the missing female Captain.

"Flight!" A call drew his attention back to his team members, a pair of them looking at a sensor instrument and the others examining the ground at the centre of the massacre. One of the team with the sensor left his partner and jogged over to Boakai.

"Sir, I can't explain exactly what happened here, but what I do know for sure is that there is evidence that a small vessel was landed here, not too long ago, and from that evidence, I would say it was Flexani in design."

Boakai instinctively looked quickly upward, then made the decision. "OK people, here we go again, gather as much physical evidence as you can – we lift as soon as possible!"

++++++++++

Captain Middleton stood on his bridge, watching his efficient crew at work around him as they searched for signs of the Flexani's listening post in the sector.

The S&R shuttles were on their way back up from the surface, one of the shuttles was already docked. He had been delighted at the news that one of the poor crew members of the Intrepid Star had been found alive by the Cephisso, but worried by the news that the Flexani had also been on the planet surface, killing the local fauna for some reason.

Even though the surviving crew member had been close to death, and adrift in space, the man had somehow survived. When the shuttle had landed onboard, he had been rushed to the Medical Wing, and was already under the careful ministrations of Doctor Clayton his chief MD.

The Captain had observed from the preliminary reports, that the man was suffering from hypoxia and asphyxiation, his O^2 levels nearly depleted with a high CO^2 toxin count in his blood.

The young man - apparently the Intrepid Star's pilot and named as Alain Brock - had unfortunately been exposed to vacuum before his flight suit sealed around him.

He was extremely fortunately though that he had been wearing it, the Captain thought, knowing that even short exposure to vacuum could be fatal.

"Excuse me, Captain....?" came a voice that broke him out of his pondering. He turned to see one of the young signal officers standing behind with a Padd in her hands.

"Yes Ensign Huett, what is it?" He asked the young female bridge officer.

She proffered him the Padd and said, "Our preliminary scans have failed to show anything conclusive regarding the whereabouts of the Flexani listening post sir. However, I can confirm that we do have a strong suspicion regarding the location of the Torrak drone base. I managed to track a weak trail to a small asteroid cluster along the outer rim of the system. As you are aware sir, the Torraks are known to use a form of fusion reactor of some sort to heat and accelerate particles of heavy metals from their engines, along with other accelerants. I was able to trace some of these exhaust emissions away from the encounter point, using the main sensor array. From the return vector I've extrapolated a likely course leading to the asteroid field."

Taking the Padd from her, he read the brief report. It was very clear and concise. They had a good sense of where the Torraks were probably secreted in this system.

"Good work Ensign," he said seeing her smile at the praise, "you may indeed have just found the base for the Torrak drones."

Nodding slightly and passing the Padd back to the Ensign he called up details on the bridge holographic display, quickly reviewing the layout of the sector and the location of the asteroid cluster. He made note that all of the shuttles were now docked.

Decision made, he spoke to the ever-present AI on the Kydoimos bridge "AI, prepare the ship for an in-system approach vector to the asteroid cluster designated CV-78-J and go to battle stations."

<Command received. Kydoimos now at Battle Stations.>

Immediately the bridge lights turned a dull red and all throughout the ship the AI alerted the crew to their mission.

Within minutes, the four main engines of Terran Task Force warship known as the Kydoimos were accelerating it towards the calculated hiding place of the Torrak drones.

++++++++++

Captain James Bernard Middleton sat quietly in his chair, in his ready room, or office as he preferred to look upon it as, located immediately off the main bridge. He stared intently at his personal display.

He read and re-read various updates and reports from his senior team as he tried to prepare his intentions for the conflict ahead.

If they found trace of the Torrak base within the asteroid cluster, they'd have a real fight on their hands and this would be the first time that most of his crew would actually face real combat.

For some reason, the phrase 'This is NOT a drill' would not stop echoing across his thoughts.

I do hope to God the men don't buckle under the pressure was his predominant thought. They had acted well up until now, but it was about to 'get real'.

He had already briefed his busy Flight Leader to ensure all Reaper crews were on high alert - their Reaper ships fuelled and prepared to launch as soon as needed. Boakai and his flight team had only just got back from their search and rescue mission before being told they were needed again. Boakai had voiced concerns over the limited amount of rest his shuttle pilots had had before they'd be getting back into a cockpit again, but grudgingly acknowledged it was necessary in this instance. Still he did have a right to grumble a bit and Middleton knew he'd owe his senior fighter pilot a bottle of whiskey, or two, after all this was done.

The plan he had devised was that on final approach to the asteroid field, they would deploy a series of scanning drones in order to get a more detailed search of the field without risking lives – yet. Maybe the unarmed drones would be a tempting target for their Flexani armed counterparts, in which case the Kydoimos and her crew would be waiting for them.

Pilots were too valuable to risk sending into the asteroid field itself at this time, which is why the Flexani probably felt it was a safe bet to hide their Torrak drones there.

The complicated nature of the asteroid paths as they spun on wildly random axis, meant that it was too risky for human pilots - and he had so few on the Kydoimos to risk. It was far simpler to send drones, each one equipped with an advanced Smart Mind with its faster-than-human reactions times.

It was far easier to lose a few drones than men and women of his crew. As well as the potential loss of expensive military hardware he thought.

The irony of that was not lost on Middleton.

If, in the event that they found the hidden Torrak base, then he would plan to use the main railguns on the Kydoimos as a first level of attack in order to destroy the Torrak base and surrounding asteroids.

This, he planned, would be doubly-effective, as the debris from destroyed asteroids in the cluster would create further obstacles and he hoped this would slow down the Torrak drones enough for his team to get weapons locks on them with the smaller weapons.

He had no doubt that a Torrak's shielding would prove no match for the firepower at his disposal, but he first needed to be able to smoke the Flexani drones out of their cover before his crew would be able to fire.

Each of the railguns possessed by the Kydoimos was controlled by an independent Smart Mind. Their operation was in turn, managed by a crewman slaved to the equipment.

Each of the fourteen railgun hard-points around the ship was managed directly by an artillery officer who was connected via a spinal link interface and via the Smart Mind controller to the railgun itself. It was a highly efficient solution that allowed for near instantaneous target locks to be confirmed at the speed of thought.

The Smart Mind assisted the human officer and managed the operational control of the miniature fusion reactors that powered the magnetic systems, as well as the targeting scanners through which the artillery officer could identify multiple hostile targets.

It was a very effective and simple solution that allowed man and machine to interact together at their most optimum.

At present, they were just minutes away from the outer edges of the asteroid cluster and their first deployment in anger.

Middleton knew he would be needed on the bridge so he stood up and walked quickly over to the doorway, leaving his small place of solitude to be with his officers.

+++++++++

battle was violent and aggressive.

Superior human technology and military might against the highly effective Flexani drones.

As they approached the asteroid cluster, their active sensor net started to react as they detected seventeen Torrak drone ships hidden within the mass of rocks at the outer edge of the system.

Many Torrak ion trails were detected by the Smart Minds in those first few seconds - the Torraks obviously having multiple bases within this asteroid cluster rather than the one Middleton has first assumed.

The Kydoimos had no need to deploy its own search drones after all, as the Flexani Torrak drones scattered like seeds in the wind when they knew they had been located.

Seventeen drones were also more than Middleton had considered would be hidden here, but he and his First Officer Jenna Brookes would work the battle like conductors at a concert, controlling the flow of battle so that the warship's flanks would be kept as protected as possible, whilst providing maximum firing arcs for the railgun crews. That would be the plan.

The first inkling the men and woman of the Kydoimos had of the impending attack was the alert sounding throughout the ship and the AI informing the bridge crew, in its calm voice, <Multiple target's detected on randomised trajectory paths within asteroid field sector G7A5. Initial scans indicate twelve Flexani Torrak-class drone ships on an intercept course with a further five similar vessels on an escape vector towards Flexani space.>

Middleton and Brookes stood at the holographic table, together with several junior bridge officers.

All closely watched the live 3D feed from the Kydoimos sensors, translated into the ten-foot by six-foot space in front of them.

They observed the unfolding attack and analysed it for any weaknesses or areas of concern.

The whole extent of the vast asteroid field was currently displayed on the holo-table, with numerous asteroids annotated and classified by the shape, density and mass by the warship's AI. Several had been highlighted with additional icons of varying colour and these showed the launch sites of the drones. Finally, the drones themselves were tagged by icons accompanied with data updated in real-time showing status and speed, their flight trajectories and any other tactical data that the AI thought the officers needed.

Some of Middleton's bridge crew wore thin VR glasses which overlaid specific details - or simply highlighted only the information pertinent to them.

The VR glasses contained embedded nanoscale circuitry in the lenses, with advanced quantum processors in the frame, and gave the user essential access to the data in real-time - virtualised augmented reality that was overlaid onto the physical world. In essence, the glasses enabled the user to view and interact with virtual objects in the real world. Captain Middleton however preferred to see the whole battleground in its entirety using his own eyes.

Within moments, the Kydoimos opened fire on the numerous targets approaching the vessel.

Like fireflies buzzing around a glow lamp, the Torraks ducked and weaved around the vast warship even as it manoeuvred itself. The holo-table lit up as the railgun ordinance fired out into the dark void.

The artillery officers, in their enclosed zones, spun the railguns to target the ever moving drones in an effort to destroy them before they could get close enough to inflict damage on the Kydoimos.

A separate section of the holo-table was dedicated to the Kydoimos itself - with many detailed indicators and icons showing details of speed, direction and the status of the warship's weapons, as well as the areas on the shielding that were taking damage. A few red points started to glow on the display and as the seconds ticked by more appeared. Tiny points along the hull of the warship where the Torraks' weapons were inflicting damage. The TTF Kydoimos was using vast energy reserves to power her crude energy shielding - but this was to simply slow the hypersonic fletchette rounds and to reduce their effectiveness before they impacted with the hard alloy shell.

Even so, the incoming fletchette rounds were still able to create modest impact craters along the hull.

The Kydoimos was one of the first ships in a new line of Terran Task Force warships that had the capability of self-healing. Carbon-bonded laminated metals in the hull, combined with advanced carbon fibres and smart nano-plastics gave the hull a unique ability to self-heal - capable of sealing small hull breaches.

Any significant damage however, would require a more dangerous and extensive repair by maintenance crews performing an EVA along the damaged sections in order to manually perform patch work welded repairs on the hull, until it could make it to a space dock once again. Any damage of that nature would have to be repaired after the battle though, no human would survive outside in the bombardment the Kydoimos was shrugging off currently.

Captain Middleton watched intensively, his green-brown eyes flitting over the digital model in front of him, searching for a weakness or break in the attack that he could exploit.

He knew that the Torrak drones, while powered by an advanced Flexani Smart Mind, were only capable of calculating and analysing attack angles, options for best kill ratio and resource management based on a fixed set of algorithms and protocols that had been programmed into them.

His crew had a distinct advance of human intelligence and adaptability. That could not be recreated electronically.

Every so often, he had occasion to issue orders, but his crew knew their jobs well, even if they were a little inexperienced in his mind, he rarely had to challenge the way they responded to way the battle was unfolding.

The bastards are aiming for the ventral railguns he thought observing as several of the Torraks joined forces to concentrate their attack on the four main guns on the underside fin, deep below him.

Each of the four railguns along the ventral fin under the ship defended their positions and even managed to take out two of the five drones before concentrated fire from the remaining three drones damaged the railgun emplacement and he saw with frustration the alert icon appear on the holographic display.

He felt a small tremor through the vessel.

The AI stated in its emotionless voice, <Ventral Port Railgun Two now inoperative.>

Damn. Not good.

"Assessment?" He demanded from the junior Lieutenant standing opposite.

It took a moment for the officer to review the report coming in from the emergency response crews before responding to the Captain. "We've got wounded sir. The port upper ventral railgun is offline. Fletchette rounds have destroyed its tactical Smart Mind processor and have penetrating the railgun fusion reactor. It led to a small explosion on Deck Five with minimal structural damage and some low radiation leakage. I've got several injured personnel now on their way to Medical but the port lower ventral railgun was also affected."

"Affected? In what way?" He enquired. Two guns offline, shit – that's a big concern.

The Lieutenant studied his VR visor before saying briefly, "The Smart Mind was temporarily blinded from targeting but now seems to be fully operational again sir."

"OK, thank you." Considering his next command carefully he said to his First Officer, "Brookes, have two Reapers launch immediate to defend that weak point. I want to ensure no further damage is done to that section. Have them take those other drones out if they can without baulking the railgunners."

"Understood Captain." she replied relaying the order to the Flight Leader waiting in the cockpit of his Reaper.

The Reaper was a two-man vessel created from centuries of battle experience - both in the air on

Earth and now in space. Mankind had developed and engineered the fast little ships - and the technology that powered them - with the single purpose of intercepting and killing. Each Reaper pilot was joined in a symbiotic partnership with the on-board Smart Mind, the same type as the railgun operators on the Kydoimos were now using.

Each Reaper became an extension of the pilot, becoming his eyes, ears and limbs as it drove him through space. The co-pilot was also linked to the flight controls and weapon systems in a similar manner, allowing him to control the firepower at his fingertips and release it by thought alone.

The Reapers were powered by twin COX G-6 hyperstar engines for high speed and rapid acceleration. They did not have the manoeuvrability of the smaller Torrak drones - since the Flexani vessels had no human cargo to worry about and protect from excessive G forces - but they were still fast and deadly.

Small 25mm calibre fletchette railguns with a hundred-thousand-round ammunition stores were the primary weapons of the Reaper but the vessels also had a multitude of hardpoints spaced around the hull to support various unguided and SM-guided

Autumn Wind missiles, as well as more specialised weaponry such as cluster mines.

To improve survivability in combat, the Reaper was equipped with numerous tactical countermeasures - ranging from electronic pods mounted under the 'wings' through to smart chaff for use when in atmospheric combat.

Turning back to the other officer Middleton said to the man, "I'm assuming repair crews are already working on the damaged railgun?"

"Yes sir." came the curt reply, the man distracted by reviewing details on his VR visor that only he could see.

Glancing back at the holo table, Middleton noted with satisfaction that one of the five escaping Torraks had been destroyed by one of the just launched Reapers, however four drones were still rapidly withdrawing from the active battle zone, on the far side of the asteroid cluster.

"Can we target those escaping drones at all?" he enquired.

"Negative Captain, they're now out of range of the main railguns and the Reapers are not fuelled to go on an extended run. It may be too much of a risk to go after them now." said Brooke, his FO.

Dammit he thought we should have dealt with those Torraks before defending the Kydoimos. They are hell bent on getting out of here for a reason, so what's so important about them?

Each space battle was unique and no simulation or planning could ever predict the way that each battle unfolded.

He was therefore very frustrated he hadn't sent out further Reapers with sufficient fuel to pursue the fleeing drones - heaven knows where they were going.

"Trace their escape vector for as long as you can," he ordered. "I want to try and extrapolate their trajectory and bearing if we can. If we have any chance of finding this Flexani listening post, we can hope they may be heading that way. It's a long shot, but we might get lucky."

"Understood sir. I'm on it."

The remaining Torraks were no match for the overwhelming firepower that was raining down upon them now from all directions.

The TTF Kydoimos' railgun crews took out four more drones in as many seconds.

Of the seventeen first identified in the asteroid cluster, only seven remained, and four of those had fled the immediate vicinity leaving just three drones remaining to be dealt with.

A tight dogfight between the two Reapers and one of the drones led to its demise.

The final two exploded in silent flame as the railguns around the Kydoimos found their targets.

The holographic display above the holo-table displayed the final tally and Captain Middleton gave the order to the Reapers to return to the warship.

Excellent work, he thought.

He smiled grimly at the final outcome and would give credit where credit was due later.

His crew continued to work hard over the next quarter of an hour to finalise and lock down the ship after the battle until Middleton issued the order, "All crews other than active repair crews, stand down, and well done all."

Shuttle crews were dispatched in order to collect any remains of the drones to see if anything could be salvaged and learnt.

He wanted to find out if any drone Smart Mind or tech had survived – he desperately needed any clue as to the whereabouts of the listening post. That data would be extremely valuable to the Task Force.

All that was left for Middleton to do then was to prepare his report to the Admiralty, and to visit the injured in Medical. He had done this on all his missions in the previous war, whatever the outcome, wanting to guarantee he kept connected with the men and women who worked under him, and make it clear to them he cared about their welfare.

His report would commend the TTF Kydoimos and her crew. He would ensure the injured artillery officer gained special mention. Captain Middleton was justifiably proud of the way his crew had responded to the battle.

CHAPTER TWELVE
Battlezone

Kath'ryn and the Flexani alien she knew as Gen6aC, sat in his shuttle, heading away from his hidden base and on a trajectory towards the TTF Kydoimos warship and - hopefully - a way home for her.

They had chosen to fly in the Flexani's small shuttle, knowing the approach of the larger Sentinel Post vessel might spook the warship.

Kath'ryn was unsure of Gen6aC's personal future - knowing he was about to revolt against his own powerful leadership in an effort to confront them about their role in the destruction of the Intrepid Star, and the resultant loss of almost all of her crew.

Knowing this, she felt extremely uncomfortable about leaving him to his fate.

Gen6aC had talked about what would happen to him on Flexani Prime. She was afraid for him and felt confused in herself. During the few hours that had passed since his explanation to her, she had struggled morally with her choice to leave him and re-join her own kind.

Kath'ryn was acutely aware that the news he had shared with her would impact the already fragile relationship between the humans and the Flexani.

She was being tormented by the knowledge that she would soon need to decide to whom this knowledge needed to be passed.

We humans have a way of overreacting, she admitted to herself, as she watched Gen6aC at what passed for the controls of the shuttle.

She'd been initially very disappointed at seeing the Flexani flight deck for the first time when they had boarded the vessel.

The last time she had been aboard the shuttle, she had either been unconscious or she had been denied the opportunity to see, first-hand, the shuttle controls.

She hadn't missed much - they were virtually non-existent.

Flexani ships, it seemed, were controlled in a similar manner to that of the human Reaper ships - via an interface link with their pilots through its subspace tweeter controls.

Gen6aC had carefully explained this to her when she first entered the small flight deck. All the surfaces were flat light grey smooth panels with limited holographic displays. It seemed that even though the Flexani pilots were slaved to their vessels the same way Reaper pilots were, they had no need for external displays - the data being beamed directly to their hind mind.

Gen6aC had laughed at her confused face when she looked around at the blank walls.

There was not even an outer viewport - external cameras and sensors on the shuttle's hull projected a 3D view directly into Gen6aC's mind so effectively he became the ship, fully immersed in space as he flew.

Gen6aC however acquiesced to her frustrated demands and had enabled one of the walls to display the external sensor net images. She was now seeing the same view he was observing in his mind, on one of the blank walls of the small bridge space. The technological differences between this small vessel and the poor old lumbering Intrepid Star were immense.

At least she was beginning to feel more comfortable knowing they were now leaving behind the small moon on which the Sentinel Post had been hidden, and were heading towards the last known location of the Kydoimos.

They had agreed between them that the best approach was, when in sensor range, the Flexani vessel would send out a subspace communication on Terran communication channels in order to avoid any misunderstanding.

They would approach the warship under a virtual flag of truce.

Then, the plan was for Kath'ryn to speak with the warship Captain, and hopefully he would allow her to board and the Flexani vessel to leave unharmed.

Tensions would be high - so she prayed that nothing would go wrong with this plan.

She had some hard and awkward talking to do with the Captain in order to make him understand the events that had taken place and the self-sacrificing risks being taken by the Arbiter in bringing her here.

She was interrupted from her thoughts by Gen6aC speaking to inform her they were now within communication range of the Kydoimos. He opened a channel as planned, but before she could even establish contact with the warship, audible and visual alerts blasted out all around the small cabin.

"Fuck! What hell is that?" she turned to Gen6aC.

"Holy Hixx!" he exclaimed, "The Terran warship is under attack by one of our own warships. The Flexani Fleet Empirical Cruiser, Horaxx."

"Damn! What can we do?"

"I am not sure if we can do anything. We have limited firepower on this shuttle and there is no way we could fight against either vessel."

Unbeknown to Gen6aC, after admonishing him for his perceived reluctance, the Servitor Gen7cD had not trusted him to undertake the task of destroying the Kydoimos. He had also realised, after reports of the drone base battle had reached him that the drones alone would be insufficient to effectively eliminate the threat, and so had instructed the Flexani warships nearest to the border to engage, even if the Arbiter failed to perform his allotted task.

The Horaxx had in fact observed the Kydoimos attack on the Torrak drones in the asteroid cluster and now it had the authority, acted. Its engines powering it towards the Kydoimos for a battle that would now prove to be the opening shots in the latest war between the two races.

"We can't just let them fight it out!" Kath'ryn said, obviously highly agitated. "We must do something to stop it."

Gen6aC activated his sensor net and changed the view on the visual display so that Kath'ryn could see the battle unfolding in front of them.

The two ships were at the limit of the shuttle's sensor range, however, both seemed evenly matched in scale and size.

Kath'ryn noticed that both had launched smaller ships and she assumed these were short-range fighters or drones. These smaller craft were speeding away from their own vessels towards the opposing other, the gap closing fast.

Meanwhile, Gen6aC had managed to contact his Servitor through his subspace link and was utterly shocked by the response.

All of his personal holdings throughout Flexani space had been annexed and he was unable to access any of his accounts.

He had been completely severed from his Caste and was now logged as a criminal with a bounty on his life for disobeying the Council in a time of war.

Further review of legal proceeding against him had been registered on the subspace Flexani network. It cited many breaches of Council law including collaboration with the enemy and dereliction of his duty as a citizen of the Flexani homeworld.

Completely unknown to Gen6aC, the Servitor had his own hidden set of sensors installed on the Sentinel Post. He had been spying on the Arbiter continuously and had observed him bring Kath'ryn aboard the Post and then discuss with her his moral issues, seen him perform the searches on the Treaty and question the Council of Elders.

The Servitor, angry at the betrayal of his junior Caste member, filed the legal proceedings himself against Gen6aC for his disobedience and treachery.

He would eliminate this threat to Flexani space, he would not tolerate traitors in his Caste.

Gen6aC was stunned into inactivity.

The smaller fighters had now engaged in battle and Kath'ryn could see dogfights commencing even as the two warships drew ever closer to each other.

"Gen. Gen... Arbiter!?" She was trying to get his attention.

She now grew extremely concerned and reached over to his exosuit to shake him. The Flexani seemed to have entered a catatonic state.

He was in a fugue and unresponsive to her touch until he turned slowly to her and said "I am no longer Arbiter Kath'ryn."

"What?" she was confused by this statement. "Shit, whatever - listen. We need to stop this battle."

"I cannot help Kath'ryn. My people will no longer accept any communications from me. I have been tagged a criminal in Flexani society," he said, his voice heavy with defeat.

She sat speechless.

"Wha... What happened?"

"It seems that my actions in assisting you and then failing to attack the warship, have resulted in the loss of my status. My subspace links to the Homeworld have been severed and my rights within society revoked. To all intents and purposes, I have become a non-entity in Flexani Caste so I cannot speak to any Flexani on the Horaxx to prevent this attack."

Kath'ryn sat dumbfounded as the battle intensified on the screen beside them both.

Gen6aC initiated an unspoken command to the small shuttle and suddenly the view changed.

"What...?"

The shuttle started to turn away from the battle.

"Gen, what are you doing?" Kath'ryn was confused.

"We are returning to my vessel Kath'ryn, we can achieve nothing here. We must return to the Sentinel ship before my access codes are completely restricted, and my belongings seized. I feel we will be requiring the safety of the main ship in the immediate future. We will need all the protection we can get. My Sentinel Post ship has a lot more defensive and offensive capabilities than this shuttle and, in addition, it has an IMD drive capable of taking us out of this sector if needed. And it is my home… my only home now."

Kath'ryn thought about what he had just said and knew that Gen6aC - no longer an Arbiter but a criminal on his homeworld - would have to seek comfort in the only place he knew, or hoped, was safe.

She could not begrudge him this one act so sat quietly, worrying about the battle they were leaving behind them.

++++++++++

James Middleton was resting in his quarters when the ship's AI triggered the red alert.

He struggled to wake from sleep as the alarm rang out.

He'd been on active duty for nearly eighteen hours since they had first entered this sector and he had literally stumbled into bed from fatigue, upon the insistent advice of his FO.

He was not getting any younger, that much he acknowledged.

He tried to brush the tiredness aside and he contemplated the matter at hand.

"OK AI, I'm awake. What is the problem?"

<We have detected an alien vessel on approaching vector. Scans indicate that this is the FFC Horaxx designation FC-78-HG. It is a warship of comparable size and firepower to the Kydoimos and is equipped with short-range fighter craft, Torrak Drones and has standard Flexani shield technologies. Known weapons are standard fletchette but this data is presently six years out-of-date. I am running active scans on all frequencies to detect any changes in their configuration but the range is presenting a challenge.>

Wide awake now and already out of bed, he started to button his tunic as he started to head to the bridge.

"Ship status?" He enquired.

<We're at Red Alert status and all teams and crew report lock down.>

"Do we know what the Horaxx wants yet? Have they made any attempt to contact us?"

<Negative Captain Middleton. My scans indicate that the FFC Horaxx is currently in battlemode with their primary shields at full capacity and I am detecting weapons activity. They are actively conducting scans of the Kydoimos and seem to be preparing to attack.>

"OK. I'm heading to the bridge. Have the senior officers meet me in my ready room."

He exited his room, glancing wistfully at his bed as he left. He checked his antique digital chronometer - a gift from his grandfather. *Well, I suppose four hours sleep isn't too bad.* James thought. I can get away with drinking caffeine for the next few hours to try and stay awake.

Within minutes he was back on the Bridge, having taken the fastest route through the main decks and up two elevators, to the section of the ship where the bridge was located. While he passed many of his crew on the way, no one stopped him on his journey. The crew all knew that the Captain did not need to be distracted under a Red Alert situation.

While he stood in the elevators, he took a few moments to read his personal Padd to update himself on the status. What he saw worried him greatly, the Horaxx was approaching at full speed. The Kydoimos would be within its range in less than seven minutes.

The bridge was guarded by two sentries wearing full battlesuits as per Red Alert protocol but they both stepped smartly aside and let him enter without a word.

Pausing for a fleeting moment to survey the bridge, he noted that most of his senior officers were not present - they must already be waiting in his ready room. He immediately headed over to the door and entered.

"Hello everyone."

There were nods, yawns and brief greetings from the four officers standing in the room - First Officer Brooke, Doctor Francis Clayton, Flight Leader Borgia and Chief Engineer Allen Van Roekel.

"Well it seems that our attack on the Torrak drone base we located in the asteroid cluster has provoked our Flexani friends. I need a tactical assessment on the Horaxx before it comes into range - which will be in about ... six minutes."

Brooke was the first officer to speak up, "From what we know of the vessel, it is pretty evenly matched to the Kydoimos sir," she said. "We know that it carries less firepower overall than us but it does have some formidable shield technology - far greater than the Kydoimos."

Chief Engineer Van Roekel added, "They are using better shield generators than we have in the TTF and they do consume less energy but - this makes them structurally weaker. From our intelligence we do know that they have less physical hull plating."

"What about their manoeuvrability. How versatile are they?"

"We're uncertain Captain," replied Brookes. "They're running at full speed now - or so we assume from their engine capacity output - but it's not known how manoeuvrable they are. We have no tangible data to base any assumptions on and our scans are unable to get any more detailed information on their engines due to sensor interference."

"Right. Well, we have less than five minutes to decide our plan here. Flight Leader, I hope the Reaper pilots are sober enough to fly because we will almost certainly need them out there. I'm authorising them to launch - now."

Boakai nodded, smiling ruefully, knowing some of the pilots had been drinking since they had landed from their previous S&R op, but they'd be fine to fly on this mission. He hoped they just weren't too drunk.

Tapping his own Padd, Middleton gave the order to launch the Reapers.

<Three minutes to contact.> The AI stated clinically to the room, interrupting the officers.

"OK. Let's focus. I want the ship at maximum attack profile, minimal aspect. Also, where are we at with repairs for the damaged railgun?" Middleton asked his Chief Engineer.

"The ventral railgun is still going to take a few days to repair I'm afraid Captain. We've got to replace the main energy compression unit, as well as the magnetic induction coil and since the Smart Mind was destroyed in the attack, we need to use one of the spares from the store and program from the backup file. That process is underway but the software team need time to test before we connect up the SM to the hardware."

"Hmm. Alright. We'll need to compensate then for the loss of the railgun."

<Two minutes to contact.>

"Alright everyone. To your battle stations. Doctor, I'm sure you have already prepared for this but have all of your Medical crews ready for potential wounded."

Doctor Clayton nodded stoically and said simply, "Certainly Captain. Good luck."

The men and one female officer all filed out of his office, the Captain following closely behind.

The main bridge was abuzz with tension.

They had been drilled well for battle, but this would be the first time that the crew would face a real opponent - the recent attack on the drone base had been very uplifting for morale, but this encounter could be a true test of the men and women of the Kydoimos, as well as the ship itself. Captain Middleton was still worried that in the heat of battle, some of his crew might crumble as they lost friends and colleagues. He knew they would not come out of this battle unscathed.

"AI, send a message to TTF Command informing them that we are about to engage the Flexani."

<Yes Captain.>

Middleton watched the central holographic display as it showed the Kydoimos and the Horaxx closing in on each other - still half a sector away and the distances between them was calculated in millions of miles - but he knew that time had run out.

Long-range sensors bleeped alerts as the main display lit up - the Horaxx was firing its main forward railguns in the first volley of this battle.

The Second Stellar War had begun in earnest.

++++++++++

To any observer, James Middleton presented a calm and collected exterior. He exuded the confidence that a warship captain was expected to exhibit in front of his crew and bridge officers.

However, this calm exterior did not completely hide the trepidation he was now feeling as he watched his Reaper pilots close upon the Flexani fighters and drones.

Both the larger vessels fired volley after volley of lethal railgun rounds at each other over the vast distance that separated them.

At this range it was minutes before the hyper-accelerated and smart mind guided fletchette rounds struck the shielding, but with no atmosphere to slow them down, the rounds fired from the massive cannons aboard each ship struck their respective targets with concussive force making the warships shudder with each strike.

The TTF Kydoimos had less effective success with its railguns than the Horaxx, as the superior Flexani energy shielding dissipated the kinetic energy, preventing their vessel taking any significant damage.

In amongst the rounds flying between the two warships, dogfights ensued between the smaller fighters.

While the Flexani fighters were slower and could change velocity less rapidly than the more advanced Reapers, the Torrak drones more than made up for it by their agility and effectiveness. Many of the Reaper pilots were distracted by avoiding the Torraks, leaving the Flexani fighters with a lot clearer path towards the TTF Kydoimos than Middleton would have preferred.

He watched, along with his First Officer, as their range closed.

When they were ready, he gave the order to ready the main Plasma weapons in preparation of targeting the approaching warship.

There were five Plasma Beam hardpoints along the exterior hull of the Kydoimos. One on the ventral wing under the ship's belly, and four along the port and starboard sides. All five were independently powered from banks of storage batteries that are charged from the main engine fusion drive. They need time to power up to capacity before firing however - which is why they could not fire as frequently as the railguns - but their output and destructive power was significant.

"Prepare to fire forward Plasma guns when target lock acquired." He watched pensively as the power levels peaked, and the smallest plasma gun fired first.

The Horaxx was presenting a minimal aspect view of its bow, the smallest possible area for targeting by the Kydoimos. However, the warship's sophisticated target lock Smart Minds sought out the most effective impact point, and an invisible stream of highly polarised plasma particles raced across the void.

These particles of charged plasma carried their energy payload through space and struck the forward energy shield of the Horaxx in a brilliant glow of electrifying discharge. The alien ship immediately suffered significant damage as their shielding buckled under the esoteric energies being applied.

Since the quasi-neutrality charge of the plasma was incompatible with the Flexani shield energy frequencies, the effect was such that their shield generators momentarily overloaded, sending fluctuating currents through their defensive shields that rippled and buckled under the onslaught.

Excellent, thought Middleton as he watched the data stream show a significant loss to their forward shield strength. "Fire railguns. Hit them while they're defences are down!" but even as he gave the order, he already knew his crew had fired. He was proud of their response.

The fletchette rounds took far longer than the Plasma beams to traverse the distance between the two vessels and Middleton watched with disappointment as the Horaxx's shields started to recover.

God their recovery time is fast, we need to be closer.

The Horaxx too, started to turn, unusually exposing its port flank. Before Middleton could reason the Flexani tactics, a bright flash along the side of the Horaxx betrayed the firing of some form of energy weapon discharging towards the Kydoimos.

This attack was more deadly than the preceding fletchette railguns.

It seemed that the Flexani also had beam weapon capability. This was not a plasma weapon - but something similar - and the exotic particles fired were more visible to the naked eye, but just as fast and deadly.

One of the Reapers was caught in its path as the beam sought out the Kydoimos and was instantly vapourised. The unfortunate pilot and co-pilot had no chance to react as the Reaper simply vanished in a small explosion. The Kydoimos bridge crew saw the alert on the holo-table scant seconds before the warship was struck by the force of the beam.

The Kydoimos fared better than the Reaper. Its weaker energy shields instantly failed but its superior hull plating took and withstood the brunt of the beam's energy. Metal and carbon fibre alloys warped and twisted under the intense radiation burst and several small hull breaches appeared as the physical shield plating broke free from its mounts along the superstructure.

However, this was not as serious as it might have been.

The TTF Kydoimos' limited self-healing capabilities proved their worth and the smaller breaches were sealed within moments of the blow and no one was directly affected by the sudden loss of pressure within the sealed off areas of the ship.

Despite this, warnings and alerts were ringing out and Middleton listened as his bridge officers dealt with the fallout from the unknown weapon's damage.

"Atmosphere restored on Deck E. Fire suppression systems active."

"What the fuck was that!?"

"Energy generators FG6 through to FG9 offline. Engineering Repair crews to Deck E immediately."

<Radiation spike detected at zero-point-four sieverts. Rate dropping. Nominal readings predicted within ten minutes.>

"Reaper Kilo Five not responding to hails and I'm getting intermittent comms dropout from the radiation burst."

"Coming about, zero-four-zero mark five. Increasing our Delta-vee to 750kph."

"Firing portside!"

<Three Torrak drones on intercept course.>

"Captain..." James Middleton turned to his lieutenant who had spoken, "I'm detecting an incoming subspace communique from the Imperial Rose. Captain Naro is requesting to speak with you – in strictest confidence and utmost urgency."

"I don't need this now, for fuc.....oh, ok, I'll take it in my Ready Room. Route it through to my personal Padd – stat!"

He strode quickly to his office as another barrage of fletchette rounds struck the hull.

The torrent of fire was relentless from both vessels now.

As the doors sealed behind him, Middleton was left disorientated for a moment by the relative silence in the room after the frenetic activity on the bridge.

He sat down heavily at his desk and the ship's AI detected his facial ID before opening the encrypted channels between the two warship captains.

"Captain Middleton. Good to see you."

"Captain Naro. Same here. Sorry to be blunt but we're in the middle of a firefight. What can I do for you?" he said with a pained smile.

"Well you'll be glad to hear we are aware of your situation and will be within range in about five minutes. We're ahead of Captain Boskowitz in the Vanguard by about fifteen minutes - so we're entering the sector and will come within attack range at full delta-vee."

Nodding, Middleton replied, "That really is good to hear - we're taking a battering right now from some form of new Flexani beam gun. It's something we've not seen before."

"You can hold on until we arrive?" The other captain enquired, concerned.

"Yes, I think we can hold our own for a while, but any assistance would be more than welcome to tip the balance."

"Understood. We will arrive shortly. Imperial Rose out."

With that the comms channels closed and Captain James Middleton rose wearily, straightened his tunic and exited his office into the cacophony of noise that was the main bridge of the Kydoimos.

CHAPTER THIRTEEN
Changing Tides

Kath'ryn and Gen6aC had flown the rest of their journey back to the Sentinel base ship in depressed silence.

Kath'ryn struggled with her own conflicting emotions as she sat trying to digest the significance of the information Gen6aC had shared with her.

She had been close, so close, to being back with her own people that she felt she had been torn in two when Gen6aC was forced to turn the small shuttle around.

She felt desperately alone, lost in the vastness of space with this alien.

An alien that was even now, being alienated from his own people. The irony of the situation was not lost on her.

Two individuals thrown together in a storm, both from different cultures, created and forged under different suns but both now buffeted by the same storm.

How the fuck did I end up here?

As the Flexani controlled the docking procedure from his link to the ship, she at last spoke. "Gen, may I ask a question?"

"Yes Kath'ryn of Terra. What is it you wish to know?"

"I want to try and understand why you felt so strongly that something was wrong with your orders. It is something that has been bothering me since you told me about this earlier. I had the impression that Flexani do not normally question their Caste Council members, is that not right?" She raised her eyebrows questioningly.

"Yes, that would normally be the case, Kath'ryn of Terra. Unlike you Terrans, we obey the orders of our Caste leaders without question, which is why it was so vexing for the Council of JurTan to negotiate with your own leaders when the Treaty was negotiated and signed. Flexani all felt that it would be impossible to come to an agreement with Terrans as we perceived you to be a complex and conflicted race, unable to adhere to any rules or regulations."

"So, what happened for you to change that perception?"

"Over the period of treaty negotiation it was decided by our leadership, that they should compromise with just a select few individual Terrans whose ideals most aligned with Flexani ideals. In essence, we found allies within Terran influence that helped to get the Treaty ratified."

The shuttle entered the small hanger of the larger Sentinel base vessel and the doors sealed behind them.

As the shuttle settled to the floor of the hanger-bay on its landing struts, fluidic Flexani atmosphere began to fill the interior of the hanger compartment.

Gen6aC powered down the shuttles engines and silently ran a check on the shuttle's systems before disconnecting from the link.

He turned back to Kath'ryn and resumed the conversation.

"I had long since learnt that there are few Flexani that possess the kind of fortitude it takes to question our leaders. In my assessment, Terrans and Flexani are no different when it comes to this. An individual will always be more concerned with calculating his or her personal outcome in any situation rather than making that situation a success for all. I am, of course, describing the state of selfishness, something I believed not to exist in Flexani culture – until now."

"But that's why it's so important to fight and sacrifice for what you believe in, because tomorrow it could all be gone! You have to take what you have today, hold onto it and protect it." she argued. "You have to treasure it and love it and fight for it, because we might never be around to worry about the consequences of our actions."

Nodding his carapace slowly in an almost human gesture, he said, "I agree with you Kath'ryn, but regrettably though, I am coming to the realisation that many Flexani would rather to lose a war if it meant they could be head slave, rather than win the war and be equal with everyone else. I do not see peace between Terrans and Flexani in the foreseeable future."

"The same could be said of humans. We do not like to be subservient to others and I feel this battle is the start of something bigger." replied Kath'ryn.

He bowed his head, "I too believe we are facing a war between our two peoples that will significantly unbalance the interstellar political landscape in this region of space. We have a saying on Flexani, *'Blood in the water will draw attention'*. This is exactly my fear and why I sought answers."

"I'm not sure I understand…" Kath'ryn stated, a little confused as to what he was alluding.

"Kath'ryn, if our two races enter into another war, I fear that other races such as the GurKaav Protectorate whose own galactic influence borders Flexani space far from the Terran border, would then be in a position to attack a weakened Flexani homeworld on another front. It would then not be too much effort for them to enter your Terran space from there and then eliminate your own race."

"Who are the Gur Kaav Protectorate?" she asked, "I'm confused, I've never heard of them."

"GurKaav." he said, correcting her. "They are a race we encountered approximately ninety of your Terran years ago. Their homeworld lies on the far side of Flexani space from here. It seems they have developed in ways culturally similar to your own - in that they have art, technology and interstellar travel. They are a young race like yours. We Flexani have been trading with them over this period and have sporadic, but mutually beneficial, commerce and trade negotiations between our two races."

"So why are they considered a threat then?"

He seemed genuinely pleased at this question, and responded, "Ah! Well as a Watcher for the Flexani, it has been my role to assess all threats to our continued existence, and I know that the GurKaav Protectorate is eager to grow. As I said, they are similar to you Terrans in this respect and they are never satisfied with their own borders. They have been expanding along the uncharted territories outside of Flexani space for a while. It is my assessment that they would welcome a war to strengthen their own position in the galactic sphere."

"But war is so destructive. Why would they choose to fight a war knowing that it would destabilise the local space?"

"For gain. My people have always had strategic plans and a long term vision of the future." he said simply, knowing that the Council of JurTan had whole Flexani Castes working on this one task.

"But you just said you have trade deals with these GurKaav Protectorate people. Why do that with a potential threat?"

"We learn. We observe. We plan."

"Oh. So that is why your race were so welcoming to mine in the early years?"

"Yes indeed Kath'ryn of Terra. By working with our enemies - like we did with you Terrans - we were able to learn a great deal about your history, the way you interact with other cultures and how you reacted to the knowledge that Terrans were not the only creatures in the universe." He sounded smug at this statement.

"In the beginning we had whole disciplines of Flexani society together with many of what you would call universities studying your Terran history. We understand what drives you Terrans better than I think you understand yourselves - because we had a unique and unbiased perspective. We learnt then that if provoked you were more likely to fight to a bitter end rather than capitulate, so it was decided to leave Terrans alone, rather than fight battles that would leave both our races perpetual enemies."

He paused for a moment.

"But I now feel we have forgotten our own teachings. We seem to be blind to the past. I am confused. I see my race seeking a war with the Terran homeworld but it serves no benefit and puts Flexani at risk. This loss of life is cannot be beneficial to either Flexani or Terran greater goals."

Kath'ryn was curious as to what those goals might be but didn't press him for an answer. Instead she asked, "Do you think that maybe Flexani's now believe that they can win a war with Earth?"

"Yes, I believe that in our arrogance, we might have changed our reasoning. See here..." he pointed to the information on the display screen. "I am seeing some strange information here in the energy sequence of the beam that the Horrax deployed against your warship as we left. It is leading me to conclude that we must have a new weapon that the Council feels will win a war for us."

Kath'ryn studied the information data curve and energy output signature and saw something in it that seemed very familiar - but she couldn't quite place it. *I'm sure I've seen something like that before...* she mused.

Her Smart Mind interrupted her, <*Kath'ryn, I can identify the energy curve you are viewing. I am able to ascertain the origin of the beam's signature.*>

Surprised that the SM had the information, she asked it to explain further.

She was therefore extremely concerned when it stated <*The energy signature generated by the new Flexani Beam weapon contains waveform matrices similar in frequency and amplitude to Corismite crystals when exposed to a neutrino burst.*>

Explain yourself!?

<You studied a report fourteen months ago which is stored in my long-term storage. The report showed the waveform curves for Corismite crystals exposed to a range of different energy sources. You requested this information as it pertained to your desire to further understand the operating principles for the engines on the Intrepid Star. I can match the waveform to one of the tests conducted in this report to the one you are seeing now.>

"Gen... I think I know what this new weapon is."

He rotated in the low gravity to face her and said, "You do? Explain."

"My Smart Mind has seen this before. Well... let me explain. I've seen this before. About a Terran year ago in a report on starship FTL engines and some scientific tests performed on Corismite crystals."

"Corismite? The same as the main element of the ore your own ship carried?" He turned back to his panel quickly and started to operate a new set of controls. Within minutes he stiffened and exclaimed "Holy Hixx!"

"What's wrong!?"

"In my misplaced attack upon your own vessel, I observed six cargo pods ejected from your main ship before it was destroyed by my Torrak drones. The drones determined there was no strategic threat presented by those pods and so did not take action, but I did perform a scan of the cargo to check if any lifesigns were present." Displaying a report on screen he pointed and said, "They did not contain life. Only Corismite."

"Yes, I know that." She responded a little exacerbated. She already knew what was in them. She was the one who had ordered their abandonment. Three-hundred thousand metric tonnes of ore destined for Earth.

"Kath'ryn of Terra. They are no longer where they were," he stated simply, pulling up a representation of the planet and its orbit where the Intrepid Star had crash-landed.

The region around it now showed empty space where the six pods should still have been still drifting in space.

"Fuck."

"Indeed. I am assuming 'fuck' is an expletive in your language. If so, then yes. Fuck is the right colloquium to use in this context."

"Don't joke. Those pods contained one hell of a hell of a lot of Corismite. Where the hell are they now!?"

"My Flexani brothers have them." He showed her a timeline display of the sector from the historical logfile. It replayed the recent timeframes to show several, presumably Flexani, craft enter the region, lock onto the containers as they floated aimlessly in space and, once secure, warp away into subspace.

"I now believe that the real reason the Council of JurTan have annexed this sector and approved the destruction of your vessel is to control the ore mine on this planet here." He pointed to the origin of the ore.

Oh my God. Andrew! In horror, she thought of the fate of the commander of the mining station.

++++++++++

Gen6aC's master, Servient Gen7cD floated patiently, waiting in the Great Council Chamber on Flexani Prime.

Surrounded by Vorrax servants who swam between the participants, serving refreshments, he gazed in adoration out of the beautiful crystalline window overlooking the peaks of Mount Urlak, under the shallow oceans of Flexani Prime.

The JurTan Window as it was known, was thought to be over one thousand-jrafs old, and was carved by skilled Maestri, from thin panels of coloured crystals found at the base of the mountain it now silently framed.

Each panel had been meticulously created, smoothed to a highly polished finish with natural sands, and basic tools of the time. No engineered or manufactured processes had created its splendour.

Few Flexani had the opportunity to witness - first-sight - the fantastic detail contained in the crystal window, so the Servient took the opportunity to study it as closely as he could. He was proud of his heritage and this window represented an accumulation of that history.

Paetron craftsmen from ancient genetic lines had created the Window to quantify the Council of JurTan's position. To demonstrate that Flexani leadership watched benignly over all Flexani society.

Images and scenes depicted many areas of Flexani life, from the early battles fought between clans and Castes before order had been imposed, to the study of genetic and cybernetic embellishments of their own DNA. It was an amazing piece of art and creative design, far surpassing - even now – the art work made by modern Paetrons.

The request for his attendance at the Great Council Chamber had come through to his office a si-krec ago and it was an invitation he could not ignore.

He had been summoned at the behest of his Caste Leaders to attend this private session of the Council, specifically to discuss progress of the preparations for the burgeoning war against the Terrans.

As he was floating near to the Window and studying its detail, he felt another Flexani approach, swimming gracefully despite his age.

He was not surprised by this meeting, as it was this Leader who had sent him the summons.

"Ah, Lord Gen7cD, I welcome you to our humble session." He was greeted in the formal manner by Atticis Gen9fG, a much older Flexani who had been part of the Council of JurTan and was a very powerful Council Member, having served on it for most of his hundred-jref life.

Rumour had it that Atticis Gen9fG also maintained a private genetic maceration chamber in order to keep his genetic decay to a minimum, but this had never been proved.

Maceration technology was a very expensive and power-consuming. Normally only a full Caste could employee the Maestri technicians to maintain them. The MECS70-B Stasis Pods on Earth had been created using some of the basic principles of the technology - but a Flexani Maceration Chamber was far, far more advanced.

Genetic cell manipulation - including the transfer of genes within and across species boundaries to produce improved or novel organisms - sat at the heart of the devices' system.

An organism's genome could be altered using this biotechnology. Arguably the best example was the Vorrax - their genome being changed over time to enable them to breathe underwater.

So, keeping his thoughts about the Council Member to himself he said "My Lord Atticis Gen9fG, I am rewarded beyond measure to be part of today's proceedings. My life is the Council's." Replying in the standard formal response.

"Your lifeblood is accepted."

Pleasantries complete, Atticis Gen9fG gestured to a remote spot in the chamber, and together they swam a little way from the others for privacy.

In previous generations, Servient Gen7cD would have been expected to actually bleed over this small ritual, allowing Lord Atticis to cut him with a ritual knife so his blood merged with the waters of the Chamber. Now, words sufficed.

The session would start soon, but it was abundantly clear that the Atticis Gen9fC wanted to talk privately beforehand.

"Servient Gen7cD, I understand that the bait has now been released. Do tell me how it progresses."

Glancing around to ensure they would not be overheard by the other Members who floated nearby he replied through a personal subspace link, "My Lord Atticis Gen9fG, I can confirm that we have taken decisive action against these vile Terran creatures. We destroyed one of their transport ships in sector 45H-56 and the Arbiter in that sector is unaware of the true plans being currently implemented. In fact, we have removed him from his post due to some unforeseen actions on his part but this has played nicely into our schemes. Due to overstepping his mission parameters, the Arbiter in question has now been stripped of his rank and we are now able to prove that indeed it was he who instigated the actions that have resulted in war, should we need a sacrificial someone to take the blame."

"Most excellent Servient. That is interesting and beneficial news," the Atticis crowed. "And what of the Horaxx?"

"The Empirical Cruiser Horaxx is currently engaged with the Terran warship in that sector. We anticipate that the Horaxx's new weapons will be overwhelmingly effective against the Terran's inferior vessel and their presence will be eliminated shortly."

"I want to be kept appraised of the progress and report to me once the vessel has been destroyed."

Bowing the Servient complied. "Yes Atticis."

"I have one last task for you Servient Gen7cD. I need for that Corismite mine that is infected by these Terran creatures secured. Dispatch sufficient ground troops to that mining colony to exterminate them. It is imperative however, you leave as much infrastructure in place as possible so we can continue to mine the Corismite ore. We can use the Terran machinery to help bring about their destruction, I will take great delight in the irony of that. To that end, instruct the battle troops to go cautiously. I cannot stress how important the Corismite crystals are to our new weapon technology."

"Yes Lord Atticis Gen9fG. With my life I will ensure your orders are undertaken."

"Good, be sure you do. Come, let us join the rest of the Council for the session. You have been very helpful with our plans Servient and shall be rewarded during the next Competitions. I shall guarantee that."

Servient Gen7cD turned to follow his superior, back toward the gathering Council Members and, as he did so, he took one more lingering look through the JurTan Window.

++++++++++

At another window, light years away, the Secretary of Defence Joshua Stormont stood, gazing at beautiful clear skies.

Through his picture window, he saw diplomatic shuttles flying overhead, ferrying visitors to the White House and other government building surrounding his own.

He had just received the report about the engagement of the Flexani and the Terran Task Force warships in battle near the border of human space, and knew that at last, this was the beginning of his plans towards the success of Project Valkyrie.

He had spent the past two decades preparing for this day.

He had used every bit of his political clout and influence to retain his position, whilst working to establish support - both financially and politically - across the globe.

World Leaders and business leaders alike had met with him in many secretive sessions over the past years and he had slowly, but surely gathered the support he needed.

Billions of credits in black budget projects had been appropriated, misappropriated, acquired, redirected and funnelled into Project Valkyrie.

Stormont was now satisfied that all his work was now bearing fruit.

He knew that the Flexani leadership would attempt to slowly strangle the human expansion throughout the universe. He had observed Treaty change after Treaty change over the past few years, all affecting the ability of the humans race in its desire to explore the stars.

The latest round of restrictions was tantamount to a demand for mankind to curb its advance out into the universe.

The SecDef was also well aware that the Flexani Caste responsible for the Council leadership were bred specifically for the sole purpose of evolving Flexani rule - at the expense of other races. *Well, mankind is one race that will not tolerate these curbs* he told himself.

He was interrupted from his thoughts by his aide, who passed him a secure Padd.

"Thank you Denise," he said, taking the device from his attractive PA.

Reading carefully the message on the Padd, Joshua smiled to himself and erased the message.

Good, the plan was progressing well.

Walking over to his desk he touched a panel on his deskPadd, opening a secure encrypted communication channel to his counterpart in Europe.

"Good afternoon Madame Piche, I trust you are well?" Blancheflor Piche was head of the European Defence Agency. The EDA formed a key part of the Terran Tactical Force globally and provided many of the resources to maintain the defensive capabilities of Earth and its protectorates.

She was a mature woman who had served in the French armada during the battle over Jupiter, and was an advocate for Project Valkyrie. She and Stormont had worked together for mutual gain for many years.

"Bonjour Joshua, comment allez-vous aujourd'hui?"

His AI instantly translated her French into English //Hello Joshua, how are you today?// and he responded "I am well thank you. I have news."

"Partagez donc. Je suis impatiente d'entendre la dernière mise à jour." //Do share. I am keen to hear the latest update.//

"Our plans are progressing well and the TTF Kydoimos is currently engaged with the enemy. Two other TTF warships are inbound to the sector and I feel that we will soon be in a position to test the new weapons against the enemy shortly'" he replied, sharing with her the latest intel he had on the whereabouts of the other vessels.

"Ce sont d'excellentes nouvelles! Avez-vous donné l'ordre pour autoriser le test d'armes?" //This is excellent news! Have you given the order for the weapons test to be authorised?// she enquired.

Nodding he said "Yes. Captain Naro and Captain Boskowitz have both been given the authority to fire if they have the opportunity."

"Des très bonnes nouvelles. Je vais le laisser dans vos mains capables." //Very good news. I will leave it in your very capable hands.//

With that she terminated the connection and Joshua sat back in his chair, staring at the official TTF logo and call log report on his screen.

His network of allies across the globe was wide and far reaching. Madame Piche though, was one of the strongest supporters of his cause. With a far-right political background in her distant past, she had been an extremely key advocate from the very beginning.

Her work in Europe had help Joshua forge some important alliances that would have otherwise been difficult to get approved in those early days.

Now, with the network insinuating itself into every government and global business on the planet, at the most senior of levels, the SecDef's role within the TTF was such that he only had to ask, and the task would be done.

He was well aware he possessed more power and influence where it mattered than his own country's President, and as he redirected his gaze back through the window he allowed himself a brief smile of satisfaction. *As for the fate of the crew of the Kydoimos,* he thought grimly, *it's unfortunate, but you can't make an omelette without breaking a few eggs.*

CHAPTER FOURTEEN
Removing a thorn

Doctor Amita Kluska sat slumped at her desk - exhausted and overwhelmed.

She had not slept now for over eighteen hours and was at the limit of her physical abilities.

Her cognitive reasoning was failing and even with her own Smart Mind assisting her, she knew she must sleep soon.

It had been nearly a week since her rancorous meeting with the Admiral and she had been driven to try different, risky and more novel approaches to the way in which the nanites were coded, structured and assembled.

For days, she and her team had worked around the clock in order to assess and evaluate new routines, discuss new ideas and at time, to scream and shout at each other in frustration.

Her body was now screaming at her for rest, but there was the wait for the current test to complete. She needed to see the results before she headed to her bed.

As she sat there waiting, she thought back to the Admiral's visit and how she had crumbled under his scrutiny.

He really is a nasty shit of a piece of work she thought.

Amita had been forced to make compromises in her team's approach to Black Snow following that last meeting. She knew the Admiral would not accept any further delays to the final project, he had made that more than clear, and she had driven her team hard to redouble their efforts in search of a breakthrough.

She was confident they had achieved their elusive goal with the latest batch of nanites, but then, she had said that the previous time, and the time before.

And the time before that.

The science they were developing and using was just not an exact process and the results that the Admiral demanded had never been recreated before outside, and so far even inside, of a lab.

She and her team needed to take the abstract science behind Black Snow and turn it into a weapon that could be mass-manufactured for the missile warheads.

Her eyes heavy and stinging with fatigue, she started to succumb to the siren call of sleep. The warmth of the room and the hum of the air conditioning was lulling her into a stupor when the sudden intrusive bleep of the machine running the tests woke her with a start.

Blinking rapidly and rubbing her eyes with her hands to force herself to focus she started at the display in hope, and sighed with immense relief.

The data on screen was showing a positive indication that the most recent release of software code for the nanites had been programmed correctly and was performing as expected on the biological sample in the container on the table beside her.

"Thank God!" she exclaimed to the empty room. *I couldn't have faced that bastard again with any worse news.*

Unknown to her however, the AI watching over The Nest complex was currently dedicating a large portion of its processing abilities to watch and report back on her activities to the Admiral.

The AI had already performed a vastly superior analysis of the data from the test sample and had concluded this sample was a viable Black Snow code-base.

It automatically started a waiting subroutine to copy all of the files pertinent to this latest batch - both current and backup storage - and send them in an encrypted data packet to the Admiral's private server as it had been ordered to do.

With its hidden cameras it observed the Doctor copy the data to her own Padd and then head off to her sleeping quarters for her much delayed rest.

Later, when Amita had slept a relieved sleep and had woken and freshened up, she returned to the science bay and discussed the successful results with her colleagues. Between them, they too concluded that the sample was indeed viable and agreed it was good enough to send it to the Admiral, unaware the Admiral had already seen a much more detailed report and was very well aware of the successful result.

Doctor Kluska was very surprised therefore to get an encrypted vmail from the Admiral within a just a few hours of sending him her report.

She opened the message and viewed it immediately.

"Doctor Kluska, I am very satisfied you have been able to successfully create a viable Black Snow solution. This is excellent news and I am now confident we have a weapon against the Flexani

that they will be unable to counteract. I am visiting Central Command in the morning and I will require you to attend. Be on the first shuttle to Earth. Your clearance has been granted to leave The Nest, and your flight orders are attached to this vmail. Admiral Varnava out."

As his face disappeared from the screen, her itinerary was displayed.

Shit, I've less than four hours to make the shuttle.

She had to get packed for Earth immediately and then head across the planet to the shuttle port.

++++++++++

Doctor Kluska stepped into the elevator, past the two guards, wheeling her small flight case behind her.

It contained her clothing for her trip to the centre of the seat of power on Earth for all of the Terran Task Forces' operations and an encrypted set of Padd's with all of her research and conclusions for presentation to the appropriate committees, as she assumed the Admiral would demand she explain her results. Politicians and shadowy men of power that worked behind the scenes to ensure that projects like Black Snow would forever be clandestine would demand to see the results of their investments.

As the doors opened, and she entered the lift, the wheels of her case stuck momentarily in the groove of the elevator doorway and she cursed before lifting the case slightly to get it inside.

Not once did either of the two guards in battlesuits offer to help.

Bastards. She thought as she finally got inside and leaned back against the wall.

The Smart Mind closed the doors and she felt the elevator start its ascent toward the surface.

Between floors, the smooth ascent was interrupted as the elevator suddenly stopped and she stumbled a little, her balance thrown.

"Err... What is going on?" she asked of the AI that controlled the base.

A calm neutral voice responded, <I have detected an illegal weapon within the elevator and your ascent has been stopped. Please wait while I conduct further intensive scans to verify.>

An illegal weapon? She was confused. She was carrying no weapon.

In fact, she had not even bought a sample of the nanites out of the lab, as that was against protocol and knew of the actions that the AI would take if anything was removed from the lab without clearance.

<Scan complete. Thank you for your patience Doctor.>

"That is OK. Please continue as I need to catch my shuttle," she ordered, concerned that time was passing and she needed to catch the public hyperloop transport to get across the Sisyphi Planum basin, and board the shuttle to Earth.

<I cannot do that Doctor Kluska. The weapon I have detected in question is secluded within your flight case. It is a small fletchette blaster and is not registered to you.>

"What!?" she started to panic now. She didn't know about any weapon.

Amita clawed at the lock on her case, trying to operate the fingerprint ID to open her case and see what the AI was talking about. As her case flew open, the contents spilled out across the elevator floor, the AI said calmly, <Lethal action protocol will

be taken in ten seconds. I am sorry Doctor. Goodbye.>

She looked on in horror and saw no gun in amongst her personal effects.

Realisation struck her with the force of a hammer blow. *That bastard Varnava!*

She collapsed in tears on the floor of the elevator as the seconds ticked by. As the countdown continued, she sobbed and just had enough time to wish she had never taken the role as senior scientist at The Nest.

The AI initiated microwave transmitters hidden within the walls of the elevator and Amita Kluska was erased from existence - her molecular structure instantly made unstable and falling as dust to the elevator floor. Her flight bag and spilled contents fared no better. The microwave energy intensified and the dust that had, only seconds before, been an eminent human scientist was almost instantaneously vapourised. Soon no residual trace remained.

Empty now, the elevator continued its smooth ascent.

++++++++++

...on Commander Andrew Terris sat back in his ...ded chair and smiled as he looked at the empty wine bottle on his desk.

It was a reminder of the wonderful evening he'd had with Kath'ryn Kass, Captain of the Intrepid Star. They had wined and dined the previous night, and he had been disappointed to see her go.

It was certainly lonely on the station. As Commander he didn't fraternise with his operators and certainly didn't partake of the services of any of the prostitutes on the station. He knew that such a life was always going to be hard but he normally preferred to keep himself to himself.

He had ended up – at just thirty-four years of age - the manager of this small but important mining operation in a distant part of the galaxy. It was far from Earth but he liked it that way.

For the past three years, Andy Terris had worked hard to ensure that the base ran at the highest possible efficiency levels, and he rarely had to worry about visits from his senior managers.

He worked over ten hours a day, sometimes almost every day of the week on this planetoid. A day here was twenty-two hours long and a week was six days long in Earth terms but still, he had little otherwise to occupy his time. The mine practically ran itself.

His one hobby that kept him sane, was his illicit trading.

Headquarters frowned on any illegal betting or market trading, but after a failed marriage had driven him from home and had left him almost bankrupt, he dabbled on the stock markets and found he'd had a remarkable aptitude for it.

Surprised by this skill, he had spent a little time building up some capital before earning this role as the Station Commander at Raven Ore.

Once he had found himself far from Earth, he diligently worked to cover up his trading activities.

No one was aware of the encrypted computer system he had smuggled at great expense, into his personal rooms on the Station. The initial trading capital he had made had been well spent on the Pech XT60e computer which had a dedicated subspace tweeter communication system and secure protocol software installed.

It allowed him to make trades to Earth in near-real-time.

Any network traffic that Raven Ore's IT systems saw, was merely logged as social media activity, so he was safe from discovery.

His only other real expense, was the bribery of that slimy engineer Coulson from the Intrepid Star. The drunken slob had once blundered into Terris's office just as Terris was in the bathroom. He hadn't bothered to secure his computer, as everyone on the station normally respected each other's desire for privacy.

Everyone but Coulson that was.

So it was that Coulson had realised, even in his alcoholic daze, that what he observed on Terris's computer monitor screen could be his opportunity for free booze.

When Terris realised what Coulson had seen, he reluctantly agreed that he would supply him with a few cases of whiskey each trip in return for his silence. It wasn't the best quality whiskey, but hell, Coulson didn't care so long as Terris paid for him to have some time with one of the local prostitutes at each visit.

That had been a few years back, before Kass had joined as Captain.

So for the past three years, his private time had been spent in the evenings trading on mining stock and ore. He mainly focused on Corismite which was mined by his very Station - enabling him to essentially manipulate his dealings with prior knowledge of new ore entering the markets.

Essentially, he had insider knowledge of the size and quality of shipments heading back to Earth in ships such as the Intrepid Star, and worked hard to manipulate the trades so as to buy low, and sell high.

Right now, Corismite crystals were superior commodities to trade in and he had made a fortune in investing wisely.

Driven by advances in experimental techniques such as neutron diffraction and available computational power, the latter of which enabled extremely accurate atomic-scale simulations of the behaviour of Corismite crystals, the science had expanded to address the needs of interstellar travel and drive systems. In particular, the field had recently made great advances in the understanding of the relationship between the atomic-scale structure of Corismite minerals and their potential uses. The accurate measurement and prediction of the elastic properties of minerals, which was leading to new insight into warp field and dark matter quantum space folding was an exciting new prospect.

Well aware of this need for the crystals in space travel, Terris had made nearly 7.6m credits in the past three years by trading cautiously.

He'd had a few miscalculations over the years though, one of which resulted in him losing over two-hundred thousand credits in one afternoon. He had been in a black mood for days after that debacle much to the puzzlement of the rest of the station staff.

Still, he was happy that the rest of his money was safe. He had plans to buy a small ocean-going yacht back on Earth and then to spend the rest of his life floating round the Bahamas soaking up the sun, fucking the female tourists and generally enjoying his retirement.

It was during one of his trading sessions, whilst seated at his desk that he got the comms alert though his terminal.

Annoyed by the interruption, since it had come during a particularly fruitful trade that was going to net him another forty-two thousand credits, he took the call.

"Yes. What is it?" He said irritably.

"Sorry Commander," came the voice of Darleen Stiers, one of the young females who managed the communication rig. "I've got an incoming vessel without any ID. What would you like me to do about it?"

"Damn. Is Harris not around?" John Harris was his second-in-command.

"Not right now. Think he's in the rec having some food."

Frustrated, he replied to the younger officer "OK. Give me a few minutes, I'll be right there."

With a sigh he ended his trade early still netting him a profit of thirty-six thousand, seven hundred and nine credits and headed out of his apartment to the main control room.

Damn, just shy of eight million creds now. He smiled at the thought of his retirement and what that money was going to be spent on.

All trace of Kath'ryn Kass forgotten in this pleasant daydream.

++++++++++

The Flexani troop carrier penetrated the atmosphere of the planet known as XT-67-C at a steep angle, with full shields to protect it from the re-entry and atmospheric buffeting.

The battesuited Flexani infantry within the shell of the vessel were protected inside their fluid filled suits and the environment of the small vessel, strapped to their holding pods.

They all wore the same configuration of suit, the black blended fibres that formed the suit's outer surface reflecting no light. Weapons at the ready, as soon as the cruiser touched down hot on the surface they flooded out like a horde of Fordinel fish when disturbed.

The strategy of the attack had been planned well in advance. The Empirical Cruiser Horaxx had been sent on a mission specifically to keep the Terran warship Kydoimos occupied whilst the attack on the mining station took place.

More ships were inbound to the system to prevent any further Terran interference, and would arrive not so many si-krec's from now to defend their new territorial border, and to help transport the now Flexani owned ore away from the planet.

The invaders arrived at the mining station and almost without slowing, commenced their bloody task. Domes and building walls were breached by the simple expedience of running through them such was the speed and mass of the exosuited Flexani.

Meanwhile, the unarmed miners fell uncomprehending under the fletchette rounds and plasma fire that spat from the guns of the marauding alien infantry.

Death befell all the mining base crew as their pockets of resistance grew fewer in number as the minutes passed.

Some of the miners did have personal weapons on the station, and they tried in vain to protect the others. There was a small cache of guns on the station too which Andrew Terris barely had time to share out among his junior staff, but they'd had little or no training and experience - certainly not against trained warriors.

The thirty-six year old commander died himself in a dirty mining colony station corridor with his colleagues and staff, on a distant planetoid. He bled out, leaving his wealth hidden, never to buy his yacht, nor to sail off into the sunset as his dreams had promised him.

Merely thirty-seven minutes after the Flexani craft had landed, no Terran was left alive to offer resistance.

The Flexani infantry had killed one hundred and seventeen human men, women and children in their attack, firing with economic precision and rooting out any people hiding in the vast complex with ruthless efficiency.

When he was alerted to the news, Servitor Gen7cD was delighted that he had once again completed the orders that his masters had demanded of him, and revelled in the knowledge that he would be rewarded well for his efforts.

The Corismite mining facility that was a remote part of the Raven Ore Confederated Logistics operations, had now become a very strategic part of the Flexani in the war with the Terrans.

By annexing the sector - first by Treaty amendments and then by force - the Flexani could now plan to mine as much crystalline ore as they could.

Servitor Gen7cD now sent out the command to other Flexani craft in orbit about the planetoid. Those ships carried the working caste members who had the expertise and experience to mine the ore. It was imperative that they performed any mining operations as expeditiously as possible.

Back on the Flexani homeworld, the Council of JurTan knew well that the Terran leadership would not standby and ignore this attack and would certainly send other warships to investigate, further embroiling the planet in war but - this time the Flexani could base the war on their own borders, far from Terran space.

The Terran battle-lines would be stretched extremely thin, and they would be fighting far from their supply lines.

With the crystalline ore refined, the Flexani would then have access to enough Corismite crystals to use in their new energy weapons.

The Servitor had enough contacts in the field of weaponry to know that the new weapons had been developed when the scientist subCaste had discovered, completely by accident, the effectiveness of the Corismite crystal when harmonious dark matter energy waves were sent through its crystalline structure.

They had successfully produced the first example of a unique form of neutron diffraction energy - one that had some essence in the realms of subspace and therefore, could cause extreme disruption to anything in its path.

The Horaxx was the first of the great Empirical Cruiser ships to be fitted with the new technology, and from the contact subspace reports of its potency against the Terran warship Kydoimos, the Servitor was sure they would win the new Stellar War.

This was the mysterious weapon that was causing so much damage to the Kydoimos during the current battle.

++++++++++

Empirical Cruiser Horaxx continued to fire both its conventional and the new energy weapons at the TTF Kydoimos whilst trying to defend itself from attack by the Terran warship.

Both vessels vied for the best tactical attack vector, moving through space as their more agile and smaller fighters weaved and dodged each other, firing their own weapons at each other.

Aboard the Horaxx, the confident Commander of the Flexani Cruiser was suddenly shocked and surprised to see his ship's AI suddenly alert him via their subspace link, that another Terran warship had arrived into the sector - unfolding subspace and arriving at high speed on a direct parallel course to the Flexani vessel.

"Chells Eye!" He exclaimed in shock as the second vessel started to pound his ship with weapons fire, weakening their energy shielding along the port side.

With now two enemy warships firing at the Empirical Cruiser, he started to re-assess this new threat and rapidly, his Smart Mind concurred with the ship's AI to arrive at the conclusion that they were losing tactical and defensive options by the Ac.

The Flexani ship lurched as fletchette rounds and plasma particle beams, directed from this new enemy invader, struck the Horaxx's hull.

He sensed decompression in several compartments as the fluidic atmosphere escaped, killing the crewmembers within instantly by exposure to the dark void.

"We will have to disengage and withdraw." He gave the silent order and initiated their escape command to the pilot on the main deck. He felt the ship's engines start to fold space.

He would have to leave his drones and fighters to their fates - they would sacrifice themselves to the Caste he knew, but he was disappointed at having to lose trained fighters.

A strike to their main IMD drive suddenly caused alerts to populate his inner vision and the AI immediately shut down the subspace engines before they could overload. Their escape route was suddenly blocked, and the Commander felt real fear for the first time.

Aboard the Imperial Rose, for it was that vessel that had turned the tide of battle, Captain Naro watched his holo-table assessing the damage his undetected approach and subsequent broadside had caused to the damaged Flexani ship.

Moving the Rose into a new position above and behind the enemy vessel, he ordered the crew to prepare their very own secret weapon. The Flexani's weren't the only ones in this new war to improve their offensive capabilities.

Only a small select team aboard the Imperial Rose really knew what the new weapon was capable of and now that team sat deep within the hull of the warship, activating the exotic material batteries and devices that would fire the new weapon against their enemy target.

As energy levels increased towards full capacity, the team awaited the signal to fire.

Captain Naro studied the best strategic point on the alien vessel on which to deploy the new weapon.

Known as *Hellfire*, the new guns had been installed a few months ago upon the orders of Admiral Varnava. The Imperial Rose had remained hidden near a clandestine military base while the Hellfire guns were installed, and this was the first true test of their capabilities.

The Captain had only a skeleton crew aboard at the time, the minimum necessary to run the ship, as he did not want his whole crew knowing of their new deadly weapon until it had been proven in battle.

Scant hours before, Captain Naro had received the orders that he would be the first to fire this new weapon against the Flexani. He had been looking forward very much to testing its capabilities against a real target.

"Fire when ready." he commanded.

The new Hellfire gun was not a traditional weapon. It fired no physical missiles nor did it fire plasma beams or standard energy pulses.

Instead it was a weapon that had the ability to manipulate space-time.

As the weapon was locked onto the fleeing Flexani Cruiser, exotic mathematic equations - controlled by a very uniquely evolved and programmed AI - calculated the necessary power to fold and crease space around a single locus.

Using the basic principles designed into the FLT engine drives on most deep-space starships, the Hellfire guns subtly altered the four-dimensional aspect of unidimensional space within the fixed focal point of the guns.

However, unlike the FLT drives which formed a field around the vessel in order to protect the ship from the effort of translating into a subspace layer below normal space-time, the Hellfire gun instead effectively reversed the principle, twisting the targeted region of space inside out, cruelly ejecting particles of matter out from one universe into another.

Molecular bonds and weak electro-magnetic fields that held the atoms in place, were suddenly irrelevant, as the weapon's effect altered their very nature. Their three-dimensional analogy which formed their cohesive connection to this universe was immediately altered; particles of unstable alien matter from other universes transposed themselves with the material in its place in this universe causing fragility and annihilation at the molecular level.

The net effect of the weapons' destructive force was such that the gates of Hell had been opened and the hell hounds inside unleashed.

The Empirical Cruiser and its Flexani crew suddenly found themselves in a maelstrom of subspace turbulence.

Matter, anti-matter and subspace all vied for the same point in space-time. Something had to give.

Flexani technology was no match for the universal energies being released and converted by the weapon's devastating effect.

On the bridge of the Kydoimos, Captain Middleton stood confused at the sight of the Horaxx suddenly ripping itself apart and exploding in a cloud of bright purple-green fire before vanishing entirely. Not one atom of the once proud ship remained. It was if it had never existed.

Kydoimos' AI was confused and struggled to identify the reason why the Flexani cruiser had destroyed itself so entirely. The AI finally theorised that the Flexani FTL engines must have failed just as they translated into subspace.

This, it reasoned, was substantiated by the fact that the ship had instigated its IMD drive moments before it had exploded. Captain Naro had timed his weapon test well, very well.

Captain Middleton however, was none the wiser.

CHAPTER FIFTEEN
White Flag

Gen6aC and Kath'ryn sat stunned.

They had watched a remote view of the battle between the opposing warships using the advanced long-range sensors aboard the Sentinel ship and had observed the strange weapons fire from first the Flexani Empirical Cruiser Horaxx and then the sudden appearance and frightening response from the TTF Imperial Rose, destroying the Horaxx in an amazing blaze of destructive power.

Through his advanced sensor net, Gen6aC had been able to record and show Kath'ryn the exact nature of the weapons.

The demise of the Horaxx though was terrifying. What was more important though, had been the origin of its destruction - the other Terran Tactical Force warship.

Kass had looked on with shock at the attack and had been bewildered by the immense significance of what she had seen. It was conclusive proof the humans had a new type of weapon in use against the Flexani.

What was also very clear to the both of them, as they sat within the main observation chamber aboard the Sentinel Post ship, was that the Flexani too, had deployed a new type of beam weapon - but it was nothing like as effective or deadly as the human weapon.

Running analysis and studying the data logs, Gen6aC quickly concluded - with the help of his Smart Mind - that the new type of exotic energy weapon deployed by the Terran warship used some kind of space-time manipulation, but beyond that, he was baffled.

Because he was now designated a criminal in Flexani society, and ostracised from all digital links to his data cache sources, he was limited in the information he was able to correlate and cross-match with his data.

"Kath'ryn of Terra… I do not understand what has just happened here. I am at a loss. My fellow Flexani – the sorrow I am feeling right now for their Caste's loss of the precious life force and genetic material is hard to bear."

"I am sorry too Gen. I just don't understand why we continue to fight the way we do," she said, lost for words.

"It is clear to me that some of our leaders are playing a dangerous game."

She nodded in agreement, "I think so too. I believe something is going on here that we're not aware of."

"You can see here from the scans," he bought up a new view on the flat surface so she too could see the information "That new warship designation - TTF-167453 - clearly using the new energy weapon against my kin. They never had a chance judging from its effects." His voice, even after translation by Kath'ryn's Smart Mind, sounded disconsolate.

Kath'ryn realised that deep down, even the Flexani had relationships and companionships like humans did. They forged bonds and wrote love poetry to each other - or so she believed - and she saw in his manner right now the impact of the total annihilation of the Horaxx was having on him.

Just scant hours before he had been labelled as a criminal in his society - stripped of everything he had, apart from this vessel they now found themselves in. Now, he had had to watch hundreds of his own kind destroyed in a manner so outrageous even to her, and she could not understand how he continued to function.

The psychological pressure and emotional strain he was under must be tremendous she thought.

She reached out to touch one of his limbs in a gesture of humanity.

He turned to her and tilted his head slightly in acknowledgement.

Gen6aC had changed into a different exosuit, one that left his main limbs free so Kath'ryn was able to physically touch him for the first time.

It had been an odd experience. His skin slightly rough to the touch which she was not expecting.

Rather than float in his natural environment which was seawater from Flexani Prime, he had adjusted the main chamber to fit human needs. Kath'ryn was breathing fresh air while he had to suffer sealed in his suit, other than the two free limbs, in order to support his mass.

However, Gen6aC had adjusted the gravity plating to a value approximately twenty percent of Earth's gravity, at Kath'ryn's best guess.

They both stood in the low gravity field which helped offset his own weight and avoided him becoming incapacitated by any higher gravitational force.

"What can I do?" she said quietly.

"I am unclear as to what our next move should be," Gen6aC replied thinking, "I can only reason that we must try again to pass our knowledge onto someone trustworthy in charge, so that we can stop any more unnecessary bloodshed and prevent more lives from being lost."

"I total agree," she acknowledged. "Both sides are obviously using new weapons technology. Call me a cynic but I've just seen enough to convince me that when you're cornered, when your back's to the wall, when you've no fight left, it's better to charge at the darkness than simply hope you'll live long enough to see the dawn." She hoped her use of all the mixed metaphors still made sense.

"What are you saying then Kath'ryn? That even if we let someone know of this atrocity, it will not change the outcome in any way?"

"Exactly! Mankind's been bitter ever since Flexani's left Earth all those decades ago, Gen. We had our narrow horizons opened to us, and many aspects of humanity were humbled by the fact that we discovered we were not alone in the universe after all. Man wanted the adventure - and you Flexani gave us that vision - to reach the stars which we had desired to reach for centuries. But we fucked it up. We could not take the gift for what it was."

"That is very astute of you Kath'ryn of Terra. I can see this perspective. Flexani also had high hopes for Terrans. There was much resentment and displeasure at the way Terrans had rejected our assistance. It was felt that Terrans had stolen the valuable gift we had granted you in order to covet it for yourselves. The First War drove Flexani to gain a better understanding of Terran capabilities and we learnt a lot. I myself, was bred from the genetic pool of several Arbiters of that first battle."

She frowned a little and thought before answering. "We tried to really understand an alien race. I don't think mankind was ever prepared for what the Flexani's gave us. We were children weren't we?"

Gen6aC nodded slowly. "Children can also teach Kath'ryn." He stated simply.

Silence lasted for a few long minutes between them as they bonded over this fact. Two alien races - one more mature than the other in terms of interstellar relationships and yet taught to learn that even a young race has something to teach them.

"I think I have a possible solution Kath'ryn of Terra. We must approach the first Terran warship, designation TTF-200869 under a flag of truce. I believe from the tactics they were operating, they knew nothing of the second warships potential. They were very nearly caught in the explosion. You too must get back to your people. I have been classed a criminal in the eye of the Council of JurTan, so I cannot go back to my own kind. Therefore, I must hope that your people will treat me well as a prisoner of war. With the information we have, it may be that I can broker a deal and ensure that I do not have to spend my life drifting throughout the galaxy as a pariah."

A tear flowed down her cheek. Kath'ryn felt true sorrow for the alien.

"You think this is the best plan?" she said.

"Yes, I do not believe that any other choice exists for us here. We must share this information with the Captain of the Terran Task Force vessel and hope that he will pass this onto trustworthy leaders. If it is true that the Flexani have taken the cargo and started to use the Corismite crystals in an attempt to create new weapon technologies, then your leadership must know this too."

"And what about our own terrible weapon!?" she exclaimed. "We must inform your people about this too."

"I agree. I will send my Vorrax back to Flexani Prime with a datacube containing all we know about this unusual Terran beam weapon, and its effect on manipulating subspace. I hope they will choose to use this data wisely."

"So then, we are agreed?"

"Yes Kath'ryn of Terra. We must do what we can to stop this war before it escalates further."

He sent a subspace command to his personal valet and ordered him to prepare the Sentinel Post's shuttle for a trip back to Flexani Prime. He called up all the data he had recorded on the new weapon used by the Imperial Rose. He copied the material to a datacube and waited for the Vorrax to arrive before handing it over, and gave his last orders to his assistant.

Gen6aC felt sad to see him go, knowing he would never see the poor creature again. He had been a good and useful presence around the Sentinel Post.

He hoped to Hixx that the Vorrax would succeed in handing over the datacube to one of the Flexani agents who would be able to take action at the hopefully right levels in the Council.

An hour later, the shuttle had departed for Flexani Prime, and Gen6aC set a course for the two Terran warships still in this sector of space.

++++++++++

"Terran Task Force Kydoimos, this is Captain Kass of the Raven Ore transport vessel the Intrepid Star, sending a distress signal from the approaching Flexani ship. Please do not fire. Repeat, please do not fire. We are approaching under a flag of truce and seek asylum. I wish to talk to Captain Middleton."

Kath'ryn's voice wavered slightly as she spoke the words into the subspace transmitter.

As they entered within sensor range of the Kydoimos, they knew that the warship would have had gone to full alert.

The second TTF vessel was also coming to bear and she was genuinely afraid for her life knowing that they could be blown to smithereens in seconds by either vessel.

God, please let them hear me she said in silent prayer.

"Alien vessel, this is the Terran Task Force warship, Kydoimos. Captain Kass, please transmit your ROCL personnel ID for verification," came the response a few moments later.

Not realising she had been holding her breath, she exhaled and took a new deep breath before reciting her personnel ID number, issued to her by Raven Ore headquarters.

Moments passed and she started to panic again, thinking she must have made a mistake in the number, when the acknowledgement came. "Thank you Captain Kass. Good to hear you are alive, please wait for the Captain."

"Captain Kass? This is Captain Middleton. I must say I'm extremely surprised, and not to say relieved, to hear your voice again and coming from an enemy alien vessel! I'm sure you have a long story to share. I'm keen to debrief you. Can you guide the Flexani ship to our dorsal docking port? Be aware, weapons are still trained on your craft. Please do not make any unusual manoeuvres."

Captain Middleton was terse and succinct with his order but she was actually glad he had recognised her voice.

"Yes Captain, I have some information to report. Err... one thing I need to say is that I have one of the Flexani with me," she stammered, not sure how they would take that statement.

Middleton was silent for a moment before he said over the voice channel, "I see. Thank you for being so open and honest, and letting me know. Can we assume the Flexani will comply with a security search?"

Gen6aC nodded in assent.

"Yes Captain. He will."

"Very well. Be aware that *any* act of aggression towards the Kydoimos or the Imperial Rose will result in immediate and deadly action being taken. Two Reapers will escort your vessel into range. I hope you understand my situation here Captain Kass, but we've just been involved in a firefight with a Flexani cruiser and are currently on a war footing, so any and all Flexani vessels will be treated with the highest threat assessment protocols right now."

"I can assure you my Flexani companion will comply," she stated, seeking to calm the tension.

Companion? Gen6aC wondered.

Middleton heard murmuring all around him as his crew on the Bridge spoke amongst themselves, wondering what was going on. He knew they would be concerned for the ship's safety and the whole ship would know the scuttlebutt even before the alien ship docked.

<Assessment on the approaching vessel complete. Scans show weapons systems and shields offline. Full technical assessment has been archived for review in file CV78N. I can confirm the vessel is no threat at this time.>

"Thank you AI." Brooke said as she approached the Captain.

"Sir. I've ordered one of the infantry squads to the dorsal airlock just in case this is some form of trick. Should we seal off access to the main sections until we are sure this is safe?"

"You think we might encounter problems?"

She considered this and said, "I think we need to be overly cautious right now sir."

"I agree," he said. "Secure the deck and post squads at core sections of the ship until we know we are safe. If this is a trick, then we would be right to be a little paranoid."

The next few minutes were tense as the crew of the Kydoimos prepared for the Sentinel ship's arrival.

Gen6aC piloted the Sentinel Post vessel slowly towards the Terran warship, marvelling at its construction.

He did not use any active sensors but noted through the visual processors on the surface of his ship, the numerous railguns tracking them as they moved closer.

The two Reapers also kept parallel to them as they approached.

As he manoeuvred the vessel towards the docking port, he followed the directions and orders from the Terran command to the letter.

He complied without hesitation - knowing one mistake would result in their deaths. His vessel's defences were good, but would almost certainly not protect them for long if Kydoimos was threatened.

He rotated his ship to align the two airlocks and slowly moved his ship to dock.

Magnetic couplings sealed the two vessels together, and he and Kath'ryn felt the clunk as the seals engaged and they docked.

Gen6aC powered down the engines as he was ordered to, and disconnected himself from the ship.

However, he did initiate security protocols first as a precaution against tampering. He did not want the Terran crew to discover the secrets of the Sentinel Post vessel just yet.

++++++++++

As the airlock door slowly opened, Kath'ryn made sure that she stood in front of Gen6aC in the airlock chamber.

She was the first to face two armoured officers - a man and a woman - holding fletchette rifles pointed directly at her and the alien behind.

She also saw more battle-suited warriors behind them in the corridor and she felt the sweat trickle down her back before her Smart Mind repressed the levels of fear in her system.

She heard one of the infantry officer speak in a slightly artificial voice, their suit's speakers conveying the order. "Step out of the airlock slowly, with your arms raised above your head."

She complied.

Stepping gently across the threshold, she and Gen6aC entered the Kydoimos.

She was directed to step to the left towards a collection of armed officers.

Gen6aC was directed to move to the right - the number of armed officers awaiting him was significantly greater.

"Come with me Captain," said one of the armed officers taking her arm and as she was led away, the last thing Kath'ryn saw was Gen6aC being ordered to the floor so that he could be restrained.

She struggled a moment seeing this being done to him but the officers around her were insistent on leading her away.

"Wait! Leave him be! He saved me!" She tried to pull back and help but the grip on her arm was strong.

"Captain, the Commander wants to debrief you. Please come with us." Kath'ryn was pulled away from the scene unfolding behind her.

As Kath'ryn was hustled away, Gen6aC felt humiliation as his pseudopod limbs were strapped up in secure restraints, guns still trained on him.

He had chosen not to wear any exosuit that would appear threatening - Kath'ryn had advised him on this and he felt very vulnerable at this moment. He wore just the most basic of exosuits that could protect him from the toxic Terran atmosphere and gravity level on-board the warship - but had little else in terms of technical superiority.

Kath'ryn and he had agreed, as they approached, that it would prudent for him not to appear threatening to the crew in any way.

One of the senior officers stepped forward and approached the restrained Flexani as he lay on the floor. "Do not make any attempt to struggle or action will be taken Flexani. Do you understand?"

"I understand Terran." He responded through his suit speaker, looking up at the human in front of him.

"Good. My name is Lieutenant Walker and this is what is going to happen next. You will be taken from here to a holding cell where you will be interrogated. You may or may not be aware, but we are currently on a war footing with the Flexani who have violated the Treaty of JurTan. You are now a prisoner of war and will be treated as such. Is this clear?"

"Yes Terran. I understand my situation completely." He felt dejected inside but he knew that he was far safer here than he would be back on Flexani Prime. His "crimes" would certainly mean his execution if he returned there. At least with these Terrans, he'd be unharmed under the terms of the Treaty.

"I'm not a fucking Terran, you Squiddie. I'm a human." The Lieutenant growled quietly as he pulled the alien up from the floor.

Gen6aC heard and understood this perfectly but chose to remain diplomatic, not running the risk of saying anything that could provoke this tense situation further.

He was then carried unceremoniously down corridors within the warship, and the ex-Arbiter observed that the decks had been cleared of personnel.

His passage was unobstructed as he was led by the guards deep into the interior of the ship.

They arrived eventually at what were obviously the holding cells. It was very clear that this was going to be a place he would be held for a while.

A series of other humans stood around the cell and he was guided into a chamber before his restraints were removed, and the large cryo-glass door sealed shut.

"Hello Flexani, my name is Doctor Clayton," spoke a mature man who stood in front of the holding cell. He was dressed in what Gen6aC surmised was a scientific outfit and carried some equipment with him that he assumed was for the purposes of interrogation.

"We have configured this holding cell for Flexani requirements and, in a few moments, the room will be filled with a fluidic environment which will be compatible with your pulmonary system. After the room fills you will be expected to remove your outer exosuit garment and place it in the compartment to your left." He pointed to an open panel in the wall.

"I trust your suit will be able to confirm whether the environment is compatible before you undress?" he asked.

"I can confirm this, yes Doctor Clayton. You are a medical doctor?"

"I am. I have a Xenomorphic Technical Doctorate from Mars University, and have studied Flexani physiology, so will be able to assist you in any medical requirements you may have while on board the Kydoimos. Whilst you are technically our prisoner, you still have rights and entitlements as agreed under the Treaty of JurTan."

"Thank you Doctor Clayton. Once the fluid enters the chamber I will check its suitability and comply on the order to remove my exosuit." Gen6aC stated to the professional officer.

"Then I will begin."

The Doctor moved to a console nearby and within seconds, fluid began to fill the chamber. They both stood watching as the oxygen/nitrogen atmosphere was slowly replaced with a substitute for Flexani seawater.

After confirmation from his suit on the voracity of the liquid and its suitability for him to breathe, he unsealed the rear compartment to the suit. Swimming free from the exosuit, he gathered it up and folded it into the indicated side compartment before stepping back.

Gen6aC felt naked for the first time and exposed to the Terrans watching him on the other side of the glass.

It was a highly embarrassing and disconcerting situation.

"Thank you. Do you have a name?" Doctor Clayton asked the alien as he floated in the chamber.

"I am known to Kath'ryn of Terra as Gen6aC."

"Kath'ryn? Ah yes, the young woman you came on board with. Gen6aC, I will conduct a series of medical scans with your permission. We need to confirm that you are not carrying any undesired diseases or technology that could compromise the ship. I'm sorry, the scan is invasive but we will be quick and cause you no harm and as little discomfort as is possible."

Realising he really had no choice in the matter he subjugated and said, "Please proceed."

Moments later, the Doctor seemed satisfied with the results of the scan. Bidding Gen6aC goodbye, he left the Flexani floating in the cell.

Gen6aC watched the doctor leave. He was not left entirely alone however. Several guards were stationed outside the cell to ensure that he did nothing untoward.

He floated silently in meditation, trying to calm the turmoil in his mind and hoped that Kath'ryn had managed to share the Flexani and human weapons' technology advancements information with the Captain. He also hoped the Captain had, *what did the Terran's call it, a conscience?*

CHAPTER SIXTEEN
Sources of Information

"So, let me get my head around this Kath'ryn. In brief, you say you've spent the past few days on an alien ship after being rescued by an alien who was hell-bent on killing you and your crew. Now you bring me information on what could be a plot by both the Flexani and the Terran Task Force, about some sort of subterfuge weapons technology programmes and the contrived start of a new Second Stellar War?!"

Captain Middleton was obviously struggling to comprehend this surely concocted story, and to fathom what was real, and what was pure fantasy. Had this erstwhile transport ship captain been brainwashed?

Middleton and Kath'ryn had spent the past three and a half hours in this small room aboard the Kydoimos.

The room contained just two uncomfortable chairs, and a small desk on which were a visual screen, which was currently turned off, an array of snack and drink cans and the ubiquitous coffee pot on a heating plate. Kath'ryn had opted for a hot coffee from the pot, but had regretted this choice ever since.

Captain Middleton had sent off the datacube she had given him that supposedly held the proof of Kath'ryn's ludicrous story for analysis, but he had insisted on interrogating her himself.

He had many questions remaining unanswered and a lot of holes in his current knowledge.

Since they had spoken last, during Kath'ryn's call for help when the Intrepid Star had been first attacked, she had been missing, presumed dead. For many days since that communication, as she and her crew had tried to flee the Torrak drones, somehow she had apparently been captured by and then escaped from creatures which the Flexani alien had called the Dall, found her way to a clandestine Flexani Listening Post, befriended the very alien who had issued the orders that had resulted in the death of her crew; and finally found her way to his ship at the end of a battle only to observe so-called subterfuge weapons technology.

How was he supposed to be expected to swallow that! It was like the plotline of an early twenty-first century e-book!

It had been revelatory hearing her seemingly wild speculations, but as Kath'ryn had shared more and more of the story, he was growing to realise that maybe, just maybe, there might a grain of truth in her incredible tale.

"You say that this alien – Arbiter Gen6aC - revealed all this to you whilst you were on board his Sentinel ship?"

"Yes. I've told you that already." She was irritated by being cooped up in this small room for the past few hours with stale coffee to drink, and ship-replicated food to eat. It was nowhere near as nourishing as the food she'd had eaten on board the Flexani vessel, and she was maudlin about that. She was craving some food that had taste, not just substance.

"So how do you know that the information he gave you is not manufactured? He may have artificially created it in an attempt to gain access to this ship," Middleton pointed out.

"For fucks sake! How many more times? Listen, Captain. I saw the Imperial Rose fire that weapon with my own eyes and I studied the readouts. Gen didn't even know what the waveform was until I told him!"

"Calm down Kath'ryn." he ordered, sensing her frustration and rising ire.

<Captain. I have information that may prove relevant to this investigation> said the voice of the ship's AI, suddenly interrupting them both. It couldn't have done so at a better time, as Kath'ryn started to seek a fight with this man who was keeping her caged like an animal.

Middleton sat back in his chair, watching Kath'ryn wearily and told the AI to continue. It had broken the tension, but Kath'ryn still fumed silently as she listened to the voice of the Kydoimos' AI.

<I have studied the report that Captain Kass supplied in the Flexani datacube with respect to the unusual technology used by the Flexani and the TTF weapons. I have also been observing the interrogation of the Flexani prisoner in the holding cell by Lieutenant Brooke in order to correlate any patterns in the information being shared. I conclude that the datacube analysis is indeed valid and has not been fabricated in any way.>

Well I'm buggered - she is telling the truth thought Middleton and waited for the AI to continue.

<Furthermore, the Flexani and Captain Kass accounts of events both collaborate in terms of timeline and efficacy. From my analysis of the waveform recorded, the Imperial Rose did in fact fire a beam of currently unknown technology toward the Flexani Cruiser Horrax which caused a collapse in the subspace field matrix localised to the Flexani vessel alone, ultimately destroying it. This data was not detected at the time of deployment by our own sensor net.>

"What about the Flexani beam that took out a large part of our shields and our Reaper?"

His crew had felt the loss of the two pilots keenly. The remaining pilots under Flight Leader Boakai's command had been devastated, never having lost anyone in combat before.

<The data recorded from that weapon discharge too is accurate. I can confirm with a high probability, that the Flexani have developed and are now employing a new weapon, based on the manipulation of Corismite crystals.>

"I told you so!" Kath'ryn shouted at Middleton.

He grudgingly accepted she may have been telling the truth.

"Very well. I will contact the Admiralty about this immediately. One of my crew will escort you to our guest quarters where you can rest." He stood up and started to walk out of the room.

As he passed through the doorway, he paused and turned back to face her.

"Apologies for doubting your word Kath'ryn, but in mitigation, you have to admit, without the substantiation from that cube, would you have believed your story? Oh, one last thing Kath'ryn, you may like to know that we managed to rescue one of your crew on a Search & Rescue mission over Mirral. Unfortunately, all of your other crew-mates from the Intrepid Star have been confirmed dead or MIA presumed dead, but - we did manage to save a young pilot, name of Brock. He was found floating in space. His flight suit saved him from serious injury initially but he was close to death by the time we found him with his oxygen level critically low."

Brock! Shit he's alive?

She felt a rush of shame as she had completely forgotten, in the heat of the moment, her companions aboard the Star.

"He... he survived?" she stammered, shock evident on her face.

Nodding he said, "Yes, you'll find him in Medical. Our doctors have been working hard to stabilise him after his exposure to vacuum."

She felt the tears flow down her cheeks and her vision blur as she realised -

At least I did not lose <u>all</u> my crew.

Middleton addressed her, softly this time, "Now if you will excuse me, I am needed back on the Bridge."

++++++++++

Middleton closed the secure link with the Admiralty and considered the conversation he'd just had with Admiral Varnava.

The Admiral knows a hell of a lot more than he's letting on he thought.

That was worrying.

Middleton had shared his report and sent over a copy of the AI assessed datacube.

The Admiral had done well to fake his surprise at hearing the news about the actions of the Imperial Rose. However, Middleton was no fool, he knew when someone was lying - and Varnava had lied to his face. Claiming that he was unaware of any new weapon technology being employed without the rest of the Task Force being informed, but Middleton knew for certain this was untrue.

However, the Admiral had been genuinely surprised to learn about the Flexani beam weapon, and the news that a vast quantity of Corismite ore had gone missing.

He'd given orders to Middleton to head the Kydoimos back to the Mirral sector immediately, and to search the whole vicinity for the missing cargo pods, as well as to check on the safety of the Mining Colony.

Middleton was now suspicious that this assignment was simply a way of getting the Kydoimos out of the Admiral's hair.

Maybe he was just being paranoid, but something just didn't add up, and this irked him greatly.

Meanwhile, the Admiral was livid after closing the link with the Captain of the TTF Kydoimos.

He was worried as to whether the Captain would start asking the questions that did not need to be asked at this time. Just how much of a liability would he turn out to be?

He considered his options.

He knew that the TTF Vanguard had now arrived in the disputed sector, having lagged behind the Imperial Rose.

All three of the TTF warships now were located in that same sector of space and the Admiral was well aware that this was a tactical disadvantage if the Flexani were intent on moving on their own plans.

He made his decision and issued his orders to each of the warship's Captains.

Whilst the TTF Kydoimos would investigate the missing Corismite cargo and babysit the Colony on Mirral, the Rose and the Vanguard would head out to two different locations along the border to deter other vessels from infringing disputed border lines.

He considered taking action against the Kydoimos but was reluctant to lose a warship at such a critical time.

I just need ensure the good Captains' silence he thought. *How though? That's going to need some thought.*

++++++++++

"Terran Task Force warship Kydoimos Mission Log, date as per timestamp, Captain Middleton reporting - begin recording:

Several hours ago we captured a surrendering Flexani vessel with two individual lifeforms on board - one human and one Flexani. The human was the missing Captain from the Raven Ore transport vessel, Intrepid Star, which crash-landed on planet XT-67-F known as Heimdallr, with a loss of all hands apart from the pilot, Alan Brock,. He was recovered from open space by the S&R mission conducted by the flight team.

When I debriefed Captain Kass I was concerned by the nature of the information she revealed to me and recorded by myself. In her report, she states that she had been captured on the planet after surviving the crash by a Flexani, known as Arbiter Gen6aC and subsequently they had both been captured by an insectoid race known to us as the Dall. The Flexani is the one we are currently holding in our cells.

Captain Kass explained to me that when they both escaped and she had performed field surgery on the alien due to injuries taken during their flight to freedom away from the Dall. It seems that he now has some honour pledge to her, and took her back to his own vessel. There they seemed to have discussed at length, the situation over her crashed vessel and his part in this attack.

It is confirmed he was the Flexani operating the Listening Post that we have been searching for, and he is the alien responsible for ordering the drone attacks and the destruction of the Intrepid Star.

We have incarcerated him under article seventeen of the JurTan Treaty as a war criminal for trial on Earth.

Captain Kass has furnished with me a Flexani datacube. This datacube contains highly accurate data on the attack by the Flexani Cruiser Horaxx on the TTF Kydoimos. It would appear that the Flexani possess scanning systems capable of extreme range as the Captain and the Flexani were able to watch our battle with the Horaxx from the Listening Post, although we are still to obtain that Listening Post's exact location.

The datacube is of great significance since it contains information on the weapon that the Flexani used against us. It is uncertain at this time, but the datacube seems to contain conclusive proof that the weapon is based on Corismite crystal technology, and we are currently underway to Mirral to confirm that the Raven Ore mining colony there is safe. If the base and the ore is at risk, we are ordered to engage the enemy to protect the colony at all costs.

Open subdirectory with private encryption, access my voice only, begin:

What disturbs me the most is that further data held on this datacube proves that our own TTF Imperial Rose warship, commanded by Captain Naro, also has new weapon technology. We have not been made aware of through TTF channels.

We saw the destruction of the Horaxx in the battle and assumed at the time that it was a faulty drive system that gave out when the ship tried to enter subspace.

Now though I'm not sure that is what we saw.

I've informed the Admiralty about this information but I can only conclude that Captain Naro has a weapon on board his ship that he does not want me or any other TTF vessel to know about. An even deeper mystery to me is that Admiral Varnava seems to know this and also does not want to share its relevance.

I am concerned, very concerned.

Therefore, I shall keep a careful eye on our Flexani prisoner and Captain Kass. The Kydoimos will find out if the colony is safe before I consider my next steps.

Close and secure subdirectory.

End report"

++++++++++

At the end of her debriefing, Kath'ryn followed the Captain's order to attend the ships' Medical Bay to undergo a medical examination once she had showered and dressed.

Thankfully, she was given a clean bill of health. Gen6aC's Vorrax had healed her broken rib and repaired her other abrasions well after her run in with the insectoid race she now knew to be called the Dall.

There had been little the medical team could say about her medical state. She was in perfect health.

Whilst in the Medical Bay, she also managed to have a very joyful reunion with Alain Brock, the young pilot of the Intrepid Star - the only other discovered survivor of the drone attack.

He was recovering well and had been in Stasis for a day previously recovering from his decompression and the subsequent after effects of hypoxia as his O^2 levels were still extremely low, but rising as he recovered.

Brock had shared with Kath'ryn his dramatic experience of being sucked out of a hole in the Intrepid Star's side moments before it had exploded.

He shared the horror at seeing the ship plummet into the atmosphere of the alien planet below and how he had known he was going to die.

Kath'ryn was just happy to know that he was recovering well and would be discharged soon from Medical.

It was unknown what would happen to him next - he seemed like a changed man to her now. More mature and nothing like the flippant young pilot she had known aboard the ill-fated Intrepid Star.

Kath'ryn shared her experiences with the young pilot as well, but heavily censored the events between her escape from the Dall and the present. Until her suspicions were acted upon, the less people who knew of them, the better. Besides that, she didn't want to concern him overly, he was still in his recovery phase and she did not want that slowed.

The Doctor and the attending nurse had given Kath'ryn a thorough scan and even checked out her Smart Mind. All seemed fine as far as they could see, and she had been discharged as fit.

She had no other place to go now apart from the mess-hall, and not feeling in the mood yet for socialising, opted instead to visit Gen6aC in his incarceration.

Gen6aC had been interrogated intensely over the past six hours and was resting, when he received Kath'ryn's visit.

She stood outside the glass holding cell, dressed in the ship's attire - having changed out of her flight suit into the standard dress uniform of the Kydoimos.

"Hello Gen," she said as he floated to the glass to greet her.

"Greetings Kath'ryn of Terra. I am glad to see you are unharmed and well."

"What about you? I hope they are treating you OK. I'm really sorry to see you in here," she said, gesturing to the cell he was floating in.

"Please, do not harbour any concerns for me. I am being treated well under the circumstances and have been able to rest. It has been a very difficult time over the last few si-krec's."

This was the first opportunity Kath'ryn had had to see the Flexani without his exosuit or Battlesuit, and he was an unusual sight.

She had of course, seen digital representations of the Flexani on the net, but nothing had prepared her for the real vividness of him floating a few feet away from her.

His limbs looked so flimsy in the fluid, drifting aimlessly around his very pale coloured torso, the upper portion of which featured one large eye that tracked her movements.

It was well known that the Flexani compound eye was more advanced than human eyes. In fact, it was much like the eye found on the Mantis Shrimp on

Earth which had one of the most elaborate visual systems ever discovered before the Flexanis had appeared on Earth.

Flexani eyes, scientists speculated, seemed to be so closely related in some way to the Mantis Shrimp that lots of wild rumours about them being a distant relation to the Shrimps surfaced the net time and time again.

Compared to the three types of colour receptive cones that humans possess in their eyes, the single eye of a Flexani carried nearly eighteen types of colour receptive cones. It is thought this gives the aliens the ability to recognise as colours a wide range of radiation frequencies.

For example, their ultra-violet vision can detect five different frequency bands in the deep ultraviolet.

To do this they use two photo-receptors in combination with four different colour filters and it is widely believed they are not sensitive to infrared light.

At least one Caste has been bred with additional optical enhancements able to detect circularly polarised light.

The midband region of a Flexani's eye is made up of six rows of specialised ommatidia - a cluster of photo-receptor cells. Four of these rows carry up to eighteen different photo-receptor pigments, twelve for colour sensitivity, the remainder for colour filtering. The two other rows, it was speculated, capable of perceiving both polarised light and multi-spectral images.

The compound eye of a Flexani was further divided into three regions.

This configuration enabled each Flexani to see objects with three individual parts and imparts trinocular vision and complex depth perception.

Their minds are capable of processing this information very efficiently and combining the optical data in a centre of their brain that is so complex when compared to the brain of a human.

Looking at his naked form, Gen6aC's body was pale, very pale. This she surmised was probably due to the lack of sunlight at depth in the Flexani oceans and that much was true to the limited human eyesight. However, since Flexani eyesight had developed to such a great degree over millennia, they themselves actually saw a scintillating array of colours and shades that provided Gen6aC with patterns like that of a butterfly's wing.

Beautiful and harmonious to other Flexani - but unfortunately bland to humans.

"I trust you have spoken with the good Captain?" Gen6aC enquired curiously.

"I did, and he didn't believe me for ages but after analysing the data you provided on that cube, he really had no choice but to accept the fact that both sides of this conflict are using dangerous new weapon technology that are being kept secret. Certainly from Captain Middleton's point of view, he was as much in the dark about the human weapon as we were. I understand from what he was saying that he's informed his superiors."

"I sense the vessel is underway again. We are currently moving."

"Moving? You can sense that?" She was amazed at this as she herself had felt nothing.

"Yes. We Flexani do have the innate ability to sense motion, even in space. We are not in subspace, but we are moving, that much I am certain of."

She didn't know what to say about that but believed his conclusion. She had come to trust and like the alien over the past few days and he certainly had a sense of honour in him.

"Do you think they will free you soon?"

He considered this and said simply "I do not believe they will. I am a prisoner of war and am being treated as such. While your people are kind and are obeying rules of war, when conflict begins again, I am fearful of what could happen in the heat of battle."

"I don't think Captain Middleton would allow his crew to harm a prisoner!" she said horrified.

"You can never be sure what an individual may or may not do based on pure reasoning and logic. The Flexani have studied Terrans for decades and we understand you more than I think you would care to admit, as I have been at pains to pint out to you before Kath'ryn."

"I'm not going to get drawn into a philosophical debate with you Gen," she smiled.

He joked back "Well, I need something to occupy my incarceration here."

She sighed, knowing she would likely never see him again. "I want to thank you Gen - for saving my life."

He was silent for a while, floating around the small chamber before gliding back to the window and placing his main pseudopod arm on the glass.

She stepped forward, conscious of the guard behind watching her very closely and place her own hand on the glass in a gesture of compassion and friendship.

CHAPTER SEVENTEEN
Next Steps

Captain Middleton and First Officer Brooke consulted the ship's AI in his private ready room off the bridge.

They had spent the last hour studying the information held on the alien's datacube, and analysed its information as the Kydoimos headed back to Heimdallr.

"I must say sir, it's pretty conclusive proof that the Imperial Rose does have new weapon tech that we haven't been allowed to know about. What did Admiral Varnava say when you consulted with him? Why aren't we aware of it?" asked Brooke.

"The Admiral was actually very evasive when I confronted him with the contents of this cube," the Captain said pointing to the metallic box on his desk. "He even suggested that this Flexani datacube had been faked and I was to treat Captain Kass as a suspected collaborator."

"A collaborator!?" she raised her eyebrows, "I've met her and I watched your interview with her. I don't believe for one minute that she would be working for the Flexani sir. They destroyed her ship and almost all her crew."

He nodded "I know. Which is why I feel Admiral Varnava is not telling me the *complete* truth."

He studied his FO before saying, "You've read her file I guess?"

"Kath'ryn Kass? Yes I have sir. It makes for some interesting reading I must say. Was she really cashiered out of the service about four years ago?"

"Yes. I've actually studied the protracted report on the incident and I think now it is extremely questionable whether she actually committed the so-called crime that apparently caused the deaths of her crew-mates on the TTF Valiant. I do know that she was the only one to survive the alleged incident with the powerlifter unit. What raises my suspicions about the whole incident though, was the fact all three of them were in the cargo bay at such a late hour and why were they were using the equipment to transport something away from the storage racks in the first place. I find it strange that the report redacted any information on what the item was, and why the powerlifter malfunctioned, killing the other two crew. She was very reticent to answer questions about that for some reason, and that resulted in her losing her commission with the Task Force. I'm beginning to think she may have been coerced in giving her silence but for the life of me, I am at a loss to know why."

"Do you believe she is telling the truth now though?" Brooke asked.

"I do actually." He rubbed his hand over his eyes, tiredness creeping into his voice.

Brooke saw a very human side of her XO. He was obviously under tremendous strain right now and she guessed he was surviving on coffee and very little rest.

"Well sir, we are nearly at Heimdallr and the last known position of the missing cargo pods. If this data is to be believed," she said gesturing to the datacube, "then we won't find the pods floating in space. That would prove that the Flexani must have taken them."

"And the mining colony?" he considered.

"I don't wish to speculate Captain but I do fear the worst…"

"I'm afraid I agree with you Brooke. I think we will find we have lost the colony already and that the Flexani are there waiting for us."

"But," he continued, "I think we must prepare our ground troops for the possibility of an attack. If necessary, I want us to go in hard and fast and catch any Flexani while they are still on the ground. We have our orders from the Admiral, whether we are to trust him or not. I really do feel that we are being used as a pawn in some massive chess game, and I don't like it."

"Of course sir." She paused before continuing guardedly "May I suggest you get a good meal and some rest Captain? You do look tired and I can cover for the next few hours on the bridge."

He considered his levels of tiredness and knew she was right. He'd certainly be no good to his ship nor to his crew if he was not well rested when the proverbial hit the fan.

Acceding he said, "Agreed. You have the bridge Brooke."

++++++++++

The Flexani warrior guard was watching the

Maestri Gen8dX closely as he operated the clumsy alien machinery.

The Maestri was operating the Terran drilling equipment remotely via a series of autonomous units powered by individual Smart Minds, slaved to him through his subspace tweeter.

These autonomous units, known as GorDak Drones, were stubby machines with three legs for stability and a series of six manipulator arms that protruded from a pyramid-like torso. This compact torso contained a powerful generator and a Smart Mind, as well as a complex sensor net that enabled it to work efficiently within the dark environment of the dirty cave where the vein of Corismite ore was located.

The GorDak drones had been in continuous use since the elimination of all of the humans of the colony, in order to mine ever single gram of Corismite Crystal ore from the chamber for refinement to use in the new weapons.

The Flexani had a deadline.

They had already worked more efficiently that the human miners ever had. The advanced technological tools and scanning equipment had found richer veins of ore than the Terran miners had up to that point. To save time though, they were having to use the abandoned human mining tools to actually mine the ore.

The Maestri had tasked the GorDaks to mine the raw ore and transport it to the surface as fast as they could. Aware that Terran ships may be on their way, speed was of the essence.

The Flexani mining team had therefore been established on Mirral with many ground troops in battle armour deployed to protect their mining efforts, but only had a small number of transport vessels. Whilst two Torrak drone ships were patrolling the atmosphere as air cover, they would not be any match for a Terran warship. The Flexani team knew that, and had to work fast.

The Maestri engineer was distracted momentarily by a subspace ping from his tweeter. One of his colleagues was contacting him.

"Maestri Gen8dX, our long range sensors have detected a Terran vessel entering the system at high delta-vee toward this location. We estimate we have one frec before they will be in weapons range. I have tasked the Torraks to give us cover but I suggest you immediately start to conclude your work quickly and prepare for evacuation."

"Thank you Maestri Gen4rF. I will complete extraction of this last vein of Corismite ore and finish up ensuring the raw material is loaded onto the transport ships. Do we know if the Terrans are aware of our presence here?"

"Negative Maestri Gen8dX. I do not believe the Terran vessel is aware of us, the assumption is that the Terran's are now investigating the loss of contact with their mining base, but since the destruction of the Empirical Cruiser Horaxx we cannot consider this intelligence accurate. Furthermore, we know that they are fully capable of destroying our Transport ships easily so we must be in subspace before they arrive."

"That is an accurate assessment. Very well, I will conclude my business here and get back to the ship immediately."

He ordered each of the slaved GorDak drones to complete their current tasks, and then to exit the dirty chamber, carrying the containers filled with raw ore.

Maestri Gen8dX and his guard then also left, heading towards the mine entrance and to their waiting vessel.

++++++++++

Rested now, Captain James Middleton and his bridge officers watched as they entered the local system where the planets Mirral and Heimdallr orbited their star.

It was a bleak and deserted solar system, with only four planets of any significant size and a star that was only slightly larger and redder than the Terran Sun.

<Scans initiated.> the AI announced to the Bridge.

Middleton watched as live data from the ship's sensor net started to populate the holo-table matrix, and the display started to show the system in detail. Under the subdued lighting of the bridge the faces of the bridge crew glowed with the light from the digitally generated images.

Details were noted and information assessed by both human and artificial minds.

When the new scans of the system were compared to the extensive scans taken when they were last here to conduct the S&R, it was obvious there were significant and worrying changes.

"Have you been able to establish contact with the Raven Ore complex yet?" he asked, turning to his Comms Officer.

"Negative sir. Nothing on subspace or any emergency bands." the officer replied.

"There." Brooke pointed to the holo-display.

Middleton directed his attention to the indicated area of space on the display. She pointed to an area on the map that had before contained six floating pods of ore. Now it was simply empty space. It was close to the point where the Intrepid Star pilot Brock had been picked up, but right now the current scan was showing nothing.

Shit. He cursed silently. *The Flexani have taken them it seems.*

Brooke pulled up a timeline view to compare. The pods were definitely there a few days ago. They were there no longer though.

<Captain, I am detecting subspace waveforms that match Flexani engine technology leading away from the planetoid. Five ships of unknown mass and size have left this system and engaged their subspace

drives back into Flexani space within the past twenty seven minutes.>

Brooke looked at her Captain. She knew what he was thinking. *The miners were dead.*

Closing his eyes for a moment, trying to gain some composure before he spoke again, James Middleton leant heavily on the table, deep in thought.

He came to a decision.

"We'll send down troops to the surface. Four Reaper crews and three of our shuttles for support. If anyone is still alive, I want them off planet and aboard this ship. Do what is necessary – understood?"

She understood his order perfectly. She turned to her Padd and sent the command to the flight crew to prepare for departure.

++++++++++

"Aghhh!"

Ed DeMarco and Pete Walker, two human infantry officers encased in enhanced battlesuits were being struck by debris, flung by GorDak drones who were also wielding long metal beams in their manipulators.

These autonomous units were launching large rocks at the men, in an effort to halt their progress through the Base.

The battlesuits deflected most of the impact, but both of them were knocked violently to the floor.

Physics being the bitch it was, their battlesuits were unable to stop the force of the blows. The conservation of momentum from the rocks was transferred to their mass and the balance in the equation meant they were sent sliding along the ground as the rocks split upon their suit's hard outer shells. Small shards of debris rained down.

The Flexani had left a contingent of these independent drone units behind as a sacrificial force to defend the mine against any unsuspecting Terrans. Each of their Smart Minds had been programmed by Maestri Gen8dX and his colleague to ensure that they caused maximum damage to the intruders, in order to hinder progress and generally disrupt any Task Force members from re-taking the Base. They were not expected to stop the Terran force, but to delay it as long as possible. The longer the delay, the further into subspace the ore carriers could flee.

The first site that had greeted the ground troops on landing at the Base was that of the lifeless bodies of the Terran miners in various scenes of carnage. Those first infantrymen were left in no doubt as to the ferocity of the Flexani warriors initial attacked the base. They had acted without mercy, deliberately leaving no one alive.

Upon the discovery of the bodies, an angry Middleton ordered the squads to advance immediately into the base to investigate further.

That had been a mistake.

The first unsuspecting squad to encounter a GorDak drone suffered badly.

Two of the four-man team had been crushed to death beneath a large section of steel walkway.

The drone had weakened the structure just enough, so that when both the men stepped out onto the steel framework together in their heavy battlesuits, their combined weight caused the remaining support bolts to shear and the men plummeted fifty feet into the cavern underneath, the twisted metal walkway falling onto their bodies.

Even their cybernetically enhanced carbon-fibre and nano exosuits had been unable to cope with the impact of the fall, and the half-ton of metal falling upon them.

The drone never even had to move from its hiding place.

So the remaining two squad members, shocked at seeing their colleagues fall, had barely time to register its presence before the GorDak drone, on the other side of the felled walkway entrance, launched steel pipes at lethal speeds towards them.

Retreating to the safety of a covering tunnel corner, they regrouped and fired their fletchette rifles upon the drone. It took an agonising few minutes before they were able to finally destroy it.

Their main access route now rendered unavailable, the pair had to waste further precious minutes in backtracking and finding a new route through to the corridor beyond.

Meanwhile, in another part of the complex, another infantry team was encountering more Flexani resistance.

"Fire at will!" Sergeant Stables ordered DeMarco and Walker as he watched them sliding over the ground, rocks bouncing off them. He and the remaining squad member, Volkes, leapt into action.

With Volkes providing covering fire to protect the men on the ground, the Sergeant leapt around the end of the wall and, using handles convenient mounted on the necks of the two men's suits, dragged them with power-assisted limbs to the safety of cover behind the wall.

The two downed members of the combat team, well trained, kept up continuous fire on the drones from their own weapons, even as they were dragged to safety.

Raising his own rifle, the Sergeant fired in short bursts from behind the wall, and his swarms of fletchette rounds struck the drones, the corridor and any other object within the killzone opposite.

The drones continued to throw objects and debris at the small squad with terrifying accuracy even as they were fired on.

The men took cover behind any strategic rocky outcrops and spoil heaps, and the fight started to draw out. Neither party gaining enough visibility to get a good shot at the other.

"Sod it!" said Volkes as he slapped in another clip. "This is bloody crazy. We need to get around these bastards!"

Sergeant Stables took a moment to assess the situation, his artificial Smart Mind providing tactical assessments and strategies to compliment his own thoughts on the problem.

Only the senior ranks of the TTF infantry had Smart Mind technology. He himself, had had his own Smart Mind for only a few months and was still learning to listen to its suggestions.

When he had first been assigned to the Kydoimos, he had been surprised to learn that while the lovely First Officer had one in her sexy head, oddly enough their Aussie Captain had not. *Guess he was old school.*

"OK, here's what we're going to do. DeMarco, Walker, you two stay put, get your breath back and cover our arses. Lay down as much covering fire as you can, while I throw a little party favour into the mix." Stables reached behind and withdrew two grenades from his belt.

DeMarco and Walker grinned at each other from behind their faceplates.

"Oh yeah Sarge." said Volkes, "bring it on!"

"All ready?"

With nods all around, the two men still lying on the floor began rapid firing at the drones as best they could and tried to keep them occupied while the Sergeant prepared the grenades. Striking the firing pins, he span around the open section in the wall and threw the two grenades with superhuman strength, the suit providing power that his own muscles could not.

He whirled back behind the wall as the grenades struck the section of corridor behind the drones.

Stables had aimed for a point above the drone's 'head' so that the grenades bounced down and landed beneath the drone's feet where they might not be able to reach them before it was too late.

His aim was accurate. The suit providing him with a level of precision that he would not have attained himself.

Within seconds, the concussive force of an explosion ripped through the small section of the base, pressure from the blast forcing the drones off their feet and back into the walls.

Volkes stepped into the void, dust and smoke obscuring the immediate vicinity but his enhanced vision enabled him to see the drones clearly. He aimed his fletchette rifle and turned to full auto. Unloading round after hypersonic round into one of the drones that had a section of its outer shell torn away by the blast.

DeMarco and Walker despite their earlier knockdown stepped into the chamber too, and stood beside him, firing their own weapons at the other drone, as it struggled to get to its feet.

Several of its arms had been crushed into the wall by the explosion, but it still had four arms free and it was pulling itself up slowly.

A lucky shot penetrated the optical sensor at the front of the torso and entered the Smart Mind, destroying the cognitive function of the autonomous unit. The drone collapsed to the floor never to move again.

Volkes took another step forward towards the drone he was firing at and screamed, "Die you fucker!"

Rounds blasted holes in its armour as well as the surrounding floor and one of its arms was completely destroyed by the weapon fire.

"VOLKES! It's already dead, you idiot!"

Acrid smoke spun in lazy spirals above the destroyed drone.

His rifle clicked empty as he stood panting in exertion.

Volkes felt the red mist that had clouded his vision subside, his levels of adrenaline abating.

"Good" he said simply and turned to face the rest of his squad. "SHIT! Sarge!"

He ran back to the section of wall they had sheltered behind before Stables had thrown the grenades.

The Sergeant was slumped on the floor, one of his hands holding a section of metal pipe that stuck out of his stomach.

Shocked, his men assessed the situation.

"Squiddie 'droid got me good boys," he grunted indicating the obviousness of the blunt pipe.

They saw, through his faceplate, his mouth full of blood.

His Smart Mind had already suppressed the pain to a level he could tolerate. It had coldly informed him of its assessment of the wound and his chance of recovery - which was surprisingly good - so he knew he was not going to die, but it was exceedingly disconcerting to see a large section of steel pipe protruding from his gut.

In the split second before Stables had thrown the grenades, the GorDak drone had thrown the metal pipe like a javelin - it had struck the Sergeant in his stomach but his raised adrenaline levels had masked the impact and subsequent pain until after he'd taken cover.

He'd been more than a little surprised to see the addition the Flexani drone had made to his battlesuit.

Acting immediately thanks to the training that had been drilled into them by the very Sergeant now impaled in front of them, the rest of the squad called for medical help over the comms whilst applying pressure and packing field dressings around the wound. They knew better than to remove the pipe - the medical team on the Kydoimos would stabilise the wounded Sergeant and he'd be back in action in no time.

He'd live.

Unfortunately, that was more than could be said for the dead civilian miners in the room behind the destroyed drones.

"Take it easy Sarge," said Walker, their field medic as he pressed a small cylinder filled with morphine to a special port on the Sergeant's suit. Walker injected the medicine into his bloodstream.

It would have been too much trouble to remove the battlesuit, so they'd been designed with the ability to administer medicines in battle through the port that was connected to a cannula that the suit was able to quickly insert into a vein, whenever a capsule was plugged into the port.

His breathing slowed and the pain subsided as the morphine took effect.

"Ahhh... That's better. Wake me later guys. I need a rest now. Getting a bit old for this sorta shit."

Grinning at his own joke he closed his eyes and his team waited for the Medics to arrive and evac him out of the base, to the ship in orbit.

++++++++++

Clearing the base of the remaining Flexani GorDak drones took the better part of another four hours.

The ground combat teams only met three more drones in key sections across the base. However, these drones had been extremely busy laying multiple traps and pitfalls - so it was a cautious Team Leader that finally declared the base safe.

Captain Middleton and First Officer Brooke landed in one of the remaining shuttles, and immediately headed into the complex, flanked by battlesuited guards. They wanted to see and assess, first-hand, the damage that had been caused by the Flexani occupation.

Shaking his head with grief and silent fury, Middleton and Brooke made their way past the many dead bodies of the colonists and miners.

Thankfully, his crew had covered most of the bodies with sheets and fabric in order to give them some respect and dignity, and he knew recovery crews would be coming soon to take them back to the Kydoimos in order to return them home to their loved ones on Earth or Mars.

Stepping over some burnt furniture he said to his FO, "It's clear to me that the Flexani took everything they could before they left. I very much doubt we'll find anything relevant or of value here now I think."

She concurred with his assessment.

The mining base was a total loss, in both material terms and in human lives.

"The way I see it, we have two options here. Either we destroy the base completely from orbit so the Flexani can't mine any more without founding a new base of their own, or we leave it intact, such as it is, and station a contingent of infantry here on the off-chance they'll be back."

"You think they will Captain?"

Nodding he stated, "Almost certainly. They left in a hurry when we arrived. That means they had no serious firepower to protect their operation - this was a snatch and grab mission."

He continued with his assessment, "Furthermore, we know that there are very few places in the universe – well, that we know about at least - where Corismite can be found and mined safely in any measurable quantity. This is one of them. Now I'm sure the Flexani must be aware of all the other places and are already mining them, so they must be pretty desperate for large quantities of high quality Corismite ore to attack this base - unless they had no other option."

"That seems reasonable. I would think this is a convenient location for them too as it had a mining operation already set up. All they had to do was kill all the human miners and use the equipment they had here to mine the ore," responded Brookes.

"Exactly."

Pausing for a moment to glance at two small shapes of what had obviously been children, now concealed beneath a dirty sheet, he stated, voice full of emotion, "However, it's obvious they didn't get the chance to bleed this mine completely dry. From what we know, this mine had a lot of ore that the miners had not yet reached. So I doubt that, in just the day or so they were here, that the Flexani managed to mine every last nugget."

"I doubt the TTF and the government on Earth would appreciate us destroying the mine either. Raven Ore too would have more than a few choice words to say on the matter I guess." She smiled mirthlessly as she said this.

"Yeah. So that leaves us with just the one option. We're going to need some troops left here to protect this base until reserves from the Imperial Rose and the Vanguard can get here."

Taking a deep breath and smelling the subtle sweet odour of death mixed into the dust and smoke pervading the area around them, Brooke sighed, agreeing with her Captain.

"Right. Make sure we leave enough equipment, two Reapers and one of the shuttles with enough fuel and ammunition to protect the mine. Assume that they'll be here for a while, so ensure they have sufficient provisions - speak to the Quartermaster about that."

"How many squads shall we leave sir?"

He considered this for a moment.

"I'm loathe to leave more than we can afford. With us already down two pilots, we'll be left with what, just three shuttles and five Reapers on the Kydoimos. Speak to the Sergeant at Arms, but I think four squads will be enough."

"That's most of our current infantry complement sir. You do know that?"

"Yes, of course I do, but I think right now they are needed here and not on board the Kydoimos."

She understood the reasoning behind that.

"Shall we also leave some of the medical team here?" she enquired.

"Hmmm. I'm not so sure Doctor Clayton would like any of his team here when we might need them on the ship but he does needs to send at least one or two nurses down. If the shit does hit the fan and the Flexani's return soon, they could be required. Issue the order. I know he won't like it and I'm sure I'll never hear the end of it…"

Brooke knew that the English doctor could be abrasive, and had often had strong words with the Captain about the operation of his division on the ship.

"Understood." she said, "And Ops and Facilities - any crew from them?"

"We're stripping the Kydoimos of good people here Brooke." He looked conflicted. "Dammit. Yes, we will need engineering and facilities people on the ground to ensure we have a good defensive stance should they need it. Assign as many as you feel we can afford to spare. I hope that our sister ships can spare some men too. I don't want the Kydoimos with only a skeleton crew should we have to go into battle again."

"Very well Captain. I'll get this done as quickly as I can."

She headed off and once again, Middleton's gaze fell on the two tiny bodies lying under the sheet.

Children who'd never again know the joy of another birthday.

He felt the weight of the situation and his responsibility lying heavy on his shoulders.

CHAPTER EIGHTEEN
Red Horse Rides

Admiral Varnava and Joshua Stormont, the Secretary of Defence for the Terran Task Force, both stood watching the exosuited men load up unmarked crates into the cargo hold of a shuttle.

The shuttle was bound for a TTF warship called the Nemesis.

Named after a Deity in Greek mythology, it was a spirit of divine retribution.

Apt name thought SecDef Stormont, knowing just what was contained in the cargo was that was being loaded.

An Imperator-class ship, almost identical in design to the Kydoimos, the Nemesis however, had more Reapers in its hangers, and was equipped with a full complement of new stealth missiles as part of Project Red Horse.

However, the most important and significant piece of technology aboard the whole ship was an experimental device that, it was hoped, would shield the ship from Flexani sensors in the same way the missiles had been designed to do.

It was untested though - hiding a missile merely a few metres long was far simpler than a hiding a four-hundred-and-twenty metre long warship by the same technology.

Black Snow - the project created by the ill-fated Doctor Kluska and her team - was ensconced in the missile warhead payloads.

Each of the seventy-five missiles stored billions of nanites containing the specialised programming for the deadly Black Snow protocol.

Each missile was scheduled to be transported to the TTF-200955x Nemesis, ready for deployment on to Flexani Prime itself.

SecDef Stormont wanted to be present to see the final warhead being loaded himself. He was keen to see the long ripening fruits of his labours over the past decade, come to its final deadly conclusion.

War had begun, and was now intended to be won.

Flexani and TTF warship had already engaged by the outer borderlands of human and Flexani space, and each side was releasing the throttle on its war machine. *It was inevitable* Stormont thought, *that mankind will be the ones destined to defeat the alien ghost that had haunted mankind since the 1900's.*

History had created the alien threat in literature, movies and more recently VR.

With the first encounters with a truly alien race, man had been thrown into a maelstrom of challenges - religious, political, technological.

Today all that would change.

So far as Stormont and his compatriots across the globe and on Mars were concerned, they would finally take back their moral place in the universe, by destroying the Flexani presence that clouded the skies over Earth.

A deeply religious man, Joshua had faced his own demons when he saw the Flexani for the first time when they landed near a small hospital in County Londonderry, Ireland. It was not known why they choose this location - maybe they were unaware that the Irish were mainly a Catholic society in that area or more probably it was pure chance that led them to choose that particular landing site - but the miracles they had performed on the first day certainly shocked the world.

This simple act of healing the infirm at the small provincial hospital struck discord through the

Catholic society and the Vatican rushed to release a press release, calling for calm.

Some called them angels.

Many vilified them as demons.

Most simply chose to continue to go to work every day and try and ignore their impact on their lives.

Stormont however was in the second classification and, presumably because of his own strict religious upbringing, saw them as demons hiding as angels bearing gifts.

It was not until the first Stellar War had broken out, that he became convinced he had been right and choose at that moment to do what was necessary to eradicate these beasts from the universe.

His mind had started to daydream when he realised that the Admiral was speaking to him.

"Sorry, yes José. Lost in thought there for a moment. What was it you said?" turning to look at the Admiral.

The Admiral repeated his question, seeking reassurance for his next step.

"I am about to issue orders to send the Nemesis into Flexani territory under stealth. Captain Tonev has been chosen along with her crew to carry out this mission. What course of action do you wish us to take should they be discovered sir?"

"I'm assuming the Rose and the Vanguard are still patrolling the Border?"

"Yes sir. Both Captain Naro and Captain Boskowitz are still in the area, as is the Kydoimos. However, I've sent the Kydoimos to Mirral to investigate the mining colony and expect a report from Middleton soon. He has furnished me with a disturbing report that the Flexani have a new weapon, based on Corismite. We believe that is why they attacked the freighter – for its cargo of Corismite ore."

Pursing his lips Stormont said, "Corismite. That's concerning but not unexpected I guess. Those Flexani were always slippery bastards but you can't blame them for trying to create new weapons, after all..." and he pointed to the cargo being loaded onto the shuttle, "...we've done the same."

"No sir. However, if the Flexani discover the Nemesis for any reason, do we send our ships over the border to protect her?"

Thinking for a moment, then shaking his head he replied, "Too risky. Right now one vessel acting on its own can be put down to a maverick Captain taking action of his own volition, and we're prepared to deal with the political ramifications of that if necessary. Four ships entering Flexani space, now that would be another matter."

"No, make sure the good Captain Tonev is aware that should they be discovered, they are to take out as many of the enemy as they can, before detonating their engines. We cannot afford to have Black Snow or Red Horse fall into their slippery tentacles."

Admiral Varnava had to agree, and Captain Tonev was already aware that her mission could be a one-way trip for her and the ship. In addition to her, only her First Officer and the ship's AI knew the real reason for their foray into Flexani space, the rest of the Nemesis crew were ignorant, and would remain so until the mission was accomplished, or die in the attempt still in ignorance.

The AI on board Nemesis had been commanded and programmed to present altered telemetry to the bridge crew so that they were not aware of their real location at any time. To the men and women on board, they would think that the TTF Nemesis was still in human space. There must be no risk of any do-gooding crewmember turning traitor and forewarning the enemy.

The last of the unmarked containers was loaded into the shuttle.

The two leaders turned back to watch exosuited workmen stepped away from the hatch as it closed.

A ground crew gave the all-clear, and the shuttle rose on its thrusters, the backwash blowing across the ground as it lifted into the air, and turned toward the warship in orbit.

++++++++++

Kath'ryn Kass and Alain Brock were deep in conversation, seated in one of the mess-halls on the warship.

Alain had been discharged from the Medical Wing a few hours before, and with no one else to talk to, had sought out his former Captain.

They now ate a meal together, talking about their lost colleagues. Sharing stories about Jung and the others victims of the drone attack.

"I spoke to someone at headquarters earlier," Kath'ryn said to him as he chewed on his food.

Raising his eyebrows he said, "Really? What did they say?"

Shrugging slightly she replied, "Well you know how it is. Blah Blah ...'you lost a multi-million credit transport vessel under your command, along with billions of credits worth of Corismite, and only you and one other of your crew survived.'" Adjusting her voice slightly, pretending she was a ROCL staff minion talking to her through the comms channel.

Shrugging slightly and trying to make light of the message she said, "Needless to say, there'll be an inquiry when we get back to Mars base."

"Oh. But you didn't do anything wrong!" he blurted out, in defence of his Captain.

She smiled wearily and responded. "Alain, you're too young to know the process that the big corporates like to follow - but it's no different from the military. They need their t's crossed and their i's dotted." She took a sip of her cool beer and continued "Right now, they'll be poring over my last log report scrutinising every word and phrase. All of my comms messages with the crew and the Colony, and I'm sure any telemetry from the Intrepid Star. Looking for ways that their really expensive lawyers can find loopholes in the work we did. I can guarantee that some middle manager is running around like a headless chicken right now, as his or her senior manager screams at them for their ineptitude."

She smiled at this thought.

"A ship was destroyed and you can be sure that Raven Ore wants answers. Its unlikely they give a toss for you and I, much less the poor bastards who died on that rust bucket. I guess they'll even attempt to sue the Task Force at some point for not defending the sector well enough - but I know I will be out of a job, long before that injunction is filed with the courts."

"Out of a job?" He was confused. "I don't understand... why would HQ sack you over this!?"

"Because they need a scapegoat Alain." She sighed at his naïvety.

"I'm an easy target with my past. They will find a way to pin something on me - enough to terminate my employment. I'm sure they will pay me off a nice tidy sum to keep me silent, but it all amounts to the same result. I doubt I will have a job with ROCL much longer."

She put the bottle to her lips and drank hard. She needed another drink. Something stronger than beer...

"Cheer up Brock!" she said putting on a false smile, "you'll have all the ladies after you know, all wanting to know how you survived decompression and being cast adrift in space."

He didn't know what to make of that statement. "Not sure I want the attention," he replied shyly.

"Ha! I bet you won't say that when the women come calling. Well the good thing is that you are safe and with luck, any investigation won't be blamed on you. I'll make sure of that."

"Thank you Captain."

"Kath'ryn. I'm not even sure it is appropriate to call me Captain now. I don't have a ship to command. Call me Kath'ryn." She said warmly. "Now. Another drink?"

Hours later they exited the Kydoimos' only bar. Alain stumbled over the entrance as two of the Kydoimos' engineering crew stepped past him laughing, heading into the bar.

The two remaining crewmen of the Intrepid Star mining transport vessel had been drinking for the past few hours. A chance to drown their sorrows and for Kath'ryn to forget about the impending Review Board. They had drunk to mourn the loss of their shipmates, reminiscing on their time aboard the Star, sharing stories together. Laughing at some, becoming morose at others.

Kath'ryn had told her Smart Mind to shut up at one point as it had tried to filter out the effects of the alcohol. It had tried to suppress the alcohol in her bloodstream until she had told it firmly she wanted to get drunk. After that, she'd felt a little better as the drunken haze had fallen over her like a warm blanket.

As she was saying her goodbyes to a drunken Brock, she turned and walked immediately into James Middleton who was walking down the corridor.

"Oof! Oh. Captain. Shorry." She mumbled, slurring her words.

"Captain Kass. I see you found your way to our official bar."

"'m norra Captain…" she replied, trying to stand still while the deck swayed underneath her.

"Sorry?" he said bemused, but before he had time to ask another question, she started to collapse to one side. Middleton reacted quickly and grabbed her waist with one hand, barely managing to catch her head in the other before it struck the metal wall panel.

Unconscious from the alcoholic consumed over the past few hours, she was a dead weight in his arms.

Shaking his head wryly, he put one of her arms over his shoulder and carried her gently, feet dragging on the floor, to the nearest elevator.

++++++++++

A groan came from Kath'ryn as she felt the pounding in her head.

What the fuck...

What was in those drinks...?

Where the fuck am I!?

Trying desperately to open her eyes, Kath'ryn felt the soft warm envelope of warm sheets around her, and the embrace of quality cloth between her and her skin.

Skin!?

Panic set in and she sat upright. She was in a strange dimly-lit room - not the quarters she'd been provided by the Quartermaster - and was only wearing her bra and panties.

Fuck, who did I sleep with this time? She looked around for her clothes and saw them neatly folded on a chair opposite. Thankfully, she didn't see anyone beside her in the bed, but she couldn't remember how the hell she'd got here to the strange quarters. Last thing she remember was running into... *oh fuck, the Captain!*

"Please tell me I didn't sleep with the Captain...?" she asked the empty room.

Taking a glance around the room she now spotted a few personal effects. Taking a moment to wrap the bedsheets around her body, she sat up.

Bad idea.

Her head span in retaliation and she nearly fell back. Gritting her teeth, she reached for a glass of water that had been left on the bedside unit, and with one gulp, drank the whole lot down.

She desperately needed to rehydrate her system and her Smart Mind started to tell exactly what levels of electrolytes she was low on.

Past experience and a lot of one-night stands on Mars had taught her various tricks to recovery. Kath'ryn needed to get some food into her stomach soon. But her immediate priority was to sneak out of this room, make it back to her assigned quarters and hope she hadn't made too much of a fool of herself last night.

As she staggered over to her clothes and started to pull them on, her attention was drawn to a personal holo-pic on a wall mounted shelf. It portrayed a rather young and dashing looking Captain Middleton receiving a medal, presumably after the first Stellar War. He was smiling proudly with honour at the award in the image.

Groaning at the realisation she may have slept with the Captain, she needed to avoid him and so wanted to get out of his quarters as fast as possible. She couldn't face the embarrassment of her indiscretion.

As she pulled on the second of her boots, the door opened, and James Middleton himself stepped in.

Bad timing. As always.

"Ah. You're awake." he stated simply, closing the door behind him.

"Listen…" She began but he interrupted her.

"Relax Captain. Nothing happened. You collapsed drunk outside the bar so I bought you here. My quarters are were much nearer the bar than your own, so it was much simpler to bring you here where I put you into bed. I've spent the night in my Ready Room on the bridge, preparing my report on the mining colony massacre, and making sure you got a good nights' rest. It looked like you had a few too many to drinks with your crewmate. I thought it better you were safe and sound asleep, rather than being alone on the ship, drunk."

Thank god... she was really worried she might have had sex with him. *Not that he wasn't attractive in a mature kind of way, sort of disappointing in a weird sort of way.* She considered as she pulled the boot over her foot and stood up.

Which was another bad idea - she swayed again and felt his arms grab her.

"Maybe you need to rest a little more Captain." He seemed very amused at this.

"I'll be OK *Captain*. I just need some food."

She tried to keep the bitterness out of her voice.

Letting her go he said, "Well the mess-hall is still serving breakfast. I would join you, but I have a ship to run."

He pointed to the door and she let herself out.

Anger and embarrassment in equal quantities were burning her cheeks red as she headed towards the messhall to get some food into her churning stomach. She wondered why this man pushed her buttons and then went out of his way to piss her off.

++++++++++

Servient Gen7cD was just settling down to rest for the day when he received a subspace ping from Lord Atticis Gen9fG - the Council Leader.

Realising the import of the message, he accepted the communication from his leader.

"Lord Gen7cD, I hear disturbing news from the front. I have it on good authority that the Empirical Cruiser Horaxx has been totally destroyed, and all Flexani lost to the gene pool. I must say, I am highly alarmed as to this news."

"Destroyed! I am shocked by Lord Atticis. Do we know how they were defeated by the Terrans?" He was studying a data-packet that had been sent by the Council member which contained the last telemetry from the Horaxx.

"We do not know at this time but our Maestri Caste members are reviewing the data. It contains some unusual and disturbing information. Therefore, my purpose in contacting you now is to be sure our operation on XT-67-C at least was successful. The Council cannot afford more bad news."

"My Lord Atticis Gen9fG, it pleases me to confirm that all of the ships successfully left the planet fully loaded and are on route back to Flexani Prime with the raw Corismite ore safe in their holds. We successfully eliminated all Terran presence on the planet. We left some automated units at the mining operation to disrupt any recovery attempts. It was my intention to appraise you of this, my Lord, at a time of your convenience."

"Good. I would not be happy if we had lost the Corismite too." he conceded.

"My Lord Atticis, if I may be so bold. I would like to proffer my services to the Council to provide a strong command structure to the war effort in the production of our new weapon technology. I would be most honoured if the Council of JurTan would permit me to manage the operations."

"A bold offer." Atticis Gen9fG paused as he considered the proposal from his mandarin. "Very well, your offer pleases me. I am granting a promotion to the 8th level Servient rank. Congratulations *Servient* Gen8cD. Your blood sacrifice is gratefully received by the Council."

Servient Gen8cD immediately saw his rank status update and felt himself swell with pride in his new position.

"Your first duty as Servient then will be to ensure that production of the new weapon technology for the war can be increased by the efficient and rapid refinement of the ore. We want all of Flexani vessels fitted with the new beam weapon within as few Krec's as possible," he ordered.

"I am honoured my Atticis. My Caste is my Life. I will not fail in my duty," the newly appointed Servient added.

"I will inform the Council of your new appointment and will expect regular and favourable updates. I expect you to relocate your offices to the production facility of Flexani Seconda immediately to overview the production and refinement of the crystals."

"I shall do so my Lord Atticis Gen9fG."

"By the Council's will," he terminated the link the Servient.

Almost radiating pride as a beacon, Gen8cD took it upon himself to order his Vorrax to summon his best bottle of fermented juice from the GoKahta region to celebrate.

CHAPTER NINETEEN
Ruination

"...and so we commit their bodies back to the firmament of our Lord, so that they may join, once again, with the stars from whence they came." The voice of the ships' Chaplin droned over the small congregation.

Kath'ryn Kass, sat wearing a demure black dress and a pair of heels a size too big for her, all loaned to her by Denise Brooke, the First Officer.

She was seated in the TTF Kydoimos' small chapel, surrounded by officers and crewmembers of the warship.

Next to her sat Alain Brock, head bowed, also dressed formally in an ill-fitting suit that he'd obviously borrowed from someone on board.

They both sat silently at the memorial service for their ten fellow crew-members from the ill-fated Intrepid Star mining ship, and the poor souls of the mining colonists from Mirral.

It had been decided to schedule both memorial services together for convenience.

Attendance in the small chapel was high, although the Captain might have ordered some of his crew to attend to ensure the pews were filled.

Kath'ryn had more than simply grief to deal with though. About an hour before the ceremony, she had received the expected communique from Raven Ore HQ demanding her presence on Earth at her 'earliest convenience' for a formal tribunal.

Her rank of Captain had been formally suspended until the meeting took place and she was also barred from all ROCL operations.

Those bloody minded managers it seemed, did their pound of flesh. She knew she was expected to play out her role as sacrificial lamb in this sham of a hearing. A scapegoat was what was required, and she fitted the bill.

She had absolutely no intention of attending however - and planned to issue her resignation after the memorial service. She'd had enough of penny pinching Raven Ore and this god-forsaken part of the universe.

Alain too had received a similar communique, but he was young and his career was not tainted like hers. He would be fine, and would continue to pilot starships for a long while yet, Kath'ryn was sure.

She would make sure that in her resignation letter, the least she could do was to mention his bravery and duty and hope the stuffed shirts at Raven Ore would have at least some compassion and respect in them. It was the least she could do.

For now though, she could only feel the grief and loss of the crew she had worked with for over two years. She also had felt emotional when First Officer Brooke had informed her that Andrew Terris - the mining Station Commander - was also dead, killed in the attack by the Flexani.

Right now, all she wanted was for this memorial to end so that she could crawl back into her bunk.

She was exhausted. Not physically, but emotionally. The past week had been an immense drain on her.

"Would anyone care to say a few words?" The Chaplain's words intruded into her brooding thoughts.

Captain James Middleton immediately stood and strode purposefully over to the small pulpit lectern.

The Chaplain courteously stepped aside, and the Commander of the Kydoimos stepped up and began to speak in his soft Australian accent to the attendees.

"I'd like to read a quote that I think is most poignant here if I may… *'We must die alone. To the very verge of the stream our friends may accompany us; they may bend over us, they may cling to us there; but that one long wave from the sea of eternity washes up to the lips, sweeps us from the shore, and we go forth alone! In that untried and utter solitude, then, what can there be for us but the pulsation of that assurance, "I am not alone, because the Father is with me." '"*

He paused for a moment, and looked up to watch the solemn faces in front of him before continuing. "In our journey here to the edges of space, we are surrounded by friends. Those friends also share our fate as we share theirs. We form bonds that go beyond blood on this ship and for that we must be grateful for we undoubtedly face difficult times ahead. We must dive into that eternal sea and be prepared to continue, but not alone. These men, women and children we grieve for today all sacrificed their lives for a desire to find their place in the universe and we must honour their lives from this point onwards. We shall remember these poor souls for the joy they brought to each other and know that we too, shall bring joy to our friends aboard this ship."

After standing in quiet contemplation for a few moments, he walked back to his chair. Kath'ryn thought he looked very tense and sensed deep emotional turmoil inside him right now - his words had been very powerful.

As the room slowly emptied after the ceremonies had finished, Kath'ryn sought out Captain Middleton to thank him.

"Kath'ryn. My condolences for the loss of your crew. I know it is not much consolation for you and Alain but as Captain of the TTF Kydoimos, I am acutely aware of how important the people you fly with are to you. If I can do anything or provide any support, you know where I am."

Was that a joke made in reference to her drunkenness the other night!?

She decided that it probably was not.

"Thank you Captain." she managed to say. "That means a lot to me, although I am a Captain no longer it seems. ROCL have suspended me until a hearing can be formally held. I guess they don't like losing a multi-million credit starship."

He frowned.

"Well if you need me to issue a report to support the facts around the attack on your ship, I'm more than happy to do that."

"Thank you, but I'm not planning to fight it. I'm quitting." she replied.

"That's a shame and a loss. I think that is a big mistake on their part. You have a lot to offer any ship Kath'ryn."

"Is that personal observation then?" she asked politely.

"Yes. I would say it is. You have shown a personal and true concern for your crew throughout the disaster. You fought hard to stay alive in very difficult circumstances." He lowered his voice before continuing, "You may have even uncovered some facts that put this war in a new light, so I think you have a lot of good traits any management team would be very stupid to lose."

She felt humbled by his words.

Kath'ryn was acutely aware of the deception she had uncovered so she asked also in a suitably muted tone, "So tell me Captain, did you manage to speak to your superiors about the weapons attack on the Flexani Cruiser ship?"

How much shall I tell her? He considered carefully before responding.

"Well, I have spoken to the Admiralty back at the TTF, yes and they are investigating the disturbing news, and are reviewing the information you and the Flexani supplied. They were quite sceptical at first of course, but once I supplied them with my AI's assessment, they informed me that they passed it on to their own science team for review."

"That sounds suspiciously like you've been given the cold shoulder! What do you believe?"

"You know the TTF processes as well as I do Kath'ryn. You were part of it once. What I think is not relevant here. My orders have been made clear and those orders are to watch for threats along the border until more TTF ships can be sent into the system."

"But the fact that one of the Task Force's own vessels is using horrendously powerful weaponry no-one acknowledges exists, doesn't that strike you as strange?"

He sighed. "You should know that sometimes weapons on board a starship are classified. I've been informed by the Admiral's office that the TTF Imperial Rose is carrying a new top secret and highly classified weapon which they used to defend the Kydoimos from attack."

"You can't believe that's the whole story!? Seriously?"

"Yes, I do. I have to, I don't have any other reason to doubt my commanders. The Kydoimos was under attack by an alien vessel in a time of war, and our sister ship arrived to provide defensive and offensive support. It is as simple and straightforward as that."

She had no response.

Grudgingly she conceded. *He might possibly be right. Sometimes ships do have new tech on board that other Captains are not informed about. But all the same, it was awfully convenient that this new weapon was already available for use – almost as if someone knew the Kydoimos would be attacked where and when it happened. The Imperial Rose had arrived just at the right time, coincidence or not..?*

Quickly changing the subject Middleton said, "Well if you are quitting and need a reference for a new job, let me know. I'd be glad to provide you with one."

Surprised and pleased, she thanked him. She had not even considered what she'd do after she quit Raven Ore Confederated Logistics.

"Excuse me Captain..." they were interrupted by Brooke, the FO.

"Yes Brooke?"

"You are needed on the Bridge sir."

Bowing his head to Kath'ryn he apologised for leaving so soon, and walked out of the room.

"He likes you, you know." said Brooke quietly, startling Kath'ryn from her train of thoughts.

"What?"

"I said, the Captain seems to have a soft spot for you."

Not sure how to respond she blushed. He had to be at least a decade older than her and she was blushing – at her age too!

"He is a very remarkable man." she said awkwardly in response.

Chuckling, Brooke stated, "Well he liked my dress on you, that much was obvious."

God, I need a drink. Kath'ryn thought.

But not too many she added to herself as an afterthought.

"Care for a drink?" she asked the FO.

"I would, but I'm on duty. Maybe later?"

"OK."

First Officer Brooke left the room too, leaving Kath'ryn standing alone with her whirling thoughts.

+++++++++

Captain James Middleton walked onto the Bridge, still in his dress uniform, and saw the immediate problem. On the holo-table display a few metres away were four fiery red markers - alien vessels.

They were approaching from Flexani space at a rapid pace.

<Captain, I have detected four new Flexani Cruiser ships on an intercept course. They will encounter the TTF Kydoimos within seventy-six minutes.>

He lent over the display, sweeping his hand over the interface and zoomed into the approaching vessels.

Telemetry and scan information presented itself next to the four vessels.

He ignored the data, choosing instead to look at the vessels digital representation as defined by the computer's holo-matrix.

Shit.

"Battlestations!" he ordered. "Plot a course away from here at ninety degrees to the Mirral ecliptic and get us out of here – fast!"

The Kydoimos was no match for four Cruisers, he had no choice but to turn and run.

He could not afford to jeopardise his crew for the sake of suicidal heroics in a battle he knew they would be seriously outclassed in, especially if these four Flexani vessels were equipped with the same beam weapon the Horaxx had used.

As his First Officer entered the Bridge, he ordered the AI to send a message to Captain Naro and Captain Boskowitz of the other two TTF ships in this sector.

Whilst they were a still some distance away, if they could reach them in time, three ships against four would be better odds. *Especially if Imperial Rose could use that new weapon again* Middleton thought.

"Helm, set course for the last known position of the Imperial Rose," he instructed.

"Captain... What's happening?" the FO enquired as she too entered the bridge, but then she saw the holo-display herself and understood his orders.

She looked him in the eyes and knew they both would need the crew at their best. She nodded once and turned away, her training taking over as she moved towards the Helm officer to ensure that they had a rapid passage out of the system.

Middleton sent a quick subspace message to the TTF Command to give a situation report and then reviewed his Padd. He needed to check the status of the repairs to the damaged sections of the ship, for the shielding had taken a beating in the last fight - and by the aggressive approach being shown by the closing four Flexani vessels, he judged that for them to be this confident they must have their new beam weapon technology.

Thankfully, the reports on his Padd indicated the damaged railgun on the ventral wing had been repaired and was fully functional again - they'd need that railgun.

<Captain Middleton, the Vanguard and the Imperial Rose have responded and will meet us on route to engage the enemy.>

He acknowledged the AI.

One of the junior offices came over to Middleton and waited to be ordered to speak. When Middleton granted permission the officer said "sir, a Mz. Kass has asked if she can speak to you on comms for a moment. She did say it was urgent."

Dammit. He was busy here! What the hell did she want...?

"OK. Quickly then, put it through."

Kath'ryn's voice came through his comm unit.

"Captain, I know you have ordered battlestations. I can guess we will soon be under attack? I'm a good pilot. You're a fighter team down and I've had training on a Reaper Mark III. I'm a little rusty but can I help in any way?"

He considered this. Ever since the loss of one of his Reaper crew when they had been hit by the alien weapon, it meant that they needed every pilot they could muster – and he'd just left two Reaper crews behind at the mining settlement – damn!

He knew her record and knew she was telling the truth - but she'd last flown a Reaper more than four years ago. He could ill-afford to be choosy though and any help would gratefully received right now.

"What about a co-pilot?" he asked, but even as the question passed his lips, he knew she had an answer, or otherwise she wouldn't be calling him.

He heard the smile in her voice, "Oh, I'm sure I can sort that. The Intrepid Star's pilot, Brock. He's only a few years out of the Academy and is a pretty good pilot."

"You're a hard woman to turn down," he stated.

"That's a 'yes' then?" she teased.

"Yes. Report to Flight Leader Boakai on the hanger deck and I'll inform him to issue you flight suits and a Reaper. The ships' AI will log your new temporary flight status. Welcome to the team *Second Lieutenant* Kass."

++++++++++

The TTF Nemesis, commanded by Captain Tonev, had entered Flexani space a little over seven hours previously.

They had slipped passed the Kydoimos completely unnoticed, and were travelling at high subspace speeds.

Their stealth technology worked optimally as they passed their sister vessel orbiting Mirral, Captain Tonev smiled knowing they would not be aware of their presence.

She was even pleased as they passed the four Flexani Cruiser ships travelling in the opposite direction, for they had not been detected by the alien sensors. Captain Tonev had only passing qualms about not coming to the Kydoimos' aid, but her mission was paramount and could not be jeopardised by an early reveal of their new stealth capability. She knew, however, that their undetected flight validated the engineering and scientific teams work on Earth, for it had performed perfectly by enabling them to bypass the Flexani sensor technology.

She was confident therefore, that the missiles would perform in the same vein when it became time for them to be launched at their target.

<Captain, we are twelve hours away from being in range of Flexani Prime.>

"Good. Keep me informed. I want to know the moment we enter the system."

The TTF Nemesis was a new vessel and only just released from drydock.

In essence, this was her shakedown voyage.

A new crew, new technology and a thousand-and-one things to go wrong - but she would strive to maintain discipline as her Captain.

If they were unlucky and were discovered, she had direct orders from the SecDef of the Terran Task Force to launch all their missiles at the nearest inhabited Flexani planet before engaging the enemy – making the ultimate sacrifice if it became necessary.

They *would* take the bastards down.

CHAPTER TWENTY
Battle

Newly appointed Second Lieutenant Kass and her co-pilot Brock sat silently in the Mark IV Reaper, on the hanger deck of the TTF Kydoimos trying to take in the words of Flight Officer Bokai as he tried to explain the controls.

Although Kath'ryn was familiar with complex flight controls, this new generation of Reaper was vastly more advanced than those she had flown many years ago, so she desperately needed this necessarily fast update from their new Flight Leader.

She'd jacked into the fighters' Smart Mind when she first sat in its tiny cockpit and the sensation felt slightly unpleasant.

It was very militaristic in its communication protocols and she had had trouble at first aligning her thoughts to its rigid structures.

"So you understand the new weapons systems now?" FL Boakai asked the two of them.

They both nodded in unison, although truth be told, Alain Brock had only ever flown simulated Reapers in VR Sims back at the Academy. They had, however, had been the same specification as the Reapers he now sat in.

But a simulation was not the real thing, he fretted.

Brock was seated directly behind Kath'ryn in the cramped cockpit. With their flightsuits and helmets on, they had very limited room inside the ship once the canopy was sealed in which to move. It would be fair to say it was very snug.

The Smart Mind link, although rigid in its command protocols, was highly effective. They only had to think a command, and the ship moved. Responding instantly to their thoughts like an extra limb.

Most of the manual controls were still present but were only there as emergency back-up should the Smart Mind fail for any reason or was destroyed.

Alain sat behind Kath'ryn, examining his VR display.

It showed him detailed HUD data from all of the on-board systems - engines status, weapons and missile batteries as well as the countermeasure systems and life support.

All were in the green.

"OK. I'm going to approve you for 'flight ready' status Second Lieutenant Kass. Your designation will be Kilo Seven. Oh, and please don't break my Reaper," he added, grinning as he climbed down the ladder to the flight deck.

All around her Reaper, crewmen and women hurried, carrying equipment and preparing the Kydoimos' Reapers and shuttles for flight.

They all knew that battle was imminent and all clung onto the hope that they would all come out of it unscathed.

Kath'ryn was nervous but at least she now had a chance of taking an active part in proceedings in some way, other than having to constantly watch helplessly from the side-lines as she had done so often recently.

It was disturbing to her that the Reaper's Smart Mind and her own Smart Mind talked directly, sometimes bypassing her brain as they communicated whilst seemingly ignoring her entirely. The two Smart Minds quickly developed a communications protocol so the two artificial entities would be able coordinate flight operations between themselves unless overridden by commands from Kath'ryn herself. The only time the

Smart Minds would overrule her, would be if they determined that the craft was in imminent danger.

She considered telling her Smart Mind to butt out but, she knew it would not listen.

"You OK back there Brock?" she enquired of the former Intrepid Star pilot.

"I think so. Last time I flew in one of these was a few years ago and it was a VR sim, at the Academy. It was pretty lifelike, but nothing like the real thing – this one doesn't have a reset button! I'll do my best."

"Now you tell me" Kath'ryn joked in an attempt to calm the young man. "I'm certain you'll be fine. Just take my lead and keep any Flexani ships off our collective arse."

Alain knew just how much the late and unlamented Chief Coulson had coveted her arse so he smiled secretly in his helmet. He knew better though than to say anything to his former Captain.

Perhaps Coulson apart, he had mourned the loss of his colleagues from the Star. It had hit his young mind hard. Those colleagues had died unnecessarily in that merciless attack by the Flexani. Brock had been grateful that the Flexani being held responsible for their deaths was now floating in a holding cell securely aboard the Kydoimos, but he didn't understand why she was determined to defend the slimy Octopod.

Alain, unknown to Kath'ryn, had attempted to talk to the alien earlier that day.

He'd visited it in the cells, shortly after the funeral of his crewmates, trying to gain an understanding from the alien as to why he had ordered his friends deaths. It hadn't gone well. He'd screamed and shouted at the Flexani's responses until he'd been dragged away by the guard.

He had no love, only a smouldering hatred for the alien.

Alain was looking forward to flying in this combat ship to take part in the battle, to defend his new 'ship' and to use the dark fire burning in his heart to fuel his efforts to take revenge on the race responsible for the lives lost.

His heart carried a lot of fire.

+++++++++

"Fire all missile batteries!" Captain Tonev screamed.

The TTF Nemesis had eventually been detected.

Unknown to the designers the vessel's subspace engines had been manufactured, oh so slightly, imbalanced and her Chief Engineer had not identified the tiny variation in the field flux. It was so slight as to be almost negligible, but it was there, it existed.

Normally during a maiden voyage closer monitoring of the engines performance would probably have identified this type of problem. There would have been time factored into the trip to enable the fine adjustments that would have eliminated the tiny wobble that the resonance set up in subspace. Because of the state of emergency and because of certain egos, that time had not been allotted and the tiny error went entirely undetected.

Unfortunately for the TTF Nemesis however, even though her engineers missed the tiny fluctuation, the unusual signature she was leaving in subspace, it was large enough that one of the numerous Flexani Sentinel Posts within Flexani space did not. It became aware of the unusual perturbations and sought to identify the anomaly on its sensor net.

The Arbiter on board that Sentinel Post had been shocked when further analysis revealed the signature to be that of a Terran warship, well within Flexani territory.

She soon recovered, sending out a subspace tweet signal immediately to her Servient overlord - who took swift action to order Torrak Drones into the immediate location in order to block further progress of the intruder.

The Flexani drones - given details on the Terran Task Force ship's compromised subspace signature – were vectored to its last detected position. Since it was still virtually 'hidden' from the conventional scanners of the Torraks, they would be unable to locate the ship while it was cloaked. The Arbiter guided the Torraks to the Nemesis' location through her subspace link, using the Sentinel Post's advanced sensors as a guide.

Captain Tonev was horrified to learn they had been spotted, but remained confident however that her new weapon would be more than a match for a few drones.

Moments later, the Nemesis dropped out of subspace and into normal space, immediately becoming visible to the approaching Torrak drones' scanners.

The crew of the Nemesis assessed their situation as fast as possible, knowing they were scant moments away from battle.

"How many ships?" Tonev asked her Bridge officers, frantically manning the ship's scanning system.

Nervously the junior officer said "I'm reading .. over two hundred Drones Captain."

Two hundred! My God!

Captain Tonev suppressed her shock and horror at the sheer number of Drones approaching them, and immediately ordered the new Hellfire weapon to be fired. This was the same weapon technology that the TTF Imperial Rose had used so effectively against the Horrax.

She was, even now, still confident it would be as effective against the size of the Torrak force as they approached.

The weapon had only been used on large vessels and targets, only once in anger, and never on small ships, but since the Torrak Drones were currently clustered together in a pack, she gambled that the subspace inversion field would envelope enough of them at once to make a difference.

As the beam raged in on the centre of the drone pack, she saw the exotic field - known as Hellfire - tear into some of the drone ships and they simply vanished in a brilliant flash of light.

But, it was just not enough though, the remainder of the alien force was still approaching, but they had scattered like a flock of disturbed birds. They each zigzagged wildly on seemingly random vectors giving the Hellfire weapon's guidance system aboard the Nemesis no chance of using the Hellfire weapon again. How could you aim at countless objects when those object's predicted position in space is unpredictable?

"I'm still tracking one-hundred and seventy-nine drones!" came the shout.

The sole net benefit from the Hellfire blast, was that it had punched an opening through the centre of the pack. That opening was still devoid of drones, empty enough for the Captain Tonev to order the launch of all of the stealth missiles toward the nearest inhabited planet in Flexani space.

"Stealth missiles away!" cried the gunnery officer.

As the seventy-five specialised missiles left the ship, they each activated their subspace stealth engines and slipped into pockets of subspace that were undetectable to the attacking drones.

The missiles were equipped with Red Horse advanced technology, designed in The Nest by Admiral Varnava's scientists. They had proved successful in countless tests and Captain Tonev was confident they'd find their target without being detected.

She deeply regretted that they had been such a long way from Flexani Prime when detected. As a result, the Nemesis had no option but to rely on the back-up plan and launch all the missiles at the nearest Flexani colony planet. It was planned that by deploying Black Snow effectively, even at this distant colony, the nano-tech infection would eventually spread to Flexani Prime itself via supply routes and other communicative means.

Once the missiles had left normal space, Captain Tonev ordered all Reapers crews to launch, and all railgun batteries to fire at will.

The space between the opposing forces quickly become a zone of death.

Hypersonic fletchette rounds from both the human warship, and the Torrak drones left no visible trails between the void, but their direction was clear. To seek out vulnerable points on their target's hulls.

The Torrak drones had a much larger target to hit, but the TTF Nemesis had a lot better shielding than the smaller more vulnerable drones.

In their favour, the Drones however, had the advantage of speed and agility on their side in this battle - and they were able to avoid many of the rounds fired in their direction.

"Damage sustained on engine baffle Four."

<Power loss of 10% to Plasma Beam two.>

"Reaper crew Red seven and Black four not responding to hail."

"Engineering repair crews to the main hanger deck. We've taken a direct hit to the main hanger doors!"

Captain Tonev sensed that despite her well trained crew's valiant efforts, because of their lack of combat training, this battle was not proceeding at all well.

The TTF Nemesis attempted to fire the Hellfire weapon again and again with very limited success - they'd only succeeded in destroying a further fifteen drones and expended valuable energy. Tonev was getting frustrated as she watched the Nemesis taking a beating.

The Torrak drones nimbly avoided the main railguns and plasma beam fire from the larger human warship.

Her crew were doing everything they could to avoid major damage being taken and she considered her options. Her Smart Mind working in tandem with her own to evaluate and identify options.

The Torraks engaged in intense dogfights with the Reaper crews, often pinning the human pilots into 'killzones' where they could be picked off by groups of Drones. With well over a hundred Torraks still orbiting the TTF Nemesis, there were plenty of drones to utilise many different tactics. Their Smart Minds simultaneously collaborating with their counterparts via subspace tweeter links, each drone working together in harmony with all the members of the pack, all with the single minded aim, eliminate the human invaders.

"Reaper Red three and Red one hit!" shouted another junior member of the crew. Captain Tonev and her First Officer attempted to instil a sense of calm in the Bridge, but they were failing.

"FOCUS!" she shouted to her Bridge officers and they stopped briefly to face her.

She saw their fear and as their Captain said simply "I understand we are exposed right now but this ship will prevail. I trust in your abilities and you've been trained for this type of situation so, focus. Work on the task at hand and let's destroy these bastards!"

There were a few muted cheers at these words, but deep inside, Tonev knew her words were hollow and they might not be able to succeed in escaping. *At least the missiles launched successfully,* she reflected. She realised it was looking hopeless now, and she may have to initiate the action she had always hoped would not be necessary, the self-initiated destruction of her own ship, together with its hard fighting and loyal crew, They would have to die without ever being aware of the truth. The truth that they were the invading force and not the Flexani.

Captain Tonev moved to the nearest control panel to start the process that would ultimately destroy the ship and her secrets.

She had almost completed her reluctant task when, the Nemesis suddenly bucked violently in reaction to a sudden fuel cell explosion. Captain Tonev was thrown from her feet as the artificial gravity plating on the bridge failed. She struck her head on the side of the holo-display table, immediately fracturing her skull, fragments of bone driven deep into her brain. The severe trauma to her ensuring she would take no further part in the proceedings, and her secret orders to overload the Nemesis's engines to destroy its secrets would remain incomplete.

The same explosion also crippled the ship's AI and the warship effectively was blinded and her sinews cut.

Meanwhile, the seventy-five stealth missiles slipped in and out of subspace on their way towards their destination. It was not Flexani Prime that was their target now, but another world populated by the alien race.

Sentinel Posts within Flexani space struggled to track the missiles.

They'd been detected upon their launch from the TTF Nemesis, but since slipping into subspace using their stealth technology, the Arbiters monitoring their whereabouts were at a loss to find them. These missiles engines had been more thoroughly proved than those of the ill-fated Nemesis and no faulty emissions would give their presence away.

Red Horse had been designed to perfection.

As the missiles continued their unseen journey deeper and deeper into Flexani territory, the newest of the Terran Task Force Imperator-class ship was continuing to take a pounding.

Slowly, through attrition and continual bombardment from the Torraks, the huge warship started to flounder.

With his Captain now comatose in Med Bay, the First Officer tried to take command – but with systems down and the AI not responding he too could not complete the self-destruct command.

Just half-an-hour after they had been detected, the attacking Torraks crippled the ship.

It drifted in space, her engines' powerless and guns silent.

As multiple breaches in the hull burned and boiled off into the vacuum of space, her crew lay injured and dying behind secure bulkheads and in supposed Safe Zones within the crippled vessel.

The victorious but impassionate Torrak drones sent a signal to the Arbiters overseeing the battle reporting the fate of the invading warship, and soon several Flexani vessels arrived. Alien warriors boarded the Nemesis.

As they penetrated the ship, these battlesuited Flexani warriors killed all crew members still left alive. Anger driving them through the ship to kill these invaders.

The TTF Nemesis died with all hands lost and became another war statistic, the names of its crew would be engraved into a wall back on Earth for their sacrifice. A sacrifice they had made never knowing what they were dying for, or that they were just worthless pawns in a much bigger game.

The Council of JurTan ordered what remained of the vessel to be towed back to Flexani Prime. This new technology that had enabled the Terran ship to avoid their scans and almost pass undetected through their space both fascinated and worried them. Its secrets must be unlocked.

++++++++++

Even while, the Flexani warriors were killing the last of the Nemesis crew, the first of the stealth missiles appeared in orbit above the Flexani colonised world of Jhnuii and orientated itself toward the surface. Jhnuii was a only small colony world in Flexani space and housed mainly the House of HudSet.

The world that the missiles had targeted, unknown to their Terran masters, could not have found a more suitable world upon which to start their artificial plague.

The House of HudSet was a Caste House that had holdings on many worlds and had wealth generated by their great expertise in the creation of specialised exosuits for high gravity worlds.

Erstwhile Arbiter Gen6aC's favourite exosuit that he used for external egress on planets with a higher gravity than Earth's had been manufactured on this planet. He had purchased it at great expense after his promotion to Level Five and had kept it maintained until his assets had been reprocessed. Even now, it was being auctioned off along with his other assets on Flexani Prime and Gen6aC would never see his favourite exosuit again.

The House of HudSet's Caste members lived in cities within the seas of Jhnuii as did most Flexani when offworld. Flexani tended to choose planets with a high volume of water - Jhnuii was no different. It was fortunate, or inevitable, that most planets in Flexani space possessed more water and less landmass than planets in the Terran sector.

However, Jhnuii did possess more landmass than most planets in known Flexani space, and that was where the House of HudSet maintained its extensive core engineering and manufacturing facilities. Exosuits were designed and built here, then tested on the various landmasses under simulated environments. Jhnuii's gravity well was precisely 1.4 times that of Earth, so it was perfect for the testing of these types of suit.

Maestri Gen2wL was suddenly distracted by a brightening in the sky above him.

He had been personally testing one of the latest generational exosuits when he saw the streak of flame and vapour trail and had stopped to watch what he assumed was an asteroid fall to Jhnuii. That asteroid though was no natural phenomena – it was in fact, one of the stealth missiles entering the atmosphere of the planet.

Jhnuii had a lot of cloud cover - as did most Flexani worlds – and Gen2wL marvelled at how it had become brightly illuminated by the object as it blazed down through the dense low clouds overhead.

Maestri Gen2wL - a low ranked engineer - calculated the trajectory of the falling asteroid and realised it would strike within only a few hamms from his position. His Smart Mind warned him of the estimated force of the explosion if the assumed asteroid struck the ground and he realised he would have to move fast, towards the ocean's edge, and safety.

As he ran in his exosuit across the sandy surface, he noted many more asteroids tearing through the clouds as they descended upon his home world. It was then the savage truth struck him and he saw the missiles for what they truly were.

These were no asteroids!

Trailing flame and leaving roiling knots of plasma in their wake the missiles fell.

He desperately signalled his leaders by subspace tweeter as the first missile struck home - warning them of this attack. Before he had a chance to finish his communique, the blast threw him sideways.

Gen2wL fell to the ground, and slid on his back, propelled by the explosive blast from the missile.

He ended up against the base of a grassy knoll near the cliff edge. Battered by otherwise unharmed – or so he presumed.

The missile had detonated its low yield explosive charge a hundred metres above the surface.

Other missiles fell on their journey into the ocean before detonating.

One aspect of the Terran missile design was for some of their number to traverse to the very seabed before detonating - the Black Snow nanites in their cocoon then being released into the water initiating the infection of the Flexani in their own safe environment. There would be no escape as the Snow fell.

Unbeknown to Gen2wL, the explosion above him, although not killing him, would soon lead to the time when he would wish that it had. It had showered Black Snow nanites down over his prototype exosuit. Their programming kicked in and they began to find entrance through the seals in the suit, and to start compromising the outer material itself, in order to gain entry and burrow into the assailable flesh inside.

Doctor Amita Kluska and her team had done a successful job with batch 17A.

The design of the hyper-stimulated helical nanites permitted them to assess and adapt to the task at hand, with lightning efficiency. Once past the bulky carbon-fibre and metallic outer shell, the nanites sought out the Flexani epidermis layer within.

Their morphology was proving very effective at infiltrating themselves undetected into Gen2wL's biology,

He would never know he was infected from the blast.

His Smart Mind was totally unaware of the nanites infiltrating their way into his bloodstream, hiding themselves from its vision to commence the second phase of their programming – to seek out other Flexani life-forms and to infect them also, to begin the plague.

Gen2wL stood up and seemingly uninjured headed into the ocean, towards what he believed was safety, the Flexani unaware he was now Patient Zero. This new disease would wipe out all Flexani life on Jhnuii within weeks.

Doctor Kluska - before she had been cruelly eliminated herself by the Admiral - had perfected the most difficult part of Project Black Snow.

The third most deadly phase would now start to convert the surrounding protein and biomatter into a resinous, fast-mutating 'crust'. This crystallisation process would cause acute agony, and eventually kill Ge2wL, in a most excruciating way.

But, for now, he was ignorant of the poison he carried inside him as he slipped into the sea waters and started to swim to his home and colleagues.

CHAPTER TWENTY-ONE
Two Paths

Kilo Seven's Reaper twisted and turned, trying to shake off the Flexani Torrak on her tail.

The Torrak drone was firing its railguns playing streams of fire across her path, but she was managing so far to avoid them impacting her hull.

For now, that was.

"Kilo Four! Where the fuck are you Kilo Four!?" Kath'ryn screamed into her comms.

"On your six! Hold your line Kilo Seven" came the response, as Second Lieutenant Kass continued her efforts to shake off the Torrak drone on her tail.

"Firing countermeasures!" Brock called as they ejected chaff into the void behind and to the sides of the fighters' twin COX G-6 Hyperstar engines.

Alain Brock had already deployed several countermeasures in an attempt to fool the Smart Mind on the Torrak, but they were having no effect on the Torraks determined attack. It still had them in its sights and fired round after round at them.

"Come on, come on…" Kath'ryn muttered under her breath to her wingman.

Compared to the Torrak they just did not have enough manoeuvrability, and she was struggling to avoid the fletchette fire.

"Target lock!" she heard Kilo Four say, as it unleashed one of its SM-guided Autumn Wind missiles at the drone on her tail.

Seconds later, Brock shouted "Yeah!" as the missile struck home on the drone's engines and it exploded silently behind them.

"In your debt Kilo Four."

"Don't thank me yet Kilo Seven, we have still more fish to fry. More incoming."

Her sensor net and Smart Mind was giving her the same information.

Local space was swarming with hundreds of ships - both enemy and domestic.

Fighters, drones and shuttles as well as the large warships all occupied this sector of space, attacking each other and trying to find a weakness in the other's defences.

The TTF Kydoimos had had to drop out of subspace when it became clear that they would never outrun the approaching Flexani cruisers. With four pursuers chasing the warship, they had tried to reach the safety of numbers - heading to the last known location of the TTF Vanguard and the TTF Imperial Rose.

Captain Middleton knew the futility of running when he could stand and fight.

He and the other Captains had spoken over subspace and agreed a plan that he would initially turn and fight, and they would be at his location within minutes of him engaging the Flexani.

It was an extremely high risk strategy.

Four alien vessels with comparable firepower to his own would prove deadly to the Kydoimos - Middleton needed to focus his strategy wisely.

They had dropped out of subspace near a small gaseous cloud.

It was an area of space that would be challenging for all participants to fight in, but at least it was his choice of battleground and it would disadvantage the alien ships as much as his own vessel.

Or so he hoped.

He prepared a defensive position as close to the cloud as he dared, spreading his net of eight Reapers as wide as he could, in teams of two fighters.

He also ordered weapon hardpoints to be fitted to the few shuttles - mainly missile batteries. Any additional firepower that could be mustered would be needed in the coming battle and he would have to utilise all of his available resources as best he could.

The ship's AI had worked out their best defensive strategy - at least until the other Terran Task Force vessels arrived - but it would mean the inevitable sacrifice of some, if not all of his dedicated crew. The more that Middleton mulled over his options in his own mind, the more he came to realise that this battle would almost certainly be his final one.

Across the rest of the ship, the crew frantically checked critical systems, diverting power from unnecessary areas to increase shield efficiency. Medical Bay was fully prepared for the inevitable casualties that were expected.

<Captain, I am detecting four subspace folds in the immediate vicinity. Flexani Empirical Cruisers on intercept.>

"Fire at will." he commanded via the subspace link to all his crew - both on the Kydoimos and off ship - to the Reapers and shuttles floating in tactical positions near the thin cover provided by the nebulous cloud.

Plasma beamers, railguns and missile batteries fired volley after volley of plasma, fletchette rounds and kinetic energy missiles at the four ships that had just emerged back into normal space.

Middleton watched the digital holographic display with intense concentration. Trying to assess the vessels that attacked them, and how he might find a weakness against the odds.

The display lit up with angry red indications as the protagonists probed each other's defences, all the time raining projectiles and plasma beams on each other. Then, just as Middleton started to despair, some welcome green images appeared on the display. The two other Terran Task Force ships had arrived within moments of each other to even up the odds slightly.

The Kydoimos had managed to survive with minimal damage and loss to her fighters. But even with two other warships and their combined might attacking the Empirical Cruisers, and with many new Reaper pilots joined with their own, they faced mounting odds and diminishing returns on their investment – their very existence.

Captain James Middleton watched in frustration as his fighter squads slowly succumbed to attrition.

Each loss was felt hard by him and by Brooke, his First Officer, as they struggled to defend the warship.

The Four Flexani Cruisers had unleashed their new beam weapon on the Kydoimos several times and the TTF warship was now straining under the attack. Many crew had been lost to the deadly attacks already, and several of the Kydoimos railguns were rendered inoperative. Silenced as the deadly Corismite's neutron diffraction energy penetrated their poor energy shielding, and damaged the ships' armour plating.

Even the hull's self-healing ability was affected by the attacks, as the radiation destroyed the nanites in the carbon-bonded hull and prevented the repair function.

Desperately scanning the display Middleton noted with dismay that the Imperial Rose and the Vanguard were faring no better. It seemed the Imperial Rose especially was being singled out, probably as a result of her role in the destruction of the Horaxx. It seemed her secret weaponry was unable to help now.

"Loss of power in Section Six-Delta, Deck Three. We've lost life support!"

<Failure in generator bank Alpha-Seven. Re-routing power.>

"We've just lost Kilo Two!"

As Middleton listened to his crew calling out the death throes of the Kydoimos, he wondered how they could possibly survive the onslaught. The ship was losing power with the engines now down to sixty-five percent of output. They had several areas of decompression in the hull across several decks that prevented repair crews from getting to the critical areas of the ship.

I need a miracle.

Then, for one brief moment it seemed as his prayer was answered as the Vanguard at last managed to unleash her new Hellfire weapon and the nearest Flexani Cruiser to her was immediately annihilated in the purple green flare of universal matter exchange.

It was, however, but a brief respite, as the Vanguard paid the ultimate price. She had spent so much energy in the firing of the Hellfire weapon that her defence systems became weakened.

Weakened to the extent that a whole squadron of the Torrak drones, in a concerted attack on her midsection, literally ripped her in two.

The need for a miracle was even more paramount.

++++++++++

Kath'ryn Kass also needed a miracle it seemed.

She was running critically low on ammunition and had just a few missiles left. She had no choice but to leave the battle and head back to the ailing Kydoimos for refuelling and re-stocking.

"Kilo Four, I need to head back to base for more ammo. Cover me?"

"Affirmative Kilo Seven."

The two Reapers wove a complex path through the ever-increasing debris field surrounding the Kydoimos, like fireflies avoiding rain. Debris from destroyed Reapers, shuttles and Torrak drones - as well as segments of the Kydoimos itself - moved in the dangerously unpredictable arcs and random paths that had been imposed on them by their original velocities added to the kinetic energy of whatever blew them apart in the gravity free environment. Avoiding this maelstrom on their approach to the Kydoimos only added to their workload as they were in turn, hampered by fire from the remaining Flexani drones and fighters, and the three remaining attacking warships.

It'll be a miracle if we can get back at all – if there's anything to get back to Kath'ryn thought as she gritted her teeth and flew her Reaper past a large section of damaged hull, barely avoiding a collision with the twisted metal.

"Kilo Seven requesting secure landing. We're at bingo fuel and need a restock."

The answer came promptly "Head for Bay Two, Kilo Seven, Kilo Four you have Bay 6. Watch your landing - we have sustained damage in the hangar bay."

"Understood Deck."

Kath'ryn lined up their approach and flew her Reaper into the hangar bay, passing through the energy shield that protected the entrance, closely followed by her wingman. She gracefully swung her Reaper into Bay Two and put it down onto its landing struts, shutting off the engines as deckhands rushed over to connect fuel lines and armourers started to load belts of ammunition and attach new missiles to the Reaper's hardpoints.

"How are you doing back there Brock?" she asked of her co-pilot.

"I'll be glad when this is over," He answered and she chuckled mirthlessly.

"Me too."

They remained in their cramped seats as the crew members worked below them, re-stocking their reserves of Fletchette ammunition, and replaced their missing Autumn Wind and FGASS Widowmaker missiles.

She had the thumbs up from the Deck Controller and was about to start her engines once again when the Corismite NDE beam struck the hangar bay.

The effect was devastating.

The many deckhands and pilots within the hangar all felt its effects as the beam penetrated the interior of the warship.

As the strange beam breached the energy shielding around the entrance, the full force of the beams' effect blasted into the hangar bay. All the crewmembers that had just finished replenishing Kath'ryn's Reaper were vapourised in front of her eyes – and they were the lucky ones. The complex energies that formed the beams' intense structure were capable of stripping the atoms apart at a molecular level.

The NDE beam itself lasted but for an instant, but that was enough for it to cause substantial damage.

Fuel containers exploded.

Missiles detonated.

Power shorted.

What was left of her erstwhile wingman's Reaper, Kilo Four was thrown across her eyeline, the rear section totally missing, to crush itself against the hanger wall.

"No!" she exclaimed feeling the Kydoimos itself shudder from the terminal hit it had taken.

The after-effects of the beam however, ultimately achieved more damage than the beam itself.

Reaper Kilo Seven was tossed around like wheat chaff in a thunderstorm, and slid across the hanger bay floor until it struck the wall beside Bay Two, coming to a sudden stop.

They had been shielded from the Flexani weapon's initial blast effect by fortune of their position in Bay Two and it was very fortunate indeed that their

Reaper and its two inhabitants – although a bit bruised and shaken · survived the subsequent explosions when the nearby fuel tanks ruptured, exploding in a massive fireball that was extinguished by the sudden vacuum to space, as the energy field around the main hangar bay door failed.

Kath'ryn had had her miracle.

Her comms unit burst into life and the shipwide command went out, "Evacuation Protocol. All crew to escape pods."

"Shit. That's not good!" said Brock, his voice panicked.

Their Reaper had come to rest after the blast, lying on its port side. Its main fuselage was crushed against the wall of Bay Two, with racks of equipment mangled around the Reapers' engines. One of its landing struts had collapsed during the explosion and the crazy angle it now rested at would made it a challenge to get out.

The two occupants were shaken but suffered no physical damage.

Well, that's the second ship I've lost – so much for my new commission, Kath'ryn thought, as she ordered Brock out of the Reaper.

They needed to get to safety, and quickly.

She quickly assessed the readiness of her flight suit before she slid the Reaper's canopy silently open and unstrapped herself from the pilot's seat.

The cybernetically enhanced flight suit she had been issued as a pilot on the Kydoimos was far more advanced than the one she had worn on the Intrepid Star. This suit, with its advanced helmet with tactical display and Smart Mind integration, had the military-grade re-breather and nano-sized oxygen flow system which could enable them to survive in vacuum for days.

Therefore, she had no worries regarding the lack of atmosphere in what remained of the hanger as they both climbed out of the wreck of the Reaper. They each slid down its flank to the deck. Thankfully, the artificial gravity was still working - somewhat. The gravity field fluctuated for several seconds before settling at a level below its optimum 1G.

Avoiding jagged shards of metal, Kath'ryn and Brock looked around the devastation. Horror rose as they saw more clearly the death and destruction the Flexani weapon had wrought upon the ship.

As Brock's boots hit the deck, he looked around and in gut-wrenching detail saw for himself the effect of explosive decompression on the bodies scattered around him, and it resonated within him as he knew it was a fate he had only just recently survived himself.

"We have to get to the escape pods." said Brock.

"No, I have to get to Gen."

"The alien!? You are not serious! For fuck's sake, why?" He stood there, shocked at her statement.

"Because he'd do the same for me that's why! You can choose to follow me or not but I need to find out if he is safe!" Kath'ryn was annoyed at Brock's response – it seemed so out of character. She had, however, totally missed Brock's reaction when he had seen the dead crewmen lying about them.

Alain Brock felt his bitterness and hatred for the Flexani grow.

They had killed his friends, they had destroyed his ship and he'd nearly died floating alone in space. Now he was at their mercy again.

He held no love for the Squiddies, and failed to understand why his ex-Captain was so enamoured with this one.

As they stood arguing on the deck, the hanger entrance energy shield came back online, and the hangar began to re-pressurise.

"Go then! It's your bloody problem!" He stormed off in anger, heading with long strides towards one of the hanger personnel exits, dodging falling debris as he went.

Why was he so angry? Kath'ryn thought.

But, with no time to waste, and feeling the ship beneath her strain from the battle fatigue, she too headed toward the exit, but instead of following the emergency signs to the escape pods, she turned in the other direction and plunged deeper into the stricken ship, towards the holding cells deep in the Kydoimos' structure.

++++++++++

Kath'ryn had to divert from her route twice on her attempt to reach Gen6aC in the holding cells.

The TTF Kydoimos had suffered decompression in many segments of its superstructure, and whole areas were sealed off behind airtight bulkhead seals. Kath'ryn struggled with her unfamiliarity of the vessels' layout to find an alternate route through the damaged sections of the ship, and had

had to backtrack several more times, in order to find a safe route through.

All the while, the ship's AI was repetitively calling for all crew to get to their allotted emergency escape pods.

All around her, crew members rushed for the nearest pod to flee the stricken ship, not giving her a second look, just pushing by in their panic.

She eventually reached the holding cells.

It had taken her nearly twenty minutes - and all that time she had felt the ship ring and shudder from more explosions and weapons attack.

She was worried for the Captain but pushed her concerns aside so as to concentrate on finding her friend.

Her friend.

She would never have used that term for the alien just a few scant a few days ago, but now Kath'ryn felt an emotional bond with the alien who had rescued her.

She felt compelled to try and do the same for him. She would rescue him.

Stumbling into the holding cell area, she was alarmed to see one of the guards on the floor, very obviously dead. A large section of wall plating had fallen, striking him a fatal blow. Still, she checked his pulse and when she knew for certain there was nothing to be done for this poor soul, she closed her eyes for a brief moment in prayer, then apologised to him as she took his weapon.

Glancing around, she saw that thankfully the holding cell that imprisoned Gen was cracked but still intact. The fluid that was the Flexani atmosphere was weeping through the cracks, but still mainly contained within the glass chamber.

"Gen!" she said, rushing over, "are you OK?"

"Kath'ryn. I am grateful to see you alive. Yes, I am functioning within stable parameters, although the atmospheric systems in my chamber seem to be offline and the fluid within is quickly becoming toxic to me."

"We need to get you out but you're going to need your exosuit to supply your life support and to support your weight. Do you know where it is?"

"It was taken from me when I arrived. I am not sure." He responded, "You need to save yourself Kath'ryn. I am on the beach and will die soon."

Tears starting to flow as she cried, "Don't you fucking tell me to save myself! I am not leaving until I get you out of there!"

She glanced around and saw a data terminal toward back of the room.

Wiping her tears away with the back of her hand, she ran over to the console.

Activating the touchscreen interface, she reviewed the information presented there. Thankfully her new pilot security codes allowed her a basic level of access to the terminal, so she performed a search for the missing Flexani exosuit.

She knew that whilst the gravity generators aboard the dying ship still functioned, even at their now reduced level, the gravity on the ship would be too great for Gen to survive for long.

There. Found it!

The exosuit had been removed to a room a few doors away, apparently for some of the science and engineering teams to study.

"Wait here!" she shouted as she ran out of the door.

"I do not believe I am at liberty to go anywhere," answered Gen6aC to an empty room.

Numerous Acs ticked by and Gen6aC floated, waiting for Kath'ryn to return.

He knew he was living on borrowed time.

During his incarceration, from inside his cell Gen6aC had felt the vibrations and sounds from the intense attack, and knew that a massive battle was being fought around him. One he was helpless to participate in. He knew possible weaknesses in the Flexani shield grids, some commands that might help the Terrans fight a more effective battle but, of course, no one had listened to him when he had pleaded to be heard.

Kath'ryn returned to the room, somewhat slower than when she had left it, weighed down as she was by the weight of his exosuit in her arms.

She found it. Then there is hope.

Kath'ryn paused for a moment as another blast rocked the vessel and the deck moved under her. She steadied her feet and looked desperately around for some way to get the suit to Gen.

There. A sealed atmospheric lock door to the side of the cell.

Walking over, she thumbed the keypad, willing the hatch to open and for it not to ask for a password or security code. With a grateful sigh, she watched as the door opened and she clumsily placed the exosuit inside.

Seconds passed as the door closed once again.

On the inside of the holding cell, another hatch automatically opened. "Quickly Gen. You need to get into the suit." she encouraged.

Encouragement was not needed as he floated across and taking his suit in his many limbs, he turned it around in the liquid so it faced away from him.

Kath'ryn watched in amazed fascination as Gen6aC then started to don the strange exosuit.

He activated the suit by his subspace tweeter link and it opened neatly at the back, two panels hinging apart. *This must be how he gets inside. Neat,* she thought.

All of the lower limbs stiffened as the suit's power was re-activated.

Kath'ryn observed Gen6aC first slip his lower pseudopod limbs into the bottom section of the exosuit through the back opening, gracefully gliding into place and slotting his 'legs' into the mechanical appendages.

Next, Gen6aC pulled his upper torso and 'arms' into the main section of the exosuit, and the rear panels hinged closed. Sealing with a small swirl of expelled fluid from the now invisible joint, like a clamshell closing.

"Amazing." she proclaimed as he turned to face her from within the cell.

Bowing slightly at what might be described as his waist section, he said, "Thank you Kath'ryn."

"Stand back," she said, raising the dead guard's fletchette rifle. She had tried to find the controls for the holding cell, but her security clearance was not high enough - she would need to do this the old fashioned, more direct way.

She waited until he had swum to the rear of the chamber, as far away from the glass as he could before she fired a burst of fletchette rounds toward the bottom corner of the tank.

The effect was dramatic.

The toughened nano plexi-glass window withheld for a few seconds before the fletchette rounds - fired at over seventy-six thousand miles an hour - shattered the glass and the room was instantly flooded.

Kath'ryn lost her footing as the water swept around her feet.

Gen6aC tumbled out with the flood to come to rest a few feet away from Kath'ryn.

Sopping wet from head to foot, she burst out laughing.

"Come Kath'ryn. We must not delay, if we are to escape. I sense that this vessel is faltering under the attack."

Her almost hysterical laughter was immediately silenced as she became once again aware of their imminent danger. "Yes. You are right," she said, "But my Reaper is damaged and won't fly - but we need to get off this ship."

"What about my ship?"

Yes of course. The Sentinel ship! "If it hasn't been destroyed, I think it must still be docked. I can check."

She waded through the receding water to the console terminal and called up the manifest file.

"Thank god! It is still docked at one of the smaller airlocks. From what I can tell, it has sustained some damage - but the engines and main systems are still working."

"Ah, yes. I am now in full subspace contact with the ship. It would appear that the Terran crew were unable to bypass my security lockouts which is very provident indeed. I have therefore commanded the AI to prepare the ship for flight, but we will need to unlock the mooring clamps. They are locked onto the ship and we cannot leave until they are removed."

"Let's worry about how to do that when we get to the airlock. Let's go!"

++++++++++

The next few minutes were frantic for the two mismatched companions.

It was obvious now, that most of the crew of the Kydoimos had already left in the escape pods, but on their journey through the ship they still encountered a few tardy crewmembers desperately seeking an undamaged escape pod with room still left on board. Thankfully, they met no resistance in fleeing - certainly she expected to have someone question why she had a Flexani with her or to have had to avoid being shot at, but no. It seemed that self-preservation was the main driving force on board the Kydoimos now.

They had attempted to use the quickest route to the small airlock through which they'd first entered the TTF Kydoimos, but the airlock was located on the opposite side of the ship to the holding cells. It had been slow going through the damaged sections to get there safely, but somehow despite the eventual tortuous route they were forced to follow, and despite the continual bombardment of the ship they had managed it.

Their luck couldn't hold out for ever though, and both were acutely aware that the Kydoimos was effectively a dead animal being stripped to the bone by circling predators – and they were still trapped inside its dying body.

Kath'ryn leaned the fletchette rifle on the wall by the airlock and removed the access panel. She had to release the docking clamps hold-down mechanism so they could release Gen6aC's Sentinel Post vessel and escape from the Kydoimos warship.

Kneeling down to get better access, she saw numerous control systems and wiring interfaces inside.

Pretty standard stuff.

She started to look for the specific control components that operated the mooring clamps when she heard a human voice speak up from behind her.

"Please, take your hands away from that panel Captain."

The voice was full of spite and anger.

She knew the voice though - it was Brock.

Raising her arms slightly away from the panel she quickly glanced at the weapon she had leaned against the wall, but it was too far away to reach.

Shit.

Turning her head slowly so as not to provoke him, she saw Brock holding a similar gun in his hands, pointed directly at the two of them.

He was standing around ten metres away, that distance was enough to cover them both with the weapon but far enough that they could not get the jump on him.

"This is on full auto so don't fuck with me. Step away from the panel Captain." His voice was heavy with malice and hate.

"What the hell are you doing Alain!?" she said, confused.

I need to get to my gun.

"I'm here to kill that fucking Squiddie once and for all. All this —", he gestured at the destruction around them, "All this is his doing. He has ruined our lives for good, and killed all our friends!" Alain was clearly hysterical and very emotional. Her concern for the safety of Gen was raised exponentially.

Taking a steadying deep breath, she slowly stepped forward, trying to place herself surreptitiously in front of the Flexani.

I need to try and calm him down she thought, desperately trying to weigh up her options.

Alain jerked the gun a little higher. "Kath'ryn. I'm not stupid. Don't make me shoot you as well. You were kind to me but you've grown too soft. All these Octopods have to die. Look around you! This ship is being destroyed by his bastard kind!" He thrust the gun in the general direction of Gen6aC.

"Alain. Listen to me. You are right. But he is a prisoner of war and needs to be treated as such."

"Oh no he's not. He's a war criminal, and as soon as you broke him out of the holding cell, you're both criminals on the run. If you get killed in the crossfire, no one will question my actions but I'd rather not have to kill you Kath'ryn. You were good to me on the Star. He wasn't though. He's going to die one way - or another." he spat.

"Wait..!" she said raising her hand sensing he was about to fire.

Alain Brock's chest exploded in a blast of red mist and Kath'ryn stood there shocked as he fell to the ground. Dead.

"Wha...?"

There was a clatter of metal and turning around she saw Gen6aC drop her fletchette rifle to the deck.

As Kath'ryn had been talking to her former shipmate, Gen6aC had seized the opportunity to subtly move his body, and to extend one of his pseudopods slowly toward the weapon.

When Kath'ryn had stepped forward, placing herself between Brock and himself, he was in a better position to grab the firearm from its position against the wall.

Hidden behind Kath'ryn, his movements had been shielded from Brock.

Gen6aC had gradually moved the gun into position, and trained the weapon on the pilot.

Once his Smart Mind had calculated the optimum trajectory, he pulled the trigger and fired past

Kath'ryn's torso. The fletchette pellets grazed her flight suit, passing under her left arm, missing it by millimetres.

Kath'ryn heard the blast from behind her followed by the clatter, and stunned by the horror of what had happened in front of her took several moments to assimilate the information her own Smart Mind was informing her on the source of the weapons fire.

She span around and faced the alien.

"You bastard!" she screamed at him, "He didn't need to die!"

"Yes he did Kath'ryn. I'm truly sorry. There have been many needless deaths in this battle I know, but he would not have allowed us to escape. He undoubtedly would have killed me and almost certainly you too. He could not leave a living witness. My own death would be unfortunate, but I could not allow him to kill you too, Kath'ryn."

Stunned, she faced him in mute shock.

"You, you don't know that....?" But she already knew that Brock certainly would have killed Gen6aC.

She was not prepared to simply accept that, even if deep down, she knew it to be true.

Disgusted and confused by the alien's logic and actions, she turned back to the panel, her mind seething in anger.

CHAPTER TWENTY-TWO
End Game

The sleek Flexani Sentinel craft undocked from the TTF Kydoimos and rotated away from the larger vessel.

It had sustained some battle damage, ironically from Flexani weaponry during the battle and many systems had been affected, but the engines still functioned, so Gen6aC had wasted no time in activating the vessel's IMD engines to move it away, into the gas cloud away from the carnage that was now underway.

The Sentinel Ship was sluggish under his control as Gen6aC fought to manoeuvre the ship free of the Kydoimos, and through the debris field. The Flexani signature of his vessel undoubtedly safeguarded their flight, as there seemed to be no active Terran weapon fire left. All the activity seemed to be the almost single minded destruction of the Terran vessel that had once been the proud TTF Kydoimos, now almost unrecognisable as anything other than an unlit but glowing mass.

Of the other two Terran vessels, there was no sign. Whether they were destroyed or had escaped, Gen6aC had no indication – neither did he care, he had to get them both away from this place of death.

He was fully focused on this task and did not notice Kath'ryn leave him alone on the bridge. He had not understood the grief and pain that he had caused her though the brutal killing of her friend, Alain.

Despite the fact that Alain had had such an emotional grievance against the alien, Gen6aC was simply insensitive to the result on the young pilot's emotions that his actions in the destruction of the Intrepid Star had had, and how that act had affected the equilibrium of the young man's mind.

Gen6aC had simply seen a threat to himself and another being who he had developed a trust for, and had dealt with it clinically and efficiently – and so Kath'ryn had lost her last remaining crewmember.

Ignorant to her pain, he thought hard about their predicament. They would need to hide for a while, and the cloud seemed like the best place for this.

Gen6aC himself was now coming to terms with his own isolation and loss from being ejected from Flexani society.

He had been struggled for the past si-krec with his own grief over losing everything he had ever know, from his being removed as an active participant in his Caste and House. He was as acutely aware of his own emotional state as he was unaware of the emotional turmoil into which he had placed Kath'ryn.

His Smart Mind was even now supressing the emotional turbulence however – the grief; the anger and the fear. Most of all, his shame of now being classed as a criminal to all other Flexani's.

So he floated now, doing the only thing he was bred to do - to observe, to record. He was reduced to simple visual observation though, his ship's scanners were useless within the cloud - as the gases and trace elements that made up the cloud's core scrambled the most sensitive of scanning equipment.

The other side of this coin however, was that it would also serve to mask their presence and to prevent their discovery.

Kath'ryn had stormed off as soon as they had broken away from the destroyed warship and not spoken a word to Gen6aC since. She sat sullen in another part of the ship, refusing to join him on the main deck or to have any further contact with him. She still could not bring herself to forgive him for killing Brock. She still could not believe that he would do such a thing, to take that type of action against another, especially as he surely knew Brock had been her friend.

Gen6aC it seemed however, showed no such regrets in killing Kath'ryn's friend, but it seemed that he would have to allow her time on her own to recover from the emotional shock.

I may have made an error in my judgement, he considered, knowing that Kath'ryn had come back to save him.

But he had no time to continue to dwell on the past now.

He had other concerns and focused all of his attention using just visual information to navigate the damaged vessel past the ruins of the space battle.

As they entered the cloud, Gen6aC rotated the ship through every orientation to gather as much information on the outcome of the battle as he could. What he saw made his emotionless resolve falter.

It seemed the two other Terran warships had not, as he had first suspected, been destroyed. Neither had they left. One was in two non-functioning sections, but the other still survived. It had not been able to save the Kydoimos but had now managed to turn the battle in its favour.

The Imperial Rose had used the strange new alien weapon that folded space-time, as well and only one of the Flexani ships now remained, strangely unreactive. Of the other Cruisers, there was no sign. They - his brethren - had vanished. The only evidence remaining were a few drones that seemed to be totally out of control and a scattering of exotic particles and matter that his jury rigged sensor net detected.

Gen6aC was conflicted.

He loved his kind and but now was alone. On the run from both the Terrans and the Flexani as a war criminal.

Kath'ryn too was on the run as a traitor to her kind most likely as she had aided a prisoner of war to escape and would now be alone. The sole survivor of the ROCL-XM-78KL Intrepid Star mining transport and the sole surviving Flexani that he knew for certain in the sector were now truly alone - together.

As the Sentinel Ship drifted among the shifting gases within the cloud, both occupants wondered separately where to go from here. Why did what had happened here in this otherwise unremarkable corner of space seem so, well, unbelievable?

++++++++++

Two men stood in an observation lounge.

They stood, deep in conversation by a large glass window, a pair of matching sofas and some token pot plants tried very hard to make the room look inviting and comfortable.

The lounge itself overlooked a vast hanger-sized chamber below that stretched away into the distance.

Orderly row upon row of MECS70-B Stasis Pods, over one thousand in total, filled the chamber far beneath the two men. A wide mezzanine floor, at a first floor level, just below the level of the observation lounge, ran down both sides of the chamber. On it were installed yet more of the advanced medical Stasis Pod units, where an army of attendants monitored their inhabitants.

Advanced Medical Console systems were positioned every twenty metres or so, each one monitoring the life signs being fed to it from up to ten of the Stasis Pods.

The many trained medical staff were hard at work, carefully observing the occupants of the Stasis Pods. On closer inspection, both human and Flexani bodies could be made out slumbering within the pods.

"And these are the latest results of the experiment?" asked one of the men of the other as he pointed out some information on the Padd he carried.

Both dressed in dark grey nondescript suits with no apparent insignia or badge indicating a rank, they nonetheless carried themselves with a stance and appearance that betrayed some sort of military training.

"Yes they are, Foster. As you can see, we've had some very successful, and interesting results during the last simulation," the other man responded, indicating one of the files on the Padd that the other man studied.

He continued, "As you know, the experiment has involved seventeen very unique AI's, all networked to the minds of the one thousand plus individuals you see here in these Pods."

"Each of these souls is connected via the new type of interface link to the slaved Smart Minds embedded in their brains – we've even managed to successfully connect the Flexani to this new interface this time around."

"As you know, the AI's were tasked with creating a universe," he continued. "A place where each person and alien could interact - a simulation so advanced, no participant can possibly be aware that it is not real."

Of the over one thousand unknowing participants in this virtual war game, some seven hundred and four humans were held in stasis, and counted among them were a certain Kath'ryn Kass, Andrew Terris, Alain Brock and Captain Middleton. Admiral Varnava, his aide and a host of others stared sightlessly from their stasis prisons. The serried ranks of machines also included the Arbiter Gen6aC, his Servient master and almost three hundred more of his species. Even a few Vorrax were represented.

The humans had volunteered - the Flexani had not.

All participated however in the scenarios the two observers and their programmers had created and all were currently unaware of their past, so deep into the virtual reality as they were, their memories synthesised by the AIs.

Each occupant – both human and alien - had been sedated as they slumbered so as the further blur their grip on the here and now, and were seamlessly and, in almost all cases, unknowingly linked directly into the sim via brain/machine interfaces to the Stasis Pods and the seventeen AI's.

As the worlds they occupied were created around them, the observers had monitored the responses in the simulation, changing parameters to observe the outcome of the virtual war between human and Flexani.

The man known as Foster enquired, "Have you sent off the files to our research branch to investigate the so-called Black Snow nanite idea? I was fascinated to read your initial report on the potential real effectiveness of the tech. Do you think we can reproduce it in the lab for real? Any weapons technology we can work with and develop, even from the theoretical, and to be honest, crazy possibilities literally dreamed up here, could give us an edge in the inevitable coming war."

"Yes, I sent off the full report to our technical labs yesterday." the other man responded.

"That is great news Professor. This unusual Hellfire weapon that was apparently installed on a couple of the human warships... what do you think about its real-world development. Can we reproduce its effects in the real world do you think?"

"I really need further study into this Foster," said the professor. "I do believe the weapon could be viable but we need further research and the development of the Hellfire theory, and it will take time."

Looking through of the window again at the comatose participants below he said, "Then we should get started now. Order the appropriate teams to look into replicating the weapons' effects - if we can have a powerful weapon such as that I'd like to see its effectiveness as it could offer us an enormous advantage over the Flexani."

The other man nodded. "What are your reactions though, to the possibilities that the Flexani have also been experimenting with new weapons technologies?" This was in reference to the Corismite crystal powered beam used against the phantom Kydoimos warship.

"I think we need to take a cautious approach. It is obvious to me that, based on these results, the Flexani," he said indicating the Padd, "could well have concluded that Corismite can be used in that way to provide a medium in which to provide resonance for the beam's particles. I am surprised that the Flexani hosts below believe they could create such a weapon."

"There is just one aspect of this whole simulation that has taken me by surprise though." the professor admitted.

"I know what you're going to say," replied the one called Foster. "You are going to point out the very strange interaction between the two species when actually brought together, the Kass and Arbiter relationship, aren't you?"

"I was," confirmed the Professor, "I was not expecting that. I surmise it's just a random blip in the chaos theory we are harnessing here, it's of no consequence – although…." He scratched his chin.

"You know," he continued, "it almost stalled the sim dead – I think we should look again at those participants."

Below them, in the Pods that contained the thousand or so participants in the simulated Second

Stellar War between the Terrans and the Flexani aliens, the war continued for those whose minds believed themselves still alive. A war that was a lie.

A complicit lie to enable the Terran known as Foster and his team establish new solutions to win the war.

The forthcoming *real* war with the Flexani.

Kath'ryn's whole life on board the Intrepid Star had been a simulacrum - an illusion created in her mind by the AI's - so that her responses and interactions between the other participants could be observed and documented along with those of the remaining unsuspecting puppets.

Her colleagues had not died on Heimdallr.

She had never been rescued by Gen6aC from the Dall.

She and Brock had never fought in a Reaper. In fact, the Reaper did not exist outside the game.

The life she had known had been created for her. Her background, life experiences and relationships all were generated by algorithms and protocols that the AIs managed.

She was totally unaware that the only real part of her life was that she was an officer in the Terran Task Force, and had undergone a new surgical procedure to implant a Smart Mind in her brain nearly four years previously.

The base that contained the multitude of MECS70-B Stasis Pods and their unsuspecting inhabitants, had been built by the Global Council in secret over seven years' previous. Its only function was to run series of simulations on aspects of the future war, and to identify ways of winning.

The result was the creation of the AIs and the framework that would allow them to evolve a series of personal experiences for each one of the occupants in the Pods, and to record how their interactions led to ways or ideas that may give an edge to the human fight.

It had been a successful programme so far, especially this last run through, and the Global Council had been very happy about the investment so far.

The man Foster turned to the Professor and said, "What about collateral count. Was the latest conclusion in our favour?"

The Professor replied smugly, "Yes. We saw over five hundred and seventy thousand potential deaths on Jhnuii from Black Snow alone; another five hundred and fifty Flexani deaths on the Horaxx and other capital ships by the Hellfire and by conventional weapons. Now, compared to those numbers, we lost the crew of the Intrepid Star; the mining colony and three warships - the TTF Vanguard, TTF Kydoimos and the TTF Nemesis. In total, around about one thousand human lives in total. I think we can claim this does represent excellent results."

Foster nodded in agreement.

"OK, wrap this one up and run the simulation again. Let's see if we can get a fifth set of results that are also favourable. I suggest we ensure that human woman and that particular Flexani she 'met' do not this time!"

THE END

Glossary of Terms

Ac - A Flexani unit of time equivalent to 10 seconds.

Arbiter - Bred with the simple task to observe, Arbiters are dispersed to Sentinel ships throughout Flexani space to watch and report on human activities along the border to Flexani space. They have independence and responsibilities and typically are bred from noble genetic DNA.

Artificial Intelligence (AI) - the intelligence exhibited by complex quantum processing machines developed in early 2022. It is a digital 'agent' formed of algorithms and protocols that perceives its environment and takes actions to maximise its chance of success at an arbitrary goal. Normally used to perform or mimic cognitive functions at rapid speeds that we intuitively associate with human minds, such as learning and problem solving.

Atticis - A high Rank from the Council of JurTan within the Flexani hierarchy. They rule Flexani Prime and the outer worlds and define the rules that maintain Flexani society. Genetically modified to live for hundreds of cycles and to have the noble strength to rule over Flexani.

Black Snow - A new and deadly weapon developed in The Nest - a secret military installation. An advanced bio-weapon that would be capable of infiltrating any Flexani exosuit and then the epidermis of the alien itself. Using the host's own biomatter to replicate it convert surrounding protein and biomatter into a resinous, fast-mutating 'crust' that looked like black snow.

Caste - Flexani society is managed by Houses that are formed from numerous Castes. These are disciplinary as well as genetic and so are complex and their extent is unknown to mankind. It is understood that over 20 different Castes occur, but this may be limited and it has been speculated that over 50 Castes might exist.

Caste Competitions - Caste Councils hold annual competitions where Flexani Caste members are awarded benefits such as genetic upgrades or gifts from their Caste Council for exceptional work.

Corismite - A mineral discovered on several planets near to Flexani space. It is especially found rich in the mines of Mirral, near to XT-67. Due to the advanced uses of this mineral in stardrive technology and manufacture, it is critical to Terran expansion across the universe.

Council of JurTan - Flexani societal leadership that forms its laws, governance and controls known Flexani space. 150 Council Members are elected every 5 Jrafs from the main Castes.

Courach - A crustacean found deep within the Flexani oceans that has lethal spines protruding from its shell, and can poison and paralyse its attackers.

Dall - An insectoid race found on the planet Heimdallr. They have three main Castes – Warrior, Drone and a Leader type. Little information is known about this species but the Dall form small clans and have a strong bond with their clan mates. They are ritualistic in nature, much like the ancient indigenous races in the Amazon basin on Earth. It is known they can work metal, have advanced manual skills and construction of dwellings but no advanced technologies.

Demi-Frec - A Flexani unit of time equivalent to 50 minutes.

DNA - Deoxyribonucleic Acid, a self-replicating material which is present in nearly all living organisms as the main constituent of chromosomes. It is the carrier of genetic information.

Empirical Cruiser Horaxx - Flexani warship around the same size as the Kydoimos.

Fletchette - a weapon capable of firing small pellets of matter from a magnetically induced barrel at supersonic speeds up to 76,000 mph.

Flexani Prime - The homeworld of the Flexani race and the location of the Council or JurTan. Mostly a water-planet, the planet is rich in minerals which helped the Flexani develop space travel. Much larger than Earth, but with a lower gravity well, the planet on had a few landmasses.

Flexani Seconda - a Planet in the Flexani system where off-world experimentation and technological advancements are created. Mainly the home of the Maestri Caste.

Flexies - Derogatory term for Flexani used by humans.

FLIR – Forward Looking Infra-Red sensor system on starships and shuttlecraft.

FLT - Faster Than Light travel using engines capable of breaching the Einstein-Rosen bridge to warp normal space-time, so that a ship can travel subspace.

Fordinel fish - native fish on the Flexani homeworld that is a delicacy food.

Frec - A Flexani unit of time equivalent to 100 minutes.

Gorsac Grenade - A powerful explosive device created from volatile minerals in Heimdallr using the crushed juices of Lillan worms. Contained in a clay shell, the mixture itself is not activated until it encounters a third agent in the centre of the grenade. A small pellet of vossimite crystal which is inert until broken on impact. The three components then react together to create an explosion.

GorDak Drone - A ground-based autonomous drone used in engineering and mechanical facilities. Often controlled by a slaved subspace link with a Flexani, with three legs for stability and a series of six manipulator arms that protruded from a pyramid-like torso. This torso contained the power source and Smart Mind, as well as a complex sensor node. The arms were configurable and interchangeable for different requirements.

Hamms - A unit of measurement of distance used by Flexani, equivalent to 2.4 furlongs or 0.48 km.

Hellfire - A new human weapon that had the ability to subtly altered the four-dimensional aspect of unidimensional space within the fixed point. The Hellfire gun twisted the region of space inside out. Molecular bonds and weak electro-magnetic fields that held the atoms in place were changed, their Dimensional analogy forming their cohesive connection to this universe was immediately altered, and particles of unstable alien matter from other universes transposed with the material in its place causing fragility and destruction on a molecular level.

Houses - Flexani citizens are bred into Houses. Each House represents a genetic pool unique to others, and they maintain their own Maceration Chamber to ensure their bloodline remains pure. Houses are formed of many different Castes and all support the laws defined by the Council of JurTan but are ruled individual by their own Caste Council.

House of NorHan - Gen6aC belongs to this House. No other information is known about the House.

House of HudSet - a House that has holdings on many worlds and creates specialised Flexani exosuits for high gravity worlds.

IMD - Flexani technology - the Infusion Manipulator Drive - uses a form of fusion to heat and accelerate particles of heavy metals as well as other accelerants to create a stream of exhaust in order to move a vessel forward in space or atmosphere.

Jraf - A Flexani unit of time equivalent to 1 solar cycle or 1 year long. A Jraf on Flexani Prime is approximately 485 days on Earth.

Krec - A Flexani unit of time equivalent to 10 luna cycles or 10 days long.

Lillan Worms - luminescent worms found in caves on Heimdallr.

Maceration Chamber - Flexani technology controlled by Caste leaders that maintained and manipulated their genetic bloodlines within the

Caste society. All Caste members supplied genetic material that was combined to keep bloodlines pure.

Maestri - Scientific Caste within the Flexani hierarchy. Typically bred with different scientific disciplines they are the Caste responsible for medical, technological and engineering advancements for the Flexani race.

MEC S70-B & MEC S70-Hx Stasis Pods - Designed in 2078 by the Moneta Engineering Consortium. By 2095, it was widely used in all aspects of deep space travel, and was the standard model of choice in most starships, whereas the MEC S70-Hx Stasis Pod model with advanced medical monitoring equipment was used to preserve life for critically-injured or terminally-ill patients, until their conditions could be stabilised in a fully-equipped medical facility. Both models of the Stasis Pod units suspended all cellular activity and disease processes, keeping the patient from succumbing to their illness or injury for an indefinite period. In 2092, a law was passed to ensure that Stasis units became standard equipment on deep space starship vessels, but was optional for short range ships within the Asteroid Belt.

Mi-Frec - A Flexani unit of time equivalent to 10 minutes.

Nanites - Molecular machines with pre-programmed commands that are injected into the body to perform particular tasks. Nanites are capable of combining and can use the materials in their local environment to replicate as well as build structures and complex tools.

NDE - Neutron Diffraction Energy Beam. A new weapon used by the Flexani based on Corismite crystals capable of vaporising at the molecular level.

Octopoid - Derogatory term for Flexani used by humans.

Octoids - Derogatory term for Flexani used by humans.

Orfin - A seal-like creature found on some Flexani worlds with four fins and a stubby nose, about the size of a small cow. Flexani use them for meat and breed them in secure ocean pens near to land.

Paetron - A musician or creative class within the Flexani Caste structure bred for their ability to create inspiring music or art that enhances Flexani culture.

Planet Heimdallr - Designation XT-67-F, is the known location of the Dall insectoid race.

Planet Mirral - Designation XT-67-C, is a planet on the edge of human space, bordering Flexani space where Corismite Crystal ore is mined.

Planet Jhnuii - Flexani world also known as Flexani Seconda, location of the House of HudSet. It has slightly more -landmass than other Flexani worlds and a higher gravity well of 1.4 times that of Flexani Prime. It houses several underwater cities used in the development and design of superior exosuits.

Project Valkyrie - Term for the combined Red Horse and Black Snow projects within the Terran Task Force.

Reaper MK IV - The Reaper Mk IV is a two-man vessel developed by the Ferris Corporation on Earth. A Reaper pilot is joined in a symbiotic partnership with the on-board Smart Mind becoming an extension of the craft. The co-pilot is also linked to the flight controls and weapon systems in a similar manner. Reapers are powered by twin COX G-6 hyperstar engines for high speed and rapid acceleration. Weaponry consists of 25mm calibre fletchette railguns with a hundred-thousand-round ammunition stores. Hardpoints spaced around the hull support various unguided and SM-guided Autumn Wind missiles, as well as more specialised weaponry such as cluster mines. To improve survivability in combat, the Reaper is equipped with numerous tactical countermeasures - ranging from electronic pods mounted under the 'wings' through to smart chaff for use when in atmospheric combat.

Red Horse - Developed in The Nest, it was a new design of stealth missiles capable of avoiding detection by Flexani sensors.

ROCL - Raven Ore Confederated Logistics, the mining arm of Raven Corporation. A corporate based on Mars specialising in the refinement and production of Corismite-based engine parts for starships.

Sentinel Post Ship - An advanced Flexani vessel used solely for the purpose of passive and active scanning of local space. Located normally along the Flexani / Human border, these vessels are manned by a single Arbiter whose purpose is to use the superior scanning technologies on board to identify any intruders in Flexani space.

Servient - A senior leader within the Caste hierarchy of the Flexani homeworld. They are bred genetically for the role of management in the political realm. Their enhancements have given them the ability to manage and respond to challenges to ensure the safety of the Flexani race.

They are typically bred from pure noble genetic DNA.

Si-Frec - A Flexani unit of time equivalent to 1 minute.

Si-Jraf - A Flexani unit of time equivalent to 5 krecs or 48.5 days long, or a Flexani Prime period equivalent to a month on Earth in relative terms.

Si-Krec - A Flexani unit of time equivalent to 1 luna cycle or 1 day long.

Smart Mind (SM) - Similar to an AI, the Smart Mind is a less-evolved quantum computer processor developed within the physical brain of an individual, to enhance and control aspects of the body. It has enhanced recall capabilities and can support an individual with advanced computing of complex tasks. Most Smart Minds interface with external systems though a port in the back of the neck to control systems such as a vessels flight controls, enabling faster response times.

Squiddie - Derogatory term for Flexani used by humans.

Subspace - A part of space/time discovered by Flexani scientist and used by space-faring races including humans. Ships with subspace engines can fold spacial matter around their vessel and slip between normal layers of space in order to transverse distances. Also known as FLT or 'Faster than Light'.

Subspace Tweeter - Technology used to send signal via the subspace strings of the universe. Utilising a form of superstring theory - which posits a connection called super-symmetry between bosons and the class of particles called fermions - scientists used Flexani conceptual mathematics to create a tool that could manipulate quantum field theory. Communication across vast distances, no longer impeded by restrictions of light, were now possible if both Tweeters had the same coded string.

The Nest - A Black Ops base for the Terran Task Force located on Mars, in the Sisyphi Montes mountain range.

Treaty of JurTan - After the First Stellar War ended in 2064, the Flexani signed a Treaty with Earth. Known as the Treaty of JurTan, it ratified the borders between the occupied systems as well as certain trade and diplomatic protocols.

TTF - Terran Tactical Force. The military force responsible for the defence of Earth, the Sol system and the outlying borders between human and Flexani space.

TTF-200869 Kydoimos - An Imperator-class warship, captained by Captain James Middleton. 420m long, the Kydoimos had 6 decks, and a crew complement of around 380 personnel, including 24 bridge officers and 22 Reaper pilots. She was protected with the latest in hull technology and possessed advanced medical facilities, including the new MEC S70-Hx Stasis Pods. 4 NovaCorp DX5 Sublight Drives for deep space FTL travel propelled the ship through space, their power coming from the 4 independent nuclear hearts inside the main superstructure. The warship was also equipped with 8 short-range Reaper attack fighters and 4 shuttles for missions to planetary surfaces and ship to ship transfers. It's multi-layered hulls were very thick with carbon-bonded laminated metals, carbon nano-fibres, and self-sealing smart plastics materials embedded in them to seal hull breaches, providing sustainability and survivability in battle to make up for the limited shield technology that utilised magnetic disruption harmonics to slow plasma and solid projectiles before their collision with the hull.

TTF-167453 Imperial Rose - A Legatus-class warship, captained by Captain Naro. The older warship was the first of the Terran Task Force fleet to carry the Hellfire weaponry.

TTF-200955x Nemesis - An Imperator-class warship, captained by Captain Tonev. Designed to me maintained with a minimal crew, it had been fitted with Red Horse stealth technology and 75 Stealth Missiles together with Hellfire weapon systems.

TTF-116781 Vanguard - A Legatus-class warship, captained by Captain Boskowitz.

Torrak Drone - A Flexani drone ship - the Torrak class craft are autonomous drones measuring a little over 12 metres in length and equipped with an Infusion Manipulator Drive, artificial combat mind capability and a fletchette railguns mounted on each of the six main 'wings'. 4 spines protrude forward of the main fuselage with 2 larger wings trailing back. A vent at the rear of the main body contained the IMD driving the ship forward in space, controlled by an Artificial Mind.

VMail - Video Mail. An evolution of email typically used by humans it can be encrypted for communication via subspace.

Vorrax - A small race of aquatic animals much like the stoat of Earth. The Vorrax have sleek fine fur allowing it to travel underwater. The Flexani modified their DNA allowing them to have gills to breathe underwater for long periods of time. Larger than the stoat though at around a metre long, the Vorrax are the personal servants to the Flexani.

Vossimite crystal · Blue / green crystal found near to volcanic vents on Heimdallr, used in the creation of Gorsac grenades.

A Note from the Author

Thanks for reading Arms Race. I've been hugely grateful for the opportunity to share my work with you, and for everyone's support, which allowed me to produce this book.

If you wouldn't mind taking a few extra minutes to post a review on your favourite book website – such as Goodreads or Amazon - it would be extremely helpful and very much appreciated.

Thank you again, and remember to look for the next book in the Hostile Realms™ series.

Printed in Poland
by Amazon Fulfillment
Poland Sp. z o.o., Wrocław